The Wheels of Cady Grey

Cady Grey is invisible. One of the 'perks' of being in a wheelchair.

Sometimes it's better that way, when you're a sweary, spitty teenaged girl and all you want to do is get through sixth form in one piece. But when a sinister shell company wants to knock the school down, she's the only one who cares enough to do anything about it.

When Cady finally gives up being invisible to fight, she finds being noticed by the wrong people might get her killed.

PAUL ARVIDSON is a forty-something ex lighting designer who lives in rural Somerset. He juggles his non-author time bringing up his children and fighting against being sucked into his wife's chicken breeding business.

The Wheels of Cady Grey

a thriller by

Paul L Arvidson

ISBN-13: 9781687865465

Ed. Sue Laybourn from No Stone Unturned Editing,
nostoneunturnedediting.co.uk
Sensitivity reader, Fuschia Aurelius instagram.com/fuchsiaaurelius
Cover by betibup33 from thebookcoverdesigner.com, all with
grateful thanks.
Printed with KDP
Available online from paularvidson.co.uk and real-life bookshops.

For Cheryl, Leah, and Nenna

Contents

The Wheels of Cady Grey

Chapter 1

Cady Grey lay nose down in the soil, the wheels of her chair spun above her, the weight of the chassis pinned her down. Rain fell in great big drops all around her. She couldn't move her legs at the best of times, but she was sure her right shin was broken. She was too stunned to feel much of it yet. Everything was one great bruise. Her head felt muzzy, she must have banged it. Along with everything else.

Petrichor: the smell of rain after a dry spell.

WTF, Cady. Where did that come from?

The subconscious can properly fuck with your head sometimes.

She opened her eyes. Eye. Grass and soil close up. Some kind of edging stone, with a smear on it. Something trickling from her fringe down her nose on the right-hand side. For a moment, it felt comfortable. Like being held down by a massive duvet or hugged tight in a huge embrace. She could just go to sleep.

And... BAM, here came the pain.

Cady clenched her jaw, at least that wasn't broken. Her lips were sticky, she could taste metal and salt. The right shin: definitely broken. But good news, she could feel her toes: they hurt like hell too. Head. She couldn't pull her focus to that yet, all too stabby. Somehow she knew if she let herself focus on that too much, she'd pass out again. And that would be bad. Really, really bad.

Shit. Shit. SHIT. Focus on something Cady.

Noise. What was that noise? Straining, laboring. *Something's gonna break*. Mechanical? Not exactly, electro-mechanical. Chair wheels, running full tilt, with nothing to grab on. Flailing like a beetle on its back. The chair must've been sat on its arm, with its controller bent backward. Well, that was going to burn the motor out and no mistake. She spread her awareness out, slowly. It wasn't far from the controller and it wasn't broken. She shifted her weight from her hips to her right arm.

Shit-shit-shit

Too much weight on her to get free, but she could move her hand. The whole chair arm was twisted out of shape. She could see along the profile of the chair that plastic engine cover had snapped loose, spilling its wiry intestines onto the grass. Man, this chair was fucked up. Dad was going to be so pissed at her. She felt for the chair controller joystick. The golf ball she always had on the top of it had gone. Lost in the crash. Just a metal stick left. She pushed the metal stick into the soil, back to its neutral position. The *skree-ing* noise stopped. Good. Quiet now. Not quiet. Ringing in her ears and rain *sploshing*. She must've been lying where a puddle was gathering, because her legs felt wet.

Tic… tac… tic…

Was that in her head? She'd dreamed about that before. Was she concussed? Another part of her brain was waking up. Her hind brain, home of warnings, of fear, of fight or flight. But she couldn't fly. Her wheels were broken.

…tac…tic …tac

Shit

Now she knew. That noise. Bad brain, slow brain, now it was catching up. TicTac. A noise and a person. Bad. Bad person. It spooled out of her like an old broken film reel, images yammering from her brain on fast forward.

Flash—the glint of a gold ring on someone's little finger. Insincere smile. Not him.

Flash—the joy of the chair lights springing into life when she'd flicked the new switch, Dad was the best. Not Dad.

Flash—bright flash, muzzle flash, ringing noise. There, that was it.

Flash—flash—flash, but only one bang? Ears overloaded in a confined space. Certainly a bang first time. Ears still ringing now. A short time ago, then.

Tic... tac...

What was that noise? Getting slowly louder, slowly closer, that was important. It was an odd noise, a stupid noise. A WTF noise. A lazy noise, a rhythm noise, like a metronome.

Tic... tac...

Like blues. A walking blues. That was it. Everything.

Tic... the noise was walking.

Tac... the sound of those stupid segs on the man's shoes.

Tic... the man: greasy hair and arrogance. Tall, Thames estuary accent.

Tac... dots tattooed on his knuckles. Something black, metal held firm in his hand. The smell of oil.

Tic he was coming. For her.

Tac... and he was going to kill her.

Tic... *tac*... Bill had called him TicTac.

Shit Bill. Where's Bill?

Something made her not want to think of that. The rear brain. Fight or flight. No flight. There was another one. What was it? Fight, flight and—

Tic… tac… Freeze. That was it. Fight, flight or freeze.

The air filled with noise. Her chair back jerked. That noise. *Bang* never quite seemed to describe that noise. It filled her ears with loud. Even out here, face down in the grass. And an echo, off every hard surface of the building behind them. The town hall. No flash this time, with her face in the grass, but at least that meant she couldn't see what was coming. No wait, it also meant the chair body was between him and her. Something from deep inside her chair was fizzing.

Tic.

"Oh, there you are," the voice dripped arrogance. She hated that voice, "don't go anywhere, will you? Oh, wait, you can't!"

"Fucker," was all she could manage in return, but with her face in the grass, she could hardly hear herself.

Tic. Tac. Tic. Tac.

"I don't really want to do this, you know?" he said. God, he loved the sound of his own voice.

"Liar."

He laughed—harsh, echoing. It rang off the walls. Harsher somehow than the shock of the gun. The gun. He really was going to kill her. How many rounds had he fired? Could she remember? There was something stopping her recall. Flash, flash, flash… What was it? Flash, flash, flash… Bill. Bill falling, falling, shouting out.

Shit. Bill.

How many rounds? One just now, three at… Three from before. One before that? So… one left? Did guns even have six rounds in them these days? How did she need to know this? But one. One was plenty.

Tic. Tac. Tic.

Fight, flight or freeze. Her Dad always said, 'you never really know which you're going to do until something bad enough happens.' Something so bad that your insides have already turned to water and your brain is racing in six different directions at once. And you're going nowhere.

"Here I come, Cady! Time to pray."

He couldn't be serious? Pray? No, this cocky shit-bag would be all about that, wouldn't he? Bang, bang. Oops, sorry I killed somebody. That's okay though, right God? Bit of absolution 101 and off we go again. Tough job being a killer, but someone's got to do it. God says it's okay.

Tic. Tac. Tic. Tac.

"Nothing come to mind? Let me choose then. Seems fitting."

Cady struggled under the chair. Her arm flailed, she couldn't move it too far, besides, the chair in the way was the only thing saving her. Even if all he saw was her hand, if he shot it off that would kill her plenty quick enough.

"Bastard," she growled into the soil.

"Oh, now. Do you want your last words on this earth to be a curse?" But before she could answer, "I've thought of one, how about this?"

Good God this guy could talk. At least being shot would be a relief from his voice.

"As I lay me down to sleep... do you know that one Cady?"

"Oh, yeah, that's great." Keep him talking, probably too late now anyway. No-one here, he could talk all he liked. She was delaying the inevitable.

"I pray the Lord my soul to keep."

She heard the metallic *chick-chak* of the gun being cocked.

"If I should die before I wake."

Cady got a whiff of excited sweat and gun, oil. She wriggled, her left arm was free. That was both arms now, maybe...

"I pray the Lord, my soul—" He leaned over and stood on her left arm at the wrist. "A- ah, stay still."

She felt the metal of the gun rustle in against the base of her skull and press there.

"I pray the Lord, my soul to take..."

But no one's year began that badly, right?

Chapter 2

"Cady, get your lazy arse on the bus!" He never really got angry as such, but she let him get just to the edge of hysteria. It felt homey somehow.

"I'm out here, Dad!" she yelled from outside.

"Gaah! Then why is your chair in here with your arse not in it?"

"Man, I've just lit up."

"Cadence Grey, do not try me this morning. I've got the Jones' timing belt to do on that Renault and Betsy Stockford is bringing that stupid Beetle back in again, and you know what a cow she can be, if she thinks she's not getting everyone's full attention. Please?"

"O-kay, coming."

"Come on, you know how I feel about smoking in the house."

"You smoke, hippogriff."

"Get in the chair. In. The. Chair." He held his breath. Then let it out.

"Book bag?"

"Check."

"Homework?"

"Check."

"Lunch and tubes and stuff?"

"Check, check, check." She clicked her chair harness buckles in punctuation. The bus beeped. "All clear to launch!" she said brightly. "Love you, Daddy."

"See you tonight Cade, try and stay out of trouble, eh?"

"Where's the fun in that?"

He sighed. She bumped her chair over the threshold of the white double-glazed door and onto the concrete ramp outside. Dave le Bus leaned against the back of the van, one Converse planted against the side, one tapping slowly on the ground. The tail lift was already down.

"Come on Cady, I know it's January but…"

She even drove in a petulant fashion. How was that a thing? Her wheels reached the lip of the tail lift.

"Fag!" said Dave.

"Now you see, I'd always pegged you as Bi," said Cady, reversing. She took one last drag on her roll-up, flicked it to the ground then drove over it onto the ramp.

"I'm not even—" said Dave, bored, reaching across with the safety strap to click from one rail to the other. "All clear?" he asked, looking Cady in the eye.

"Crystal," she said, clocking a twinkle. Dave always had a twinkle. He fired the handset, and with a whine the tail lift rose. "Morning peasants!" she yelled into the bus as she got to deck level.

"Morn-ing Cady!" familiar voices sing-songed back.

"Cady!" Daisy, shouted, slightly too loud, "Don't forget it's Home Ec today."

"Oh arse," Cady said. She'd got all the ingredients out last night and put them in the square biscuit tin. Only a sponge cake, it would be a breeze, she made them for her dad all the time but since she'd not gone back into the kitchen in a rush to prove her point, the whole bag must've still been there on the table.

The ramp clunked to the top. A plastic bag crunched into her wheel. She followed from the hand that held it down into her dad's face.

"You're a hero," she said.

"And you're a muppet. Have a nice day."

****

Dave Le Bus started the tiresome business of strapping the chair down. She watched him head down, arse up clicking a ratchet into the track. He had a lower back tattoo just peeking over his boxers. Some tribal-looking thing.

Ex-roadie—it figures.

He seemed tired this morning, older than usual. She wasn't even sure she could pin an age on how old he was. Old enough to be a roadie in the 90's, what would that make him now? Thirty, forty? He looked closer to the latter than the former today.

"You gonna do this?" Dave held his face like he was trying not to tut.

"Wha?"

"Seat belt?" He flicked his fringe out of his eyes.

"Oh, yeah, sorry." She took the belt from him with one hand and reached over to find the stalk to clip it into with the other.

Daisy leaned round the edge of her seat and fixed her with a grin, "Nice holidays?"

"Daze, I've only just seen you, New Year wasn't that long ago. I thought you'd remember more of it than me. Obviously not."

A grunt came from the opposite side of the aisle.

"And you can cut that out, Mr Ed," said Cady, "you were invited."

"I couldn't," said Ed.

Daisy kicked him gently in the foot, "I thought we'd established that being paralytically shy was not an excuse."

"Muh," said Ed, moving to stand.

"No, you don't, Edward," an unfamiliar voice came from the front of the bus. Dave's new shotgun, Cady presumed. Like chopsticks, special bus staff always came in pairs.

The driver's door slammed shut and the passenger door slowly closed to a flurry of electronic warning beeps.

"All strapped in?" Dave flicked on the stereo. It flared into life with a noisy punk offering.

"Da-ve, do we have to listen to that again? It's my turn to choose."

"That your lot again, Dave?" Cady asked.

"Yeah," said Dave, wounded.

Your lot referred to the least unfamous band Dave had been associated with in his time as a roadie. An early noughties punk outfit called Bellend Sebastian.

"I like it," said Ed.

"Come on Dave," whined Daisy, "fair's fair. I've got it all cued-up and everything."

"Shoot," said Dave, swapping the stereo over to Bluetooth.

As the bus pulled away to the cheery strains of *Never Gonna Give You Up* by Rick Astley, Cady rummaged in her bag and smiled.

Chapter 3

Northfield Special School was unusual in its teaching if not in its architecture. Its faded eighties cheery optimism had dulled from the primary colours of the massive pencils stockading the playground, but the enthusiasm of the staff somehow never had.

This was in good part due to Barbara Wintle, spinster of the parish and head since 1997. Neither her kindness nor her enthusiasm had dulled in the intervening years, but her grey streaks weren't the only signs of her edges being knocked off.

From Cady's point of view, they had a sixth-form that managed both her physical limitations and her intellectual strengths. And that, she had found, was a rare thing indeed.

The bus rounded the corner, Dave as usual, skimmed the gatepost. Today some shiny new notice was stapled neatly at the top in a plastic poly-pocket. The raggedy clothed gatepost seemed to be a repository for all the bake-sale—summer fete—coffee morning ads for the school and the surrounding housing estate of Absfield. Cady's attention though, was attracted by a flash of shiny red. A spanking new, shiny red, classic Balder chair—all the bells and whistles, tilt and lift, headlights, indicators, top speed of 4.3 mph, the whole shebang—was perched on the ramp outside the school's front doors. Sat in it was a boy of maybe sixteen, glancing from under a mop of curly brown hair. Behind him, an equally new Mercedes S class with its ramp down, faced him in the car park.

As the bus screeched round and parked in one movement, Cady noticed the boy jump, "Cool," she said, "fresh meat."

Rick Astley's *Greatest Hits* stopped abruptly and Dave brought the bus to a stop, cranking the handbrake on. "Terminus! Please remove all your pets and belongings from the vehicle, as the management cannot be held responsible for what winds up on eBay."

Dave turned and faced down the bus to start on the job of un-ratcheting Cady. She'd already unbelted herself. At the front of the bus, the door opened on its own. Dave had a habit of popping the door button as he passed. He even sometimes waved at it too, like he was Harry Potter, the nobber. She was at the back doors of the van before he'd finished stowing the straps.

"C'mon Dave," she said. "People to do, things to see."

"Should've called you Patience," he muttered, opening the back doors of the van and hopping down to deploy the tail-lift. After the tortuous uncoiling and slow whine to deck level, Dave clipped across the limp safety cord, "On you go then," he said.

Cady was already moving and came to a stop square in the middle of the lift.

"Going down—underwear, garden furniture and stationery."

"Not appropriate, Dave."

"Bite me. Do not alight the vehicle until the ride has fully stopped."

Cady glanced at Dave and rolled her eyes. He unclipped the safety strap and snatched his foot away from the already moving wheel.

"Bag!" said Dave.

"Thanks Dave, my hero!" Cady said, reaching an arm out to him, but looking towards the shiny-chaired newcomer.

"See you tonight Ms Grey," said Dave.

"Uh-huh." She waved off-handedly.

The boy's head twitched between the car in front of him and the door behind him like some invisible tennis match as Cady drove over.

Cady wondered if he'd bolt. She let go of her joystick and let her chair roll to a halt an inch away from his wheel, "And you are?" she asked.

"Williams-White." He turned his head to her and it was as if a smooth mask came down, smooth to match the RP accent. "Charles Williams-White."

"Nice to meet you Charles Williams-White. Cadence Grey. All we need's a Sirius Black and we'd be set."

"Eh?"

"Never mind. Are you staying?"

"Well." His head twitched towards the Mercedes again, "that is my mother and father— they're— You know, they…"

"I have no idea," said Cady, then added, "Your folks make all your decisions?"

"No! Well, about school and the chair racing and things, but we've just moved here you understand, and they're seeing what school they want to put me in, and it's all a bit stressful for them, what with the moving to the new bungalow and all and the building work for the adaptations, the bathroom and the chair ramps and such and Father having to commute to the City now and..." He sighed.

Cady smiled, "And you?"

"Eh?"

"You. What about you? What do you want?"

"Er, I'm… I don't…"

"Don't get asked all that often? No. Thought not." She sailed past him so that he had to turn away from the main school doors to keep facing her.

"Uh?"

"Sixth form centre's this way, you coming?" Cady was already punching a code into the pad farther down the building. She shoved the door hard enough with her footplate for it to bang against the magnetic catch, and didn't look back as she rolled in.

As she reached the hall, she heard the new chair's motor behind her, "Shut the door, there's a luv, the Dep gets awful shitty if we leave the security lock open. Button. Right hand side."

Charles did as he was asked and banged on the large square metal button with a chair symbol on it. The door clunked and started to swing slowly back into place.

"Chair racing, huh?" Cady could barely be heard as she drove off. "Nice."

Chapter 4

No map was needed to reach the sixth form centre. He could hear the music from the moment the door to the outside closed. And the closer he got, the louder it got. Whatever the music system in the common room was, it was loud. He could feel the thudding through his chair wheels from across the hall.

The glass double doors were not automatic, so Charles pushed awkwardly with his chair, hoping they opened inward. A large white laser printed sign read *Sixth Form Common Room*. A small orange handwritten note below it read:

****

Do not tap on the glass.
Do not feed the animals.

****

A shock wave of noise hit him in the face.

"*I'm SPASTICUS, SPASTICUS, SPASTICUS AUTISTICUS!*" screamed the stereo system. A familiar voice, but Charlie wasn't all that great at pop music, especially old stuff. A tall boy approached, about his own age, buzz cut hair and an awkward gait as he walked. Had he got off the coach before Cady and the Downs girl?

"Awesome, isn't it?" the boy shouted into Charlie's face. "Dave Le Bus set it up for us!"

"Who?" Charlie asked.

"The music?" said the boy, taken aback, "Ian Dury, you muppet! What are they teaching the kids these days?" He headed for a door with the classic orange chair logo on it.

"No, I meant—"

"Toast?" a voice came from behind him.

He turned, "sorry?"

"No-one ever needs to be sorry about toast," Cady said breezily.

"I, uh…" he offered, but Cady was already on her way back to the countertop of what looked like a low rent sandwich bar. This seemed to comprise the heart of the common room.

"Suit yourself," she said.

The kettle behind her clicked off. Charlie noticed the music had gone off too. A door in the wall behind the "sandwich bar" opened and the other girl from the bus came out.

"Tea?" Cady nodded toward the counter. Before Charlie had chance to realise it was him she was speaking to, she rolled on, "this place runs on the stuff."

"Er?" said Charlie.

"You'd better," said the other girl, "she gets a bit like Mrs Brown if you don't."

"Ooh, harsh," said Cady.

"T-Uh!" came a deep voiced male shout to Charlie's right.

"On it, Bill!" Cady said.

He realised that the common room was L-shaped and the sandwich-bar-counter thing was at its elbow. Down the end of the cul-de-sac as Charlie peered round the corner was a ratty, unmatched three piece suite, the monster music system with speaker stacks as tall as the top of his head when seated, and the tallest boy he had ever seen. Was he two metres? Over, probably, and he was as broad in the beam as he was tall. Kneeling at his feet was a woman with wild purple hair. She seemed to be tying his laces.

"Me too please, two sugars," said laces-tying woman without turning round.

"Done yours, Linda." There was clattering as Cady fished a chaos of mugs out of the sink and clumped them together on the speckled melamine countertop. "Come on, Daze," Cady said, "it'll be cold before you've poured it."

"Perfect takes time," Daze replied, pouring from a large, dull metal teapot.

Cady drew breath to speak, but the monolithic speakers blasted the opening bars of *Loving the Alien*.

"It's a compilation," said skinny crew-cut over Charlie's shoulder. He grabbed a tea from the cluster with one hand, didn't stop for milk, and in one smooth movement, sat, unshouldered a rucksack and plonked himself into one of the mismatched armchairs, open laptop on his knee.

"Well can you knock it off a minute, Ed?" asked Cady, "I've got an announcement to make."

Ed thumped his keyboard and the music stopped.

"Ladies and gentlemen, let me introduce you all to Charles Williams-White, new to this parish and well known chair racer.

Charlie stared. "We looked you up," said Cady. "So me you've already met, provider of tea and cheer is Daisy, the D.J. there is Mr Ed." Ed waved. "And there in the corner is Big Bad Bill, the T.A with the purple hair is the awesome Linda."

"Eech!" shouted Bill.

"Good call," said Cady.

All eyes fell on Charlie. He felt the heat rise in his face. He looked at the counter where two mugs had been left steaming, "What just happened there?" he said.

"Bill said 'Speech,'" Cady said.

"Oh," said Charlie. He grabbed a mug of tea from the counter top, took a swig and then "hoo-ed" silently. When the burning heat had died down in his mouth, he spoke. "I- er- I don't know if I'm staying. I—"

The doors swung open and Mrs Wintle, the head, swept in mid-tour, Charlie's parents in her wake. He hurriedly put his mug on the counter.

"And this, obviously, is the Common Room. Morning Sixth-Form. They've got their own accessible loo here, and tea and coffee facilities. There's the library and resource centre just next door…" and she breezed on out through the other door, parents in tow.

"Wow, they didn't even stop," said Charlie.

"No," said Cady, "that's our Barbara for you. Always a bit of a moving target." She offered him his tea back.

He took it and smiled, then noticed that Cady didn't have one, "What about you?"

"Mine's the one in the jug."

Charlie had failed to notice that the last mug on the counter top had a spout. Cady flourished a syringe from under her black furry jumper with a grin. She seemed to be attached to it in some fashion by a clear tube snaking away under her top. She took the blue and white stripy jug by the handle and began to pour tea from it into the open top of the syringe. Charlie was unable to look away as she flicked a plastic clip along the tube and the level of tea slowly lowered in the syringe.

"I'm a tubie," she said, "amongst other things. I can go somewhere else if it freaks you."

"No, I'm fine," said Charlie, "you're fine. It's all fine."

"Stop baiting the poor boy," said Daisy, "he's clearly got enough on his plate."

"Oh?" said Cady.

"Well, if you had your eyes open," said Daisy.

"Oh, yeah, the parents thing?" Cady said. "I clocked that."

"Clocked what exactly?" asked Charlie. Then into the silence that followed, "They are *my* parents, you know. I am still here."

"Not for long," said Ed refilling the kettle.

"What?"

"What my less subtle friend was trying to say was—"

"There's no way in hell they'll let you stay," said Ed.

"What!"

"Hey, when did you get all touchy-feely?" asked Daisy. "You're treading on my turf there, Eddie."

Ed huffed. "He couldn't even see them," said Cady. "He was round the corner."

"On his laptop!" said Daisy.

"Mmh-hmm," said Cady.

The kettle clicked in the silence.

"I'm still here," said Charlie.

Cady sighed, "You have much to learn young Padawan."

Ed glared at her.

"What?" Cady winked at Charlie, "He hates it when I quote *Star Trek*."

Ed coughed loudly.

"Not now." When Charlie cleared his throat, Cady said, "you either. No time." She pointed over Charlie's shoulder to the doors, where his parents were on the way back in. He didn't move. "It's make your mind up time, kid," she said.

Charlie turned his chair slowly as his parents bustled in.

"Come on, Charles," said his mother, "we must go!"

"You heard your mother, let's go!"

They both turned, not waiting.

"Why?" Charlie's voice was quiet.

"Sorry?" His mother stopped.

"Why do I have to go?"

"Let's not do this here," said his father.

"Why not?" asked Charlie.

"Okay." His mother raised herself to her full height. "Let's. I'm sure your new friends won't care, or even remember." She strode back towards him, "Because, darling, we want to do the best for you and this," she took in everything with a wave, "is not what's best."

Ed bundled past them to the toilet. Everyone stared at him, "What? I need to pee when I get nervous."

"You don't, though," said Charlie.

"Sorry?"

"You don't. Want what's best. For me I mean."

"I'm sorry, I don't understand."

"You want what's best for you! What looks best to your friends at the W.I and the golf club. You want to pack me off to some godforsaken boarding school again, so I'll be out of sight and out of mind."

"How dare you, you ungrateful—" She stood hands clenched.

"I'll be in the car," said his father quietly, and just as quietly, left.

The door hissed closed. She breathed out slowly.

"No," said Charlie.

"I beg your pardon?"

"No."

"Get in the car. Now." She walked back to the doors and half-turned.

"No."

"Don't 'No' me, young man. Get into the car." She reached out to touch the door handle.

"No. I'm staying here."

"But—"

"No."

"But why? Why stay in this dreadful place?"

"Because for the first time today, in this dreadful place, someone I'd only just met, asked me what I wanted. And you never have."

She opened her mouth. Then closed it again. "Okay then, Mr. Grown-Up Man. What do you want?"

"To stay here. I'm coming to school here."

"I won't hear of it!" she shouted.

Her hand fell from the door, as it opened away from her and the head walked back in, slowly, with a young woman about twenty in tow, "Everyone okay in here?" She took in the scene briefly, and before anyone spoke, "If I may, I believe we can come to a temporary compromise?"

His mother's hands sprang open, but Mrs Wintle carried on unabated, "We are in a fortunate position today, that one of our students has called in sick, last minute so we are surplus one staff member, as it were." She indicated the woman with a hand. The woman hid under her blonde fringe.

Mrs Wintle-White stared from under knitted brows. The Head looked back, mouth held flat, "You'd be doing us all a favour. Especially Liza here."

The bathroom door creaked, Ed poked his nose out. Neither woman broke eye contact. The door creaked shut again.

"There are a couple of forms to sign, just to cover today. Shall we?" said the head, gesturing to the door.

"Your father will pick you up tonight. We look for a new school for you tomorrow. We aren't done here, young man."

She swept through the door after the head.

They all watched the door in silence. It seemed to take forever to close. They were still watching as Bill shuffled up to join them. "'Soles," he said.

"Yeah," said Cady. Then to Charlie, "Sorry."

Chapter 5

Cady looked over the head of her mop and down the corridor at her opponent. Charlie had chosen Ed, who was fussing straightening goggles and tightening wheelchair straps, as his second. In her own corner was Daisy, ever steady Daisy.

"It's okay Cady, you got this," Daisy said.

"Right, everyone know the rules?" They were lucky that Johnny B the caretaker had a sense of humour. That being said, gossip was he was ex-special forces, so he didn't take any messing. And all the kit was his. "Best of three runs, hits to the body only. Above the neck is a foul. No hits or one hit each after three runs is a draw. And make it quick, it's only fifteen minutes till the bell goes."

Daisy adjusted the straps on Cady's goggles, straightened the bin lid she was holding and gave her a thumbs up.

"Ready?" said Johnny B. "Joust!"

Wheels spun and electric engines screamed at full tilt. Cady bore down on Charlie, eyes narrowed, flecks of water from the mop spraying in her face as she flew. She was by far the faster of the two. For all that her chair was ten years older than Charlie's, it had been tweaked within an inch of its life. She held the mop firmly and pushed her joystick to breaking point with her knuckles.

Ten metres, Charlie holding the same line as her, mop aimed high, but tucked right behind his bin-lid. Five metres, she could've seen the whites of his eyes, if they hadn't been screwed tight shut. Two: she'd be bound to hit him. One: no thud. She opened her eyes where she'd shut them reflexively. No, Charlie, the bastard, had jinked at the last minute and sped past her, but her mop was right on target. Speakman, the deputy head was square in her way. Shit, where had he come from? She let go of the joystick, but the floor was slick with water, even with the motor stopped, it was too late. She hit the middle of the deputy head's double-breasted suit with a wet thud.

She looked with horror from the mop, edged up into the thunderous face of the deputy head.

"Err... hi?" she managed.

"Cady Grey," he said, "my office. Now." He turned slowly and paced away.

Cady dropped mop and bin lid in the corridor, mouthed "Not over," at Charlie and turned to go.

****

She rounded the corner to the deputy head's office, only to find she'd been beaten to the door by the head, by the faint smell of posh soap, and the door was closing on a man she didn't recognise from the back. She raised her hand to knock but stopped. There was shouting from inside the office. She pursed her lips, twirled the chair round and parked it at the front of the row of heads office chairs, where there was a gap nearest the door, with her back to the wall.

"...thought we hadn't..."

More indistinct hissing. Like someone really cross not wanting to be overheard. Then muttering. For ages. Cady considered the idea of moving her chair, but being right in front of the door when it opened would definitely give the game away. She sighed.

"…doesn't work like tha…"

"What do you mean?"

"What do I *mean*?" Mocking tone to that.

"…t's be civilised, eh?"

"…for that!"

"You had no right!"

You always know you're at the end of an argument when you hear that, thought Cady.

She turned her chair off, then on again.

Something else was hissed in anger, and that seemed to be the end of it. She flinched as the door banged open, Mrs Wintle rushed out, without even seeing Cady and stomped down the passage in the direction of her own office.

The muttering resumed in a more muted tone. Then the door opened again, just a crack.

"We'll talk soon," Speakman's voice came from inside the room.

The mystery man made a kind of 'humph' noise, then opened the door completely. Now Cady could see him properly: sixty-odd, balding but no attempt at a scary comb-over, two wedding rings? One on each hand. An expensive but worn suit fronted with a plastic *visitor* badge on a red school lanyard and a faint slick of sweat on his forehead as he turned to face Cady. He took her in, head down and not chair up, she noticed, then clocked he was staring and half-smiled, turned on his heel and left. One more to come out. Cady sat tight. The bell for assembly went. She could hear rushing and shouting from the direction of the hall.

The door of the office opened. Speakman leaned out and stared up the hall toward the noise. Then he turned sharply to look at her.

"What are you still doing here?" he said. "Get to assembly." Then when she paused confused, "Go!"

She decided to head back the way she'd come and go the long way round to assembly. She didn't fancy Speakman's company all the way back while he was in that mood. Asshole could stew on his own. When she got back to the class, of course it was empty. She breezed through the other door without stopping, and made her way round to the hall. The head was waiting to go in and turned when she heard Cady's chair. Cady noticed her make-up was thicker than it had been this morning.

"In you go, Cady."

"Sorry, Mrs. Wintle, trouble again," Cady said.

"Don't worry about that, quickly now, everyone's waiting."

Everyone was waiting for the head, enough that they thought the door opening was her and not Cady. Everyone stared as she slowly maneuvered the chair down the aisle of the packed hall. She'd worry about how odd that was when she'd stopped wishing for the wood-block floor to swallow her up. She arrived at the back of the room.

"Chair off," whispered the gravelly voice of their class T.A, Mrs Balch.

Cady complied.

"Nice entrance," said Ed in her other ear.

"Piss off," she hissed back.

"Thank you at the back," said the head.

Cady flushed again. Then the head began to speak.

Chapter 6

Miss Wintle paced, head down, hands sometimes clasped, sometimes lose, fingers twitching. Cady scanned the room to see where Nasreen, the class teacher, and Linda the TA, stood. She caught Nasreen's eye and nodded towards Miss Wintle. Nasreen shrugged in reply.

The head looked up at the room full of people, thought better of it and looked down again. Cady noticed that Speakman was staring at her. Though, so was everyone else.

She coughed, "I'm sorry," she said, coughed again and behind Cady, Linda scuttled out of the door. "I have… er, some dreadful news. I…" Linda returned with a tumbler of water and took it down the side of the room to the head. "Thank you," she said to Linda.

"I… er. I'm afraid the school… the school is going to have to close."

There was a pin-drop moment, then gasps, moans, shouts.

"What the fuck?" Cady said to Ed, who was just sitting, wide-eyed.

"Language, Ms Grey," said Deputy Speakman.

"No, now's the time for language! Why?" shouted Cady.

"I- I don't know," said Miss Wintle, "perhaps we should all just give it time to sink in and then"— she took a handkerchief out of her sleeve, went to blow her nose and then just turned and walked out of the hall towards her office—"I'm sorry…"

Like quicksilver, Speakman was in her place, "Quiet! Quiet children. If you'll be quiet I'll try to explain. Quiet. Thank you. Right. If I may, I'll try and frame this and answer some questions,"

Cady's hand was first up.

"Yes, Ms Grey."

"Why?"

"Well," said Speakman, "the simplest answer is: we are a council-run and funded school. They have chosen to sell the land we are sited on. Ergo, we must close."

"What?" Cady said. "That's just crap."

"Please try and keep some decorum, Ms Grey," he said. Then, "and whatever your opinion on the decision, that does not change it."

The general level of noise rose again. Ed shouted over the top, "C- C- Can't. Can't appeal?"

"I don't think appeal is possible," said Mr Speakman, "the council has done what is called a compulsory purchase on the land. It is, as it were, a done deal."

"Bollocks!" shouted Cady.

"That's quite enough, Ms Grey. Out!" said Speakman.

She powered up her chair and turned it in its place then pushed her stick gently forward to edge towards the door. Her cheeks flushed. In the room, though, no-one noticed her departure. There was a rising level of voices, some students had stood, some were rocking where they sat. She passed Big Bad Bill slapping himself round the waist, hard, in a gross mockery of a hug. And the volume was rising quickly. Last in the row she passed a wet-faced Daisy.

"Quiet please, children!" Speakman tried to force his voice to carry without shouting.

"'Locks!" yelled Bill.

Cady drove out of the hall. The volume behind her rose so fast, if was almost like she wasn't getting any farther away. She wasn't sure where she was going anyway, Speakman hadn't said. She was buggered if she was going to waste her time sat outside his office again, he didn't really give a toss where she went.

"Quiet! QUIET!" yelled Speakman behind her, just above the noise. Cady couldn't help but smile. She rolled out into the hallway. Then she heard the sobbing. It led her across the hall to the main offices and reception.

"Miss Wintle? Are you okay?"

"Oh… oh o…, I, I'm f… fine thank you, C-Cady." Mrs Wintle blew her nose.

Cady sighed. "How long have you known?"

"I… it," Miss Wintle took a deep breath, "It. It has been. As much. Of a surprise, to me, as it has. To you."

"This morning then?" said Cady.

"Yes," she said. *Figures,* thought Cady,

"What happens to us?" Cady said quietly.

"The younger students will be found placements in other schools, some in mainstream perhaps, but—" It looked to Cady like she wanted to wipe her nose again, but her hands were shaking too much.

"But, what?" Cady said.

"You. The sixth form. Facilities there are… scarcer… you… will—"

"We'll what?"

"If you're in the realms of adult services, well then, the authority no longer has any obligation to find you a new placement. You'll be fine Cady, you're bright, you can turn up at the local college and they'll welcome you with open arms."

"And two flights of stairs," Cady said. "But sod me, what about Daisy and Bill? Ed even? He's not going to cope in all the noise of a mainstream college."

"I don't know, Cady, truly I don't. It's not my responsibility anymore."

"What?" Cady said. "You're just going to quit out on us? Really?"

Wintle gripped the edge of her desk, "Cadence Grey! I have given my all to this school. Twenty-five years of my life and all the blood, sweat, and tears one woman can put in in that time. I'm sixty-four, Cady. It's only two years till they'll retire me anyway, would have been next year if they'd not moved the goalposts, and I'm starting to feel it. I'm tired. I'm tired of all the paperwork, and the fighting for money, and hoarding the money, and inspections and courses, and the fighting, always the fighting. Well, I'm sick of it and I'm glad it's over." The tears were falling again, splashing onto the desk, but no sobbing now.

"But Miss Wintle—"

"Get. Out."

Cady powered her chair to face the door, opened her mouth to speak, then heard a massive howl from the hall. She covered her ears. Speakman was trying to use the hall P.A.

"BACK TO YOUR CLASSROOMS!" he yelled into the microphone as it howled. "ASSEMBLY IS OVER!"

Chapter 7

The door to the sixth form's classroom banged open and new boy Charlie sped out in his chair, pursued by Bill growling and brandishing a wooden chair by one leg. Bill nearly fell headlong over Cady's chair.

"Woah, there fella!" Cady said. Bill stopped short, the chair still over his head. "Rough morning there, mate?"

"Yeh," said Bill.

"Hmm. Put the chair down and stop chasing the new guy. He looks like he breaks real easy."

"'K," Bill, slowly lowered the chair and tried to back into the doorway at the same time. And so slowly. Hell, he had some strength in that arm.

"Where's your TA, hun?"

"H- haa-" said Bill.

"Still?" said Cady.

"Yeah," Daisy was behind her in the corridor, shepherding Charlie back towards the classroom, "it's chaos down there. TAs have been roped in as riot control."

"Best-stay-out-of-the-way type chaos, or better-go-and-help-out chaos?" asked Cady.

"I'd steer clear of this one. I think they've got it," said Daisy, "'Sides, Nasreen's not far behind me."

"So let's all sit the fuck down and pretend like nothing's happening then," said Cady.

"I couldn't have put it better myself, Cady, though I'd have used more eloquent language," said their teacher, entering the room. "Ed and Jasmine are on their way, so maybe we can get some work done?"

"What are we supposed to be doing today anyway, Miss?" Daisy asked.

"Well, we were going to do a trip out to town to the Farmers Market, carrying on with the nutrition unit, but in light of today's announcement—"

"Then, what's the point?" Cady twitched her joystick.

"I wasn't going to say that—"

"Elephant. Room. Why not? You keep saying we're all grown-ups here, treat us that way."

The door banged again and Jasmine entered, yelling, driven by Ed from the controller at the back of the chair. He shuffled her chair into the class, parked it up and beeped the control button to return control to its owner. "Sorry, Jazz," he said.

"Care to tell us why you were driving someone else's chair, Edward?" asked the teacher.

"I'm sorry miss, I had to. She was just driving round in a circle yelling 'Na, na, na!' Being in there was really winding her up. I just drove her out."

"Well you're all here now," said Nasreen. "TA's on their way back?"

"I think so." Ed furrowed his brow. "Linda was helping get year ten back to their classroom and Jenny has gone to the nurse. I think someone ran over her foot in their chair. What is going on, Miss?"

"I'm not sure I know myself Ed," she said.

"What have they told you?" said Cady, watching Nasreen's face carefully for a reaction.

"No more than they've told everyone." Nasreen had a good poker face.

"Well that sucks," said Cady. She noticed that Ed to the right of her now he'd returned to his seat, was sat feet tucked up on his chair, rocking gently.

"Yes it does, Cady, but what can we do?"

"We can't just sit and do nothing!" Cady said. "Can't you call your union?"

"Well, yes I suppose I could. I've never spoken to them before, except to join."

"Today might be a good day to make friends? I'm no expert, but I'm pretty sure announcing that everyone is sacked with no consultation and no notice is not okay?"

"But what can they do, Cady?"

"I don't know, do I? But it might, I dunno, buy us all some time—"

There was a crash. The door behind her slammed. Ed's class chair was tipped over and he wasn't in it.

"Is every day here like this?" Charlie looked bemused.

"Not most days, no," said Cady. "Today is proving trickier than average."

"Why don't I find that reassuring?" he said.

"You picked us, remember?"

"Yeah."

Nasreen sighed heavily and turned to Daisy, "Go and check if Mrs Balch is now free, then get her to go and look for her student. Once you've found her and delivered the message, return straight back here, please."

"Maam, yes mam!" Daisy said over her shoulder as she left the room.

The teacher then reached down onto her desk for the interactive white board controls, booted her laptop, turned to the screen and pointed at the slowly brightening text. The headline to the slide read, *Food Groups*

"Nuurh!" said Bill.

"Sorry, Bill?" said Nasreen.

"I think he said, 'death by PowerPoint, how jolly!'" Cady chimed in.

"Well if I'm going to be phoning unions, I don't want you lot swinging from the rafters while I'm gone," Nasreen waved her phone for emphasis.

"Point taken," said Cady.

Nasreen rifled through the drawers of her desk, stopped rustling, muttered and turned to the class, "I'll be two minutes. I need to find a number, there's one in the staff-room. Don't wreck the place. Cady, I'm leaving you in charge."

She wasn't even gone two minutes before she returned, mobile poked under her headscarf. When she looked up at the board, which was now displaying a game of mine sweeper, she sighed, breezed through the classroom and out of the fire door. They waited for it close behind her.

"Okay, my go," said Daisy and picked up the remote, stared at the screen thoughtfully, hovered the pointer on a blank space and clicked. "Phew!"

"Bill's go!" said Cady, picking up the remote. She pointed it at the first unflagged square. "There?"

"Nuh."

"There?"

"Nuh,"

"The-re?" Bill nodded, "You sure?"

"Yuh."

"Okay." She clicked. The screen went red.

"BOOM!" everyone chorused.

The door crashed back open, Ed rushed in, frantically waving a poly-pocket. He'd almost made it to the other side of the room and the fire-exit when he caught himself, "This, this, this, this, this, THIS!"

"What mate?" He was wafted it too madly in Cady's face for her to even see.

Daisy, nearer to the exit, snatched the flapping plastic and brought it and Ed back to Cady's desk front and centre, and laid it out.

"Look, look, look!"

"Okay. Give us a minute." Cady smoothed down the poly-pocket and then carefully removed the sheet of headed paper inside.

"Planning Site Notice," Daisy read aloud.

"Figures," said Cady.

"But look!" said Ed, "Look!"

"What?" Cady stared. "Ed, this'd be way easier if you calm down."

He tapped and tapped at the paper, "Read, read."

"Okay," said Cady, "But get yourself a glass of water, and sit."

"Okay! Okay, okay."

And Cady read, "So, Absdown Borough Council Planning site notice, blah, I give notice, blah, application number, blah, hybrid application.' What the hell is one of those? Applicant: New Day Limited.' Whoever they are. Proposal: Demolition, Change of use and see Hybrid application at site of former Parkfield Special Needs School. Wow."

"Cady?" Daisy put a hand on her shoulder. "What's that bit?"

"Oh, sorry. Blah, blah, inspect copies of the application and any other documents at 'Barnstone House, 1-4 High Street, blah, Monday to Friday, nine to five or view on line at blah.'"

"Sing out?" said Ed, now sat with his laptop open.

"Huh?"

"Url?"

"Oh. www.absdowne.gov.uk/planning," said Cady. "If you have any observations slash representations on the application, please forward in writing or via the website within 21 days of the date of this notice, quoting app number blah.'"

"What's the date?" asked Daisy.

"Third of Jan," said Ed between taps.

"Not today, you div," said Daisy, "on the notice."

"Oh, Friday 15th December, last year, obvs."

"How many days does that make?"

"Twenny," said Ed, still typing.

"Shit! What?" Cady's eyes went wide.

"Can they do that?" said Daisy.

"I think they have," said Cady, then to Ed, "any joy?"

"Looks simple enough. But it says if we'd like to object there's a meeting about it."

"When?" Daisy frowned.

"Today," Cady and Ed chorused.

Cady turned her head as she heard banging on the emergency doors.

"Coming miss," said Daisy, sliding off the desk.

Then the classroom door opened, with Linda, Jenny and Liza coming through.

"Change of plan, folks!" said Cady.

Chapter 8

Everyone looked at Cady. Nasreen was frantically scribbling on a piece of paper. The TAs began to get everyone settled. A small window at the centre of the whiteboard read. *Something has gone wrong. Would you like to continue or force close?*

"Get any joy from the union?" said Cady.

"They can send someone tomorrow." Nasreen blew her nose. "They were lovely."

"What did they say, though?"

"Well, basically, sit tight till they get here, but at least they can help negotiate terms with the council, for redundancy—"

"What? Can't they stop it? Do anything to stop it getting closed?"

"I don't think so, Cady. They were most worried that no-one had told them earlier."

"That's because this is getting rushed through," Cady said. "No-one was intending to tell them."

"We should get back to work now, Cady," Nasreen said.

"Yeah, we should, but nobody else is playing by the rules here. Why should we?"

"What do you suggest instead?" Nasreen repinned her scarf where the phone had pushed it loose.

"I suggest that some of us, at least, go to this meeting at the council and try and put in an objection or whatever?"

"I'm afraid I can't. I've got a parents' evening at my own kid's school tonight."

"It's at two," said Ed.

"Well then." Nasreen shrugged.

"Doesn't matter," said Cady, "some of us can go."

"I'm in," said Ed.

"Me too," said Daisy.

"Charlie?" Cady turned her head.

"I guess."

"How are you going to get there in school time?" Nasreen asked.

Cady pulled out her mobile. "Phone a friend."

"Wait," said Nasreen, but Cady had already started dialing and was making her way back to the fire exit. Nasreen carried on talking, but to everyone else, "How am I going to explain everyone's absence this afternoon, please?"

"School trip?" said Daisy.

"Yes, but we need forms and consents and a risk assessment—"

"Could just blag it," Ed grinned.

"What?" said Nasreen. "I'll get sacked."

"Gonna happen anyway," said Ed.

Nasreen's mouth remained open in a kind of silent scream. She flapped her hands to get Ed and Daisy to sit at least. Charles had slowly edged his chair to the back of the room where Jasmine's T.A and Ed's had lifted her onto a bright blue kind of trolley stretcher thing. Cady watched him as he stood in silence for a while, then ran his hand along the woven plastic, hanging under the trolley. When Nasreen spoke again, he jumped.

"Joining us Charles?" she said kindly.

"Sorry, yeah," he said and drove to the front of the class, past Bill, who was balancing his chair on the front two legs, Linda was whispering something in his ear.

Nasreen clicked at her laptop. After a loud *bong* from the classroom speakers a boot-up screen began. Nasreen drummed her nails on the desk. The computer chirped, then she clicked an icon and a slideshow started. The plain black text read, *A Balanced Diet.*

Daisy looked up, "My dad says, that's a pie in each hand."

Nasreen shook her head.

"Sorted," Cady said as the fire door closed behind her, "Dave Le Bus is gonna meet us at half-one and drive us down there. He's off this afternoon."

"Er, should I, er," Liza the TA pushed her glasses back up her nose, she was quietly spoken, so everyone turned to listen to her. "It's just I'm supposed to be looking after Charles today. The head—" Everyone waited for the end of a sentence, but none came.

"You'd better come with," said Cady.

"I don't want to get into trouble," she said.

"You're not here anyway?" said Ed.

"Well my person isn't in but—"

"No-one will notice." Cady grinned.

Nasreen sighed heavily from the front of the class, , "Can we get back to,"—she took in the projector display with her hand—"you know?"

"Sure," said Cady.

"Sorry," said Daisy.

Cady steered her chair back into place and powered down. She felt a foot in her back and craned her neck round, "S'up Bill?"

Bill growled.

"Wanna come too?"

"Uh."

"Hmm, will you stay put this time and look after Jazzy for us? Just until we know what's going on."

He rolled his head on his neck and stared Cady in the eye, "mmh."

"Cheers mate," said Cady.

"Can we?" said Nasreen, staring at Cady.

"Yep."

"So, what do we mean when we say a balanced diet?" said Nasreen. "And it's not as Ms Cohen suggested, 'a pie in each hand'."

There was a loud crash from the middle of the room and deafening shouting. Behind Cady, Bill lay on the floor chair alongside him.

"Oopsy," said Daisy.

"I did tell you," said Linda, going to help him up. "Can you…" She turned to Liza who rushed to her side.

"Is he okay?" Nasreen asked.

"Yeah," said Linda, "he went down sideways. Like a sack of spuds, bless him. You're all right aren't you, Bill?"

Bill giggled in reply. Linda waited until he was re-instated on all four legs of the chair, looked down at the laptop, sighed and prodded it out of screensaver.

"Sooo, what do we think balanced means?" she said.

A loud bell rang. The shuffling of chairs and shouting erupted from all corners of the school.

"For—" said Nasreen, holding up a hand. She swept a look round the class, then breathed out slowly. "Go."

Mayhem erupted. Charlie turned desperately toward Cady. She smiled and mouthed "break" back. He nodded. Bill and Daisy were at the door already.

"Don't forget, it's Home Ec after break so we meet back in the Zone, not here."

"The Zone?" Charlie looked bemused. More bemused.

"Where the cookers are," said Cady, "I'll show you. Come on. Daze'll have the kettle on by the time we get there and she gets all antsy if there's no-one to serve it to when the kettle clicks."

Chapter 9

"Are you sure about this Cady?" Liza asked from the back of the bus, as Cady thumbed the tail lift control.

The lift made the obligatory straining noise that it did whether carrying a hundred kilos or one. As the lift slowly reached deck level of the van, Cady looked at the edge of the lift and not Liza as she spoke, "Stop being a worry wart." She lifted her head as Liza started the process of strapping her in, "Ed and Daisy not on yet?"

"Ed's in the loo, Daisy's gone to see if he's okay."

"Can you two hurry up?" Charlie said from the back doors of the van.

"On my way fella," said Dave le Bus.

"We need to be quick, y' know, before—"

Charlie twiddled his power chair joystick back and forth, but went nowhere. A loud *ping-click* noise followed each tweak. He tapped his right foot, his trainers rattled against the straps. The *ping-clicking* continued.

"You'll shag your motor doing that, you know," Cady said, over her shoulder.

"What?"

"Twitching your joystick?"

"Oh sorry," Charlie said.

"Don't say sorry, your chair. Come on Ed, hold it together mate."

With a clunk of the controller, Dave brought the tail lift back for Charlie. The van was unusual in that it could take more than one wheelchair at a time.

Dave swore it'd take six if the seats were pulled out. Cady doubted that had ever been done. He always talked a good game. Cady puffed her cheeks and made a play of blowing her fringe out of her eyes, "About time too," she said.

Ed came through the side door, shortly followed by Daisy. He walked to the van head down, hoodie up: a Punisher one today. In his hand, he clutched the poly-pocket from the gatepost, with its notice still inside. Daisy was keeping a pace behind him and kept looking over her shoulder, back at the doors.

"Okay?" Cady asked as Ed pulled himself up onto the bus.

"Mm," Ed said.

"Do anything?" Cady asked.

"Nah."

"'Kay," she turned to Daisy. "We good?"

"Yup."

"Cool let's get the hell outta here, Dave."

Dave started the engine in reply as Liza finished with Charlie's seat-belt, when she had, she sat across from Cady, turned and looked right into her eyes, "I've got a bad feeling about this."

"Someone had to say it," Cady said flatly. The van lurched forward and they were off. "Anyone been to one of these before?"

"Father— Dad has," said Charlie.

"Any ideas what to expect?"

"I think council meetings are all different."

"They don't decide on stuff today?" Cady asked, frowning.

"They need all the councilors to do that. And I don't think the proles are allowed in to those. I think this is just about information," said Charlie.

The van jerked to a halt and stalled. Everyone was thrown against their straps, "Shit, sorry." Dave looked over at the team in the back and then back out of the windscreen. "Look where you're going, Mrs."

The engine whined as it re-started. Once it had caught and Dave signaled to move off, Ed, sitting in one of the two shotgun seats at the front, reached into the rucksack at his feet and produced a CD case. He leaned forward and put it into the slot under the radio. The soundtrack from *Pulp Fiction* blasted from the speakers. Liz winced, Cady tried to work out whether it was the whiplash or the swearing that was upsetting her, but the young TA had turned her head to the window. Streaks of drizzle flecked the windows. It always reminded Cady of that crazy Einstein relativity thing. She couldn't remember how exactly, maybe she would ask Ed when he was less edgy. He had his head down. She hoped he'd be okay.

"Nearly there, guys."

Out of the window Cady saw the large red-brown gothic monstrosity that was the Town Hall looming across the junction from them like the castle of some fairy tale evil baron. It certainly didn't scream bastion of local democracy.

The bus pulled up in front and came to rest along the kerb in front of the imposing front entrance staircase, and behind some kind of sky blue soft-top car.

"Nice wheels," said Charlie.

"New BMW 4 series MSport," said Ed, from under his hood. "It says 'trying too hard'. If he was properly well off he'd have a Porsche."

"He?" said Daisy.

"Yeah, number plate says SX18ANT. I'm guessing he's an Anthony. His wife chose the colour."

"You could tell all that from the car?" Charlie had his eyebrows raised.

"Yep."

Dave le Bus put the hazards on with one hand and the blue badge onto the dashboard with the other. He strode down the bus to the strapped-down chairs, indicating that Liza should help with a flick of his head. It was unusual for Dave to be so quiet. Liza began unstrapping her while Dave worked on Charlie. Cady nearly asked whether Liza thought Dave was all right, but one look at Liza's tense face and she thought better of it. Daisy stood up but with a curt "wait" sign from Dave she sat again. Only when he'd finished unstrapping Charlie, did he speak.

"Right. Liz, you stay on the back and I'll do the lift from the floor." Then, on his way out of the bus front door, he glanced over his shoulder to Ed and Daisy, "you two stay put until the chairs are at ground level."

When Cady got to ground level, Charlie was gawping at the massive sides of the building. This place was about imposing order not asking opinions. At least it had some hanging baskets on the lamp posts outside the front. Liz stayed with the two chairs while Dave went to secure the bus.

"Come on," said Cady searching for a dropped kerb as she passed Charlie.

"Careful," said Liza.

"Always careful," Cady sighed. "Come on, we can get up on the side while Dave's getting the other two out. Christ, where's the dropped kerb along here?"

There wasn't one so far as Cady could see, but there was a section of pavement where the kerbstones had collapsed enough from years of tread and badly parked vans, for them to potentially get a chair bumped up.

"This'll do!" Cady bumped her chair up.

"Really?" Charlie said. The chassis of his newer chair was lower to the ground. He squared his chair to the kerb, frowning as the wheels spun and he failed to gain purchase.

"Dude that chair's gonna be shagged before today's out!" Cady laughed. "Didn't you watch how I did it? Come at it sideways then jink up one wheel at a time. Jeez, you might be able to race, but you sure can't climb."

"I don't get out into town much," said Charlie.

"No," Cady turned her chair towards the entrance. By the time Charlie had gotten his chair up the kerb, the others were all stood in a row assessing the staircase in the thin drizzle.

"What's up?" Charlie asked.

"No ramp!" everyone else chorused.

"Tossers," said Dave. "I'll ask," and he started to climb the stairs, "you lot wait there."

Somewhere above them the Town Hall clock made muted bongs.

"Come on Dave, we'll be late," said Daisy.

"Technically, we are already late," muttered Ed.

Dave stuck his head back out of the doors, "Clerk says it's round the side of the building, tradesmen's entrance."

"And spazzers," Ed, started to climb the steps, towards Dave.

"Edward Buckminster!" said Daisy.

Cady and Charlie, followed by Liz, started to make the long trek round the side of the building.

Chapter 10

The meeting was already in full swing by the time they had located the lift to the second floor and then made out which room it was being held in, amid all the 'previous mayors' nomenclature. The heavy wooden door to this one was labelled *Blenkinsop Room* but it was the bored-looking council bod with the clipboard leaning on the wall who gave it away. He was not much older than Cady, with an ill-fitting suit. He scratched a spot on the back of his neck as Cady approached. She coughed, he jumped and stood straight.

"Is it in here, then?" asked Cady.

"What? Sorry?" the Council bod said. His lanyard read *Jack Hobbs, Intern, Planning Dept.*

"Is the planning meeting in here, Jack?" Cady repeated patiently.

"Oh, yeah, sorry. Can I take your names?"

Cady frowned.

"Please. It's for… well, I don't know what it's for but we're not allowed to send you spam or anything, and I'll get into trouble if I don't take everyone's name who's here." He looked pleadingly at Cady.

"Cadence Grey," she said. It seemed to give permission for everyone else, so as he wrote minimum details down—address and email—and fumbled with red visitor lanyards as they all complied. Ed indicated his need to go last.

"Mr…?"

"Duck," said Ed.

Cady coughed.

Jack wrote it down. "Initial?"

"D."

"Email?"

"Don't have one," Ed said.

"'Kay," said Jack listlessly. "Go on in, but try and be quiet, I think it's already started." He opened the heavy wooden door, which creaked its age. They filed in.

****

Inside was a long thin room, connected to another by the opening of a partition that was held wide for the purposes of the meeting. A projector screen on flimsy aluminum legs showed some version of 'awful corporate presentation'.

"Take a seat…er…come on in," said a reedy male voice, way too close to them to have come from the carpet-covered lectern next to the screen. The voice had come from—a large black imposing PA speaker on an equally black stand. Cady and Charlie shuffled to sit behind the last row of plastic seats before Daisy whisked three chairs away for her and Charlie to park alongside the last row. Dave and Liz sat at the far end, the rest of the students filed in. They filled most of the row. Directly in front of them, a bald chap in a business suit shuffled over seats to the aisle. Did she recognise him? Cady sighed. A lot of the folk in here were balding and in business suits, including the speaker.

"Are we all…er…good? As we were then, I am Councilor Carver." Councilor Carver wore a grey suit with sleeves that seemed to be vying to escape up his arms, exposing a gold-coloured watch matching a gold pinky ring. "For those of you that have just come in and I'm here to take you through the new development," he scratched his nose, "on site 11.7 of the council's current local plan. Slide please. Slide."

Cady heard a 'tut' from behind her and turned her head. It seemed Intern Jack had more than one string to his bow as he now sat behind a small table in the corner furnished with a laptop. He slapped at the keyboard. Ed winced. The new slide featured an over-detailed map of what appeared to be the whole town.

"Scanned in, tacky," said Ed, slightly too loud.
"Shhh!"
"It's only 'cos they can't use Auto-Cad," he said.

Daisy turned and glared. Ed shrugged.

It had labels and numbers aplenty, but none big enough to read. Carver wafted a hand at the screen and a red laser dot followed where he wafted.

"As you can see this is the area in question, near Parkfields, and not far from the hospital." The dot jiggled over a section of town where Cady thought the school should be. Instead on the plan, the place where it should have been was outlined with a thick red edge, slightly the wrong shape to be just the school, and in the centre of the area was a label—
11.7.

"So, zooming in to the block plan. Slide." Jack was a little more on the ball this time. Cady could still hear the *thunk* behind her.

The 'block plan' was definitely where the school was, or at least the front bit. What the back edge of the plan took in wasn't entirely clear, but the area on the bigger map in red, now seemed to have been sub-divided into three sections. It had been blown-up on a photocopier and someone with a fondness for highlighters had set to on it. It made the sections difficult to look at directly. Councilor Carver seemed eager to explain. Cady massaged her temples.

"So, as you can see the block plan adjoins the hospital site at the back edge, so all those parts labelled 11.7B. We'll come back to more of that later, but the front edge of the development, marked A here, would be given over to retail developments, badly needed for the residents of Parkfields."

"Nah we don't!" A woman's yelled from the front row. She had a fierce buzz cut, and a faded tattoo of two dolphins on the back of her neck.

A woman offstage to the right, coughed loudly and said in an R.P accent, "If we can leave questions till the end. Thank you."

"Shall we move on to the main thrust of the development?" In the front row three very trendily dressed folk shuffled. Carver looked down at them, "If you'll forgive me, we'll come back to your section after, if…ah, that's okay?"

They mumbled assent.

"For the purposes of this, may I invite up on stage the CEO of Absdale General Hospital Trust, Dr. John Dean."

Carver sat again, off-stage.

Cady's eyes glazed over. She could see everyone else on the back row was losing the will to live as well. It seemed 'the main thrust' as 'Carver' put it, was an extension to the hospital, more wards for some department or other. He seemed as though he was enjoying every second of his moment in the limelight. He wasn't that great a public speaker either. The woman Carver was sitting next to, where all the bigwigs seemed to be sitting was clapping a little too loudly when he said things like: "This is an expansion this town sorely needs, and I congratulate…"

One thing Cady did notice was the PowerPoint put together by the Trust bloke seemed to be way slicker than Carver's council version. It figured. The presentation seemed largely to consist of lots of space age-looking buildings with happy green space-age trees and happy smiling people. It seemed that in all of the pictures there was a striking lack of sick people. Perhaps the new magic buildings would somehow achieve that. Cady sighed and rubbed her face. When her eyes came back into focus, Carver was back on stage.

"As you can see," Carver said, "the whole development will see a massive improvement and consolidation in the Parkfields area, along with more new exciting facilities for the residents there, with a vital, life-saving expansion to the wards adjoining the site and the two departments aforementioned." He glanced around the room before continuing, "So if there are no questions we'll move to have coffee, then the architects have I believe set up some boards at the back of the room for people to examine the plans and visualisations at their leisure—"

Tattoos was on her feet like a shot, "I 'ave!"

Carver looked taken aback, he was clearly hoping she'd forgotten, "I'm sorry?"

"I 'ave."

"You have what, I'm sorry er…Mrs?"

"Ms," she said, "Belinda Smith for the Parkfields residents association, and yeah I've got a question."

"Ah, good," said Carver, in a tone of voice that implied anything but.

"What about all the building work?" she asked.

"What about it?"

"Well, how long's it gonna take?"

"In the region of twenty months, I believe, from the last set of project management updates, why?"

"What do all of us living in the estate do about all that mess and noise and traffic twenny-four-seven? We've got kids to get to sleep, husbands to get to work, mine works nights. Who sorts out that, then?"

"I think you'll find that's all been taken into account in the er…scoping and impact documents,"

"Where are they, then?"

"They are on the council planning portal, along with all other relevant information, anything else?"

"What about my mate Mabel?" said Tattoos. "She ain't got a computer?"

"Can she not visit the local library?"

"You've shut that."

"I meant the town library, sorry."

"You're jokin' aren't ya? She can't hardly walk down 'er stairs, let alone all the way to the bus stop."

"I'm sure she'll appreciate the new development's shops then," said the woman with the R.P accent, from the wings. "Can we move on to coffee? Time is against us, I think."

"Cee!" Ed shouted, now on his feet. Daisy clutched his sleeve, mouthing 'sit down.'

"I'm sorry young man?" R.P said.

"No, let him speak," a man's voice came from the wings.

"You didn't talk about 11.7C," he said. "What's that for?"

"That," said Carver, his ring glinting as he leaned into the microphone, "is a very good question." The offstage bigwigs seemed to be conferring. Carver went on, "However, it's laid out in better detail in the architect's drawings on the boards at the back."

"I think they're worried the coffee's getting cold," whispered Dave le Bus, along the row.

"Okay. I'll look," said Ed.

"Thank you," said Carver. He took a tissue out of his pocket and wiped his forehead. Cady didn't think the room was particularly warm. "Well if that's all?" said Carver.

Tattoos was in like a ferret, "No, it's not all!"

"Well," said R.P accent woman standing, and sweeping over in front of the lectern. She mouthed something to Carver on the way past. He nodded. "How about we set up a separate meeting to address the concerns of the Parkside residents in more detail? Then we can talk properly? Give ourselves a little space? We'll grab you after coffee and make a date?"

"Yeah, okay," Belinda Smith said.

"Splendid," R.P stood. Cady could see that R.P's skirt suit was expensive. Not Armani, but some designer that was super expensive. The skirt flowed like dark blue water and she looked at home in it. There was a loud clap and R.P spoke again, "So, on the subject of coffee and biscuits, let's break!"

The coffee was being poured at the left hand side of the stage. There was a low trestle that had either been there from the get-go or had been sneaked in while they'd all been looking at the stage. A large queue had already formed. Cady didn't have the stomach for hot drinks. She found she was the only one still on the row.

"You coming?" said Daisy.

"Oh. Yeah." Cady turned her chair slowly and crept the chair towards the large array of design boards and their cheerful sketches. Ed was already there, photographing on his phone for all he was worth. One of the young flashy-suits—Cady guessed, probably, what, architects? Designers, whatever, hovered a discreet distance from Ed. He leaned in to speak to Ed, before Cady got to them.

"It's all on the website, you know," The young-flashy-suit was early twenties, and spoke from under a hipster moustache.

"Yeah, but your website's shit," said Ed.

The man opened his mouth to reply, but Ed wiggled his phone in response.

"Oh, it wasn't optimised for…"

"Welcome to the twenty-first century," said Ed. He turned his back on the moustache and carried on taking photos.

Cady cruised in, clocked Moustache, smiled, shrugged and moved towards the brightly coloured boards. What the hell was going on here? The whole room was a melee of sights, sounds, and smells. She stared at the most basic version of the plan she could find, that hadn't been adorned by fake trees and fake people, and stared. She let her eyes defocus. What was it? What wasn't she seeing?

Ed waved in front of her eyes.

"Something's not right here," she said.

"No shit, Sherlock. Shall we go?"

"You got all you need?"

"All I can get from here, anyhow."

"Where's Dave and Liza?" Cady looked round.

"Biscuits, where do you think?" said Daisy.

"Nice way to spend tax-payers money," Ed said.

In a waft of expensive perfume, R.P accent was at Cady's elbow, "Oh, don't be like that. The biscuits are lovely and," she leaned over in a conspiratorial whisper, "we got the developer to pay for them. Fill your boots."

Ed shot off, coughing. Cady found she was clenched and slowly turned the chair round to catch Daisy's eye. Daisy signed #Go?

#Quick Cady signed back.

She turned and headed towards the door. Jack-the-intern had returned to the doorway with his clip board as they approached. Cady could hear Dave le Bus having a strained conversation on his phone in the corridor beyond them, Liza was herding everyone back from the biscuits.

Jack caught Cady's eye and smiled kindly, "Okay?" he asked.

"Yeah."

"Mind if I collect your email address?"

Her eyes widened.

"Y' know, for updates and stuff."

The rustling of packets heralded Ed and Liza's return, "Come on," Liza said.

"Can I get your email?" Jack whined weakly, now half to Ed and Liza as well.

"Bite me," Ed sprayed biscuit crumbs.

Daisy kicked Ed.

"What?" Ed turned his head. Biscuit crumbs fell in a slow arc. "I don't want their spam."

"Never mind, muppet" Daisy, hustled Ed out of the door. "Sorry," she mouthed to Jack-the-intern over her shoulder.

Lisa looked at her watch, "We should go back before we're missed."

"Bit late for that," said Dave le Bus, sighing.

Chapter 11

The atmosphere in the common room was electric. Cady had spent the afternoon in the deputy's study with Liza and Dave, trying to calm Speakman's ire about the whole situation. When she was dismissed, she was content that Liza and Dave were unlikely to be, at least for the time being. General studies had been canceled due to staff rearrangements, so they only had one forty minute period following afternoon break to wait until the bus bowled up. When Cady let her chair push the doors open for her, steam was rising from the teapot on the bar.

Charlie, surprisingly, was sitting in his chair, right next to the counter, mug in one hand, left foot extended in a stretch on one of the common-room's ratty pouffes. He smiled broadly at Cady as she entered.

"Well, you've made yourself right at home," she said.

"Have you heard the good news?" Daisy asked.

"No, do tell," she said.

Daisy turned her head to Charlie.

He said, "I'm coming home on the bus with you lot!"

"Oh?"

"Yeah, the head arranged it, she's amazing!"

"She has her moments," said Cady. "Where's Ed and Bill?"

"Bill's doing physio, Ed's in the cupboard," said Daisy.

Appearing right on cue, Ed stuck his head out behind Daisy. "I prefer H.Q," he beckoned her over.

"You want me to get in the cupboard with you?" Cady said. "Not. Happening."

"You might be surprised," said Daisy.

"That's what I'm worried about," Cady, drove over.

"I'll protect you," Daisy said.

Cady glared at her at that, but maneuvered round Charlie, and under Daisy's arm holding up the drop-leaf of the counter. Ed disappeared back into the cupboard. Daisy shoved a cardboard box with her foot to allow Cady a turning circle. Then Cady nosed the chair through the doorway, and her mouth fell open.

"You have been a busy boy."

Inside, what used to be the store cupboard, not a centimetre of bare wall space remained. There were photos pinned, blu-tacked and stapled left and right, diagrams of the school, town hall and a version of the block-plan occupying all of the facing wall from the door. At the far end of the cupboard and curling round onto the walls, was a rogues gallery of teachers, some of the people who'd been at the town hall meeting earlier, and people Cady didn't recognise. Overlaid on that was some kind of mental set of string, or wool, going from one picture to another, sometimes from one plan to another. It reminded Cady of that thing she'd seen on the internet of what a web looked like when the spider was on drugs. There seemed to be some sort of colour code, but she was beat if she could work it out.

"Come in then," said Ed.

"I'm a little worried I might garrote myself."

Cady edged her chair in slowly, behind her Daisy peered round the door. Outside in the common room she could hear Charlie driving up too. For a den, this was going to prove cosy. Ed stood in the corner. Somehow, he had perched his beloved laptop on a stack of cardboard boxes. God help them if they ran out of toilet roll. Or whatever was in there. A cable trailed to Ed's bag on the floor, which seemed to be buzzing and spitting paper out.

"So," Ed said. "Dramatis on that wall." He waved at the wall with the rogue's gallery photos on it. "Maps and planning docs there, of us and the town hall."

"Dramatis?" said Daisy.

"It means cast of characters" said Charlie, rolling into place in the doorway.

"Why a map of the town hall, too?" said Cady.

"Oh," said Ed, "it was on the same website."

They all looked at the walls in silence for a moment. No one dared ask about the multi-coloured string.

Ed broke the silence, "what am I missing?"

"A few slates?" offered Charlie. "What's all this on this wall?"

Charlie waved at the wall the door was in. It was filled with symbols, each on its own little card. He had a red rose, a yellow bird, a blue torch, a pound sign, an alien, a dagger, computers, dark glasses. Magical symbols—the works.

"Motives?" Ed muttered. "We can't leave anything out."

"Templars? Masons? Aliens?" said Charlie, "we can probably leave those out."

"He loves a good conspiracy, does our Ed," said Cady. She noticed that he'd circled the card bearing the classic Masonic set square symbol, and red strings led to more photos.

"Why are the school lot on here?" Cady had tweaked her chair over to look at the photos. The school lot in question included photos of the head, Deputy Speakman, and all of the governors. It turned out the chair of governors was the balding guy that Cady had seen exiting the deputy's office after whatever kind of row, and then seen again at the planning meeting. Ed had lovingly labeled each one with a Sharpie in his spidery hand. The chair of governors was *Stephen Longman.*

"I don't know yet," said Ed. "I was trying to put up all the people who would stand to lose out from this,"

"Or gain from it?" suggested Charlie.

"Yeah, maybe."

Cady's eyes fell on the picture of the councilor, stood at the lectern earlier in the day, hands gripping the sides. Odd ring on his little finger. She hadn't even seen Ed take that one. *Cllr Anthony Carver,* the label read. There was a bit of red string going back across the room and a bit of blue string going straight left to the annoying R.P-voiced woman from the meeting.

"Oh!" said Cady, "she's his wife!"

"Yeah," said Ed, "and she's minted. She's a Hartland, or was before she married Carver."

Cady frowned, "Should I know who they are?"

"Property," said Charlie, "massive estates all over the hill. Huge hall, deer and everything. Dad knows them. She plays golf."

"Not him?" asked Cady.

"Lord no," said Charlie, "our Mr Carver couldn't hit a horse's arse with a shovel, Dad says."

Cady noticed a group of photos was bounded by yellow wool. Very posed, shiny photos, except a couple that were clearly taken at the planning meeting. The whole box was labelled *Redwell Developments*. String led from that to a file card on its own, pinned to the wall that read *New Day*. Cady prodded at it and then at Ed.

"Dunno," he said, "A shell company of some sort? I need to do a bit of poking at Companies House, cos I'm buggered if I'm paying for downloads."

Cady assumed, poking meant some kind of hacking activity that she preferred not to know about. Behind her Daisy hummed, she was staring at the blow-up of the block plan, a jigsaw of A4 sheets that Ed had drawn around the edges of in red to make it look like the one they'd seen in the presentation. "What's this say?" Daisy indicated a smudge on the plan in the middle of the 11.7C area, just under that label.

"A mark on the plan?" said Ed, "Pencil line maybe? Dunno, some of the bits lost quite a lot a definition when I blew them up. Lemme look again on the website. It's a scan on there, a version of the massive plan they've got in their office I expect."

He made a few stabs at his keyboard and screen and brought up the plan, then the area in question. Muttering, he called up another window with image manipulation software. He battered away at that for a few more minutes.

"Anyone mind if I put the kettle on again?" asked Charlie.

"Be my guest," said Daisy.

Outside, they heard the voice of Big Bad Bill's TA, Linda Balch, "Hellooo! Anyone in here?"

"We're in here," Cady shouted from the cupboard. "We'd run out of tea bags!"

Charlie looked askance at her and she shrugged, mouthing "what?"

"Want a brew, Linda?" Daisy, backed out hastily.

"That would be lovely dear," she said, "I expect Bill will have one too?"

"Yuuh," said Bill.

"Bit of a rough time in physio, lovely?" asked Daisy.

"Nnnh," said Bill.

"I don't think they went particularly easy on him, poor love," said Linda. "Did they, mate, eh?" She led Bill to an orange armchair, which he gladly flopped into. He winced as he sat.

Daisy started pottering around what she considered to be her little kitchen. Linda raised her chin in the direction of the open store cupboard door, "There's no crafty snogging going on it there is there? I know what you teenagers are like. Do I need to come in?"

"No!" said Cady, horror-struck. "We're coming out." She started backing her chair out, but Ed's hand on her arm stopped her.

"Wait!" he barked.

"What?"

"Look at this."

In the image manipulation software a massive *11.7c* was sat above centre in the screen. Below was a blown up version of the smudge that Daisy had spotted.

"What am I looking at, exactly?" Cady asked.

"I think it's rubbing out," said Ed.

"Can't be it's in pen, surely."

"But look, there's shadow on it, indents, I've enhanced them as best I can on here. And see how the smear is a slightly different colour from the paper?"

Cady looked. The smudge was positioned exactly below the numbers in the middle of the page. And was roughly the same width top to bottom, as the numbers visible above.

"Correction fluid," Cady quietly backed away from the computer and running her hand over the spot on the main map.

Daisy served tea and they sat huddled at the end of the common room, Linda talking conspiratorially to Bill. Cady stared at the curl of steam rising from the jug with her tea in. She rummaged in her bag her for a tube-feeding kit and then fumbled under her T-shirt to connect it to her port. She paused and looked across at Ed, "Do you really think Carver is—? A mason I mean?"

Before he could answer Charlie jumped in, "Or perhaps he's an alien, wooooh!" Everyone laughed at that. Except Ed, who slammed his tea down, grabbed his bag and stormed out.

"Oh Ed!" said Cady, "We were—"

But Ed had gone.

Chapter 12

Cady called Ed the moment she got home. Straight to messages. She texted him, Msgr'd him and Whatsapp'd him. He was clearly having a full-on meltdown. That could mean anything, smashing stuff, hurting himself, running away. With no sign of her dad, she made two cups of tea, one half-full to go in her joystick hand, and went to find him. The garage was the best bet since there were tinny radio sounds coming from there. She turned her chair to the door number three from the kitchen—door one from the hall and door two out to the garden. Of all the doors in the house, the one out to the garage had the smallest handle. Dad had been saying he'd fix it since Mum had left. And the squeaky back door. And that drippy tap in Cady's bedroom. She had to put her tea down on the kitchen table, go back and click the door open, go back for her tea and push the door the rest of the way with her chair, being careful not to slop any when she and the door met.

"Hey Dad!" she called out through the blare of Radio 6. No answer. There was a large tan-coloured Range Rover up on the small ramps in the middle of the large garage, as she rounded the corner of it in her chair, she could see two Converse sticking out from two blue overalled legs, which were themselves stuck out from under the car. She had to stop the chair, as his legs were right across her path. She made space on the workbench for her tea amongst the strewn tools—Dad was never a tidy worker—put her cup down and slapped the top of the faux-old radio.

"Tea up!"

"Nice," her dad said, from beneath the car. "You're a lifesaver." He shuffled on the wheelie board and an open hand emerged. Cady reached down in a well-practised move, gripping the cup from the top and leaning over the chair edge to her dad's waiting hand.

"Cheers love."

He retreated back under the car, "Nice day at school?"

"So, so."

"Eww man! There's no sugar in this, Cade."

"Make it yourself next-time."

Her dad muttered something that could've been *tetchy*.

More clanking came from under the car and a slight shift in where the inspection light was shining. Then a stream of curses.

"Shit. Pass me a twelve love, please."

"Sure," Cady rummaged on the bench, found a spanner and leaned over the chair, again tapping the spanner on the sill of the car.

"Careful you don't scratch it. This is old man Webster's car, you know how protective he is. Besides, that turd-coloured 80s Rover paint is a pig to get hold of these days." Retrieving the spanner, he disappeared under the car again. There was a *thunk*, followed by more swearing. "Concentrate, love. That's not a twelve, it's a ten."

"I can't concentrate, piss off and get your own!" she shouted, and drove back out towards the kitchen.

"Cady? Oh, Cady love," but she'd gone

By the time she'd made a peanut butter sandwich from the stuff in the kitchen, her dad had emerged from the car and the garage, brandishing a rag that was getting increasingly less white by the second. "What's up, lovely?"

"Nothing. I'm fine."

"Yes. Yes you are. I can see that." He threw the towel over the back of a kitchen chair.

Cady twitched. "I've told you a hundred times, put the sodding towels in the basket. It's not hard."

"Yes, Mum."

"And don't you dare bring Mum into this."

"Sorry, tactless."

"Yeah?"

"Look, we can do this the hard way or the easy way, Cade. I can wind you up till you crack and tell me what's bothering you, or you could just tell me."

"What do you want for tea?" she asked.

"Just chuck some pizza and a handful of chips in and stop changing the subject."

"I don't want to talk about it."

"I'm gonna guess, boys?" Cady tutted. "A boy?"

"No. Ed. Well yes, of course he's a boy, but not a *boy.*"

"Oh Ed. Right. How is Ed these days?"

"Today? Pretty shit."

She turned her chair away toward the back kitchen door and opened it. *Stupid inward opening doors. Why can't all doors open outwards?* She was headed out the door with her sandwich, when she thought better of it, turned her chair round and headed to the eye level oven to turn it on. She snagged chips and some kind of meat feast from the upright freezer and rooted round in the cabinets either side of the oven to find a couple of baking trays. She started in on the unopened bag of chips with her teeth and some pulling, too lazy to go all the way across the kitchen to get scissors. Teeth would be fine. The bag gave suddenly and sprayed chips everywhere, floor, chair.

"No, no, No! Everything's trashed now."

"It's fine sweetheart, they're just chips."

"It's the last bag," she said.

"There are shops. Some of them even deliver."

Cady's phone beeped from her bag, down the side of her chair. She jumped, then checked the text. *Daisy. Crap.*

Hey, texted Daisy.

Hey. Have you seen Ed since school?

No. I thought he'd gone home.

Well yeah, but I can't get him on his phone.

Prolly avoiding you.

Yeah.

C.U tomoz.

Ping me if you hear, ok?

Her dad had gone and got the dustpan and brush from the cupboard under the stairs and was busy sweeping up the chips when Cady had finished the brief exchange.

"So, the suspense is killing me, what happened to Ed?"

"I did," said Cady.

"I find that hard to believe."

"Well. Believe it."

"What happened exactly?"

"Well we were noodling on the internet and Ed made some kind a reference to freemasons and we all took the piss out of him, and he got upset and ran out of school, and we think he's gone home but we can't tell he won't answer his phone or anything."

"Oh. Okay. Well, we all know Ed."

"Yeah, we do Dad, that's what's worrying me. With Ed, when he gets over his head it can go either way."

"Mmm."

"Remember last time when that hopeless know-it-all TA started? When he ran home that time it was a hospital visit and he wasn't back at school for a week."

"Okay, we'll think of something."

Cady had rolled and was in the process of lighting the kind of super thin roll-up that only comes from practice. As it lit, she blew her first puff out of the back kitchen door. Dad hated the smell of smoke in the house. Despite that, Cady felt his hand on her shoulder and looked up.

"Want me to give his folks a bell and check in?"

"Aw man, would you?"

"Sure."

"You are a gem, Daddy. Sorry I shouted and gave you poisonous tea." Cady couldn't put a hand on his with the cig she was holding so she scrunched her shoulders up instead, a kind of shrug hug.

"That's okay kid," he said and left for the phone in the hall.

Cady looked out into the murky sky. The weather was so shot, it was difficult to tell what season it was. She flicked the kitchen light off so she could sit in the doorway in relative dimness. It suited her mood. Only the occasional drag of her rolly lit her face. She spat out a stray tobacco flake and stared into the gloom. A bird flew past, even darker black against the black of the sky. It made a mournful squawk. She wasn't great at animal I.D. That was Daisy's bag. She took a last drag, extinguished her cig between her fingers and flicked its corpse into the garden, to join its friends. It was lucky Dad wasn't that house-proud.

She heard the clunk of the phone hitting its cradle, "Soo, he's fine," said Dad.

"That sounds like, 'he's fine—but," said Cady.

"He's up in his room, his mum's been in to see him and proffer drinks, but she says he's in 'Flat food place'?"

"Yeah, that means he's in computer world and he only wants flat food shoving under the door," Cady smiled.

"And that's okay, because?" said her dad, raising an eyebrow.

"Because the alternatives would be much worse. We're good I think. I should go see him."

"Will he be okay with that?"

"I'll only know when I get there."

"You haven't had any proper tea yet."

"Karl Marx says it's theft, you know that."

Dad huffed. Cady grinned.

"Tell you what, if you chuck me a tenner, I can go past the chippy on the way to Ed's and I can take some with me."

"Shrewd," said Dad.

"You taught me well."

"You wanna lift up there?"

"Nah, I'll be fine, it's only half an hour. You're only offering because you want chips anyway."

"Maybe."

"Think of your waistline."

"Huff."

The Wheels of Cady Grey

Chapter 13

Ed's house was at the top of the hill from the estate where Cady and her dad lived. Luckily for Cady's plan, the chip shop was on the way. Her chair would do twenty miles on a full charge and she'd hardly been five today, her battery readout was still showing green so she didn't have that to worry about, less still since it had stopped raining and now the broken, angry orange of a sun was trying to set, despite the clouds.

Since the chippy was nearer Ed's house than Cady's, the plastic bag on her legs was still warm when she got to the massive paved driveway of the Buckmaster residence. She drove up to the door and reached behind her seat to the basket strapped to her wheelchair where she stored stuff. Holstered there was a three-foot long plastic grab arm that Cady pulled out. The Buckmaster bell pull was eye level for someone five-foot tall. Cady pulled it with the grab arm. The curtains twitched. Then she heard steps in the hallway. The door was opened by Jean, eyes all crinkled with the huge smile she had for Cady.

"Hey lovely," she said, "Ned's round back, I'll unlock the side gate."

Cady waited at the gate into the garden until she heard the clunking of bolts and unlocking of padlocks.

"Can never be too careful round here," Jean muttered and lifted the latch.

"I don't think you need to worry, Mrs B. Most burglars'll be killed off by your hill." Cady looked back down towards the estate and saw the street lights twinkle, even from there.

"He's in the den," said Jean. "Mmm, those chips smell nice."

"Present for Ed I'm afraid. Thanks Mrs B, I'll find him."

'The Den' was once a second lounge-cum-dining room with massive patio doors that opened onto the garden. Now full length green curtains screened the interior of the once airy room from view, and it was the workroom, playroom and bedroom of Edward Buckmaster. Cady rolled the chair up and knocked on the glass with the grabber arm.

"Knock, knock Ed!" said Cady. "I've brought chips."

"Beware of Greeks bearing gifts!" he shouted from the other side of the glass. He must have had an air vent open as she could hear him from outside the double glazing.

"I'm not Greek."

"Point."

"Let me in, you tit, before these chips go cold."

He clunked the door open and slid one pane to the side with a hiss. Then he clanged a portable metal ramp into place down onto the decking.

"Come."

She slid along the drawbridge, and with her non-steering hand, held the plastic bag containing the two portions of chips ahead of her with the grab arm, "Peace offering!"

Ed approached the bag carefully, sniffed around it, then prodded it. "Offer accepted."

"Sorry for being an arse," said Cady, once she'd levelled her chair into Ed's musty-smelling room.

Ed sat in a massive leather office chair with more wheels than made sense, turned on a massive monitor in the middle of his tech desk/nest and beckoned Cady over, "Apology accepted, momentarily."

He bustled her farther into the room, then, with great pantomime, went back to the patio doors, pulled in the chair ramp, looked both ways out of the door, closed it, and then the curtains. Cady shook her head. Ed glared back. It was pretty muggy in the room with the curtains shut. She felt a small mercy that the smell of the salt and vinegar drowned out the smell of circuit boards and boy.

The monitor was massive but old, and whined and complained its way to full speed. When it had finally settled, Ed adjusted a knob to improve the contrast and then rustled in the chip paper, now on his knee, produced a chip and flourished it. "Observe!"

He clicked an icon and a program churned onto the screen via various starting filler bars and whirly icons. Clearly Ed was going to make her wait. He at least threw her the second packet of chips. She peeled it open, after scavenging the abandoned plastic bag from the floor to keep the grease off her jeans, and tore into it. She had her mouth stuffed full of chips when the file that Ed was interested in opened in a window centre screen.

"See?" he said.

"Mmm-ff?" She was looking at one of the pictures Ed had taken on his phone at the council meeting.

He zoomed the window. All Cady could see was some gold and blue and flesh colours in a big blur, "What about now?" he sighed heavily.

"Nope," Cady said. She gulped down her chips, then. "What exactly are we looking at?"

Again a huge sigh from Ed, "Let's start from the beginning. The original picture of Carver. At the lectern. Where we watched him talk." A bigger version of the original picture, not too blurry.

"Right?" said Cady.

"Ok, good. Now look at his hands."

He gripped the edges of the lectern with his greasy sausage fingers. His posture said nervous, all the time his words and slides said otherwise.

"A bit white knuckles?" she said.

"Yeah, well spotted, but that's not what I mean. Look more closely at his left hand."

"Ring?" Cady said.

"Good," said Ed, "But look where it is. A pinky ring. In the UK? Is unusual, *non*?"

"Er, I guess?"

"Now back to exhibit A," he drew her attention back to the first picture. Cady could see now from the colours that it was a blow-up of Carver's left hand on the lectern. "And that's the ring. See?"

"It's a bit blurry."

"Yeah, it's quite zoomed-in. Look what happens when I ramp up the contrast though."

Some darker blurs came a bit more into focus on the gold bit where Cady assumed the ring was. It was difficult to tell. And staring at it harder just felt like one of those 3D pictures that Cady could never get to resolve into anything. Ed called up another window, this time of a very clear ink line drawing of a familiar looking angular logo. There was a passing resemblance in the shape, but Cady thought of that cloud game where one of you found a patch in the sky and said Dragon where everyone else said Dog eating a banana.

"It's not all that clear, Ed."

"Which is what I thought you'd say, which is why I followed him home. That sky blue soft-top Beamer we saw at the Town Hall? It's his, and I pinched Dad's camera, since it's a bit more jazzy and it's got a zoom lens and thirty odd thou mega pixels so it was ideal and Dad never uses it, you know, retired man's tools and all that."

"Christ, that escalated quickly," said Cady, rubbing her temple.

"What?"

"Well, you went from, thinking Oh he's a bit odd, to FOLLOWING HIM HOME AND SPYING ON HIM? That's quite a leap."

"Will you just hear me out?" said Ed.

"Then will you listen to me?" said Cady.

"Okay. I'll be quick."

"Good, because you're starting to scare me."

"Right. Look," another photo. Phone camera and the scene outside the Town Hall again, but with the van from school and the Blue BMW soft-top in shot. "That's outside the Town Hall."

"Yep," said Cady. She drew another chip from the packet, they were starting to get cold.

"This is him getting out of the same car, at his house, with Dad's camera." No doubt in the hi-res photo, it was Carver and his car.

"Okay."

"And now zoomed right in on his hand as he's opening the door."

And the hi-res did it's magic. He opened the door with the key in his left hand and there was the ring. The logo was identical to the one from the slide.

"So that tells us what? He's got a house and a ring."

"It tells us he's a Mason, Cady."

"WHAT?"

"Look at the logo. It's a Masonic logo."

"It looks like the other logo, if that's what you mean."

"Don't be obtuse Cady. Look, here's the Wikipedia page on Masons. All this stuff is well known."

"Okay, okay," she said, "it looks the same."

"It is the same, Cady. Therefore, he's a Mason."

"Okay, let's accept that he is for a moment: so what? What does that tell us? So far as I understood it you're allowed to be a Freemason in this country without falling under investigation."

"Yeah, but it's weird right? Don't you think we should check it out?"

"You've already spied on this guy's house, Ed. This is nuts. It's, I dunno, harassment or stalking, or something."

"So you think we should, what? Just bowl right up and ask him, 'excuse me Mr Carver sir, but we know you're up to something, mind awfully telling us what'?" said Ed, scornfully.

"No not that, but…"

"So what, then?"

"I don't know. What are you suggesting we 'check out'?"

"The Masonic Lodge. See if he turns up there?"

"That'll take all year."

"Nope. Won't. They meet up regularly on Wednesday nights. If we asked Dave, could borrow the bus and we could go after school tomorrow evening."

"You're insane. This is insane."

"But will you?" said Ed.

"No!" said Cady. "Absolutely not. No."

Chapter 14

The school bus sat in a dip between two street lamps, on Corporation Street, diagonally opposite where the entrance to the Masonic Lodge Car Park stood. Dave le Bus was terrifyingly more than keen to help out. It did result in a tense moment in the supermarket petrol station when Dave won the argument about whether timing for that was perfect. It was decided that taking the van home to fill it up was more important as an alibi, but Ed was beside himself by the time they got there. Cady looked at her watch—10.00pm and they'd been there an hour already. She gave Ed a gentle kick in the leg he was twitching.

"What?" asked Ed.

"You'll never take a photo of anything with that jiggling going on, you're driving me round the bend."

"Shush, you two, if you yell the place down bickering, we'll get caught," said Dave. "Quiet on a stake-out. You never watched *The Sweeney*?"

"The who?" asked Cady.

Dave sighed, "Kids."

Cady scratched her neck. Ed had insisted they all dress in black. The nearest clean thing Cady could find was a black woolen turtle neck that she was now regretting. Ed was tapping his foot again. He gazed down the viewfinder of the DSLR and tweaked the zoom lens.

"It's definitely his car. I could tell that tacky soft-top anywhere. It's just I can't get his number plate in from here, he's parked at the wrong angle."

"Do we need his number plate?" asked Cady.

"Leave it out!" said Dave.

"You're enjoying this too much," Cady shot back.

"Seriously though, if you're trying to collect evidence. It needs to be, y' know, evidence-y," said Dave.

"Urrhgh," Ed started unscrewing the zoom lens.

He fumbled in his rucksack and began unzipping and zipping up various lens bags. He screwed a short lens back onto the camera and removed the lens cap. Cady looked skywards, then back at her watch.

"The near up lens is gonna help why? Oh, wait no, no. No!" Cady's hand flashed out towards Ed's collar, but he swerved and was at the dash, banging the button. "We're supposed to be low, oh what's the use—" But Ed was gone out of the van and into the night.

"Trust him, he'll be fine," Dave closed the van door by hand so it didn't make a noise.

"Huh."

"He's a big boy now," said Dave.

"Yeah, you'd think."

The porch lights at the front of the building came on—ninety degrees round the side from the car-park, but Dave swore anyway and muttered something about needing coms next time they were out on a job. The front door opened enough to let someone out, and a tall figure in a long dark coat came out and stood beneath the overhang. After a very long thirty seconds, the person dug into their pockets, a cigarette flared into life and the smoke puffed out, spiraling into the lamplight. Cady twitched and slapped her jacket pockets suddenly, then relaxed. She fished out a tin and began the ritual that accompanied it.

"If you light that up in here, I swear I'll stub it out on your nose," said Dave.

"Killjoy."

"Seriously though, if you light up in here, someone will smell it tomorrow and I'll get sacked."

"Ok, keep your pants on. Jeez, this stake out shit is boring. Can I get out now?"

"No." Said Dave.

"Come on," Cady whined, "Ed got out."

"Ed didn't need the ramp lowering, with all the shenanigans that ensues."

Cady glared at him. Dave shrugged and proffered a tube of mints by way of apology.

"Filthy habit anyway," he said.

"Listen," said Cady, "if I get old enough for cancer to kill me, I'll consider that a result."

Now it was Dave's turn to stare. Cady held his gaze, daring him to reply. He opened his mouth, thought for a second, put a mint in it from the tube that was still pointed at Cady, closed his mouth and returned the sweets to the glove box. He slammed it shut. "Ed's coming back," he said.

Cady peeked over the dash to see the porch light was out and the dark figure had gone. *Small mercies.* Ed still took the longest possible route back to the van, trying and failing to appear nonchalant on the way. Dave kicked the panel in the right place and the door hissed open.

"Well done, Secret Squirrel," said Dave.

"Who?"

"Never mind. Did you get something?"

"Yeah," said Ed, "but I had to crouch down until that guy had gone back in from his smoke break. This is okay though, you can see the car and the hall in the background. Could do with a shot of him getting in though really."

"Aw man, how long do we have to stay here?" said Cady. "I'm starving and I'm desperate for a smoke."

"Look," said Dave, "if you can wait ten more minutes, the pub'll be kicking out and we can go to the kebab shop on the corner under cover of loads of people moving. Can you hang on that long?"

"Ye-ss," said Cady, sullenly.

"If you're all good, I'll treat you to kebabs. We happen to be having a stake-out right near the finest Lebanese take-away this side of… of… "

"Lebanon?" said Ed.

"Technically, should be a lamb-out if it's kebabs," said Cady.

"I think your Dad might want that joke back," said Dave.

They waited for the last fifteen minutes in silence, save for the occasional *clunk* as Ed kicked the seat in front. Cady booted her chair up, when she saw the first person leaving the pub just up the road.

"Just wait till this first guy passes us," said Dave, "then we'll dive out."

The guy in question meandered towards them, and then past. Then Dave hopped out of the passenger door after Ed and they both worked at the tail lift to get Cady down. By the time she was at ground level, a couple were having an impressively noisy row while they walked down the middle of the road. They used that as their cover to flee up the road to the all night take-away. Dave was not wrong about the kebabs. Cady was lost in bliss. Ed chewed thoughtfully on his, though he'd elected to have the chicken instead of the stunning gyros. Ed feared eating anything he could not immediately identify. Likewise, where Cady had her pitta rammed to bursting with whatever salads and sauces the girl serving behind the counter was prepared to put on, Ed had opted for lettuce, no sauce, no mayo. He still seemed to be enjoying himself. They sauntered back along the road, but weren't even halfway through their kebabs by the time they returned to the van. Ed laughed, a sharp bark.

"Unlucky," Ed said, "you got a ticket, Dave."

"A ticket? This time of night? You've gotta be joking." Dave walked round to the front of the van, where, sure enough there was a white envelope under the windscreen wiper. He put the kebab in his mouth to free both hands, the easier to free the offending article. Dave froze. The kebab fell from his mouth with a curse. He pocketed the envelope, opened the driver's door and started the engine. He ran to the back of the van and battered the tail lift down.

"Get on the van," Dave said.

"I've not finished my—"

"Get on, *now.*"

Cady ran the chair onto the ramp, Ed heard the urgency and helped. Dave slapped the tail lift control box into Ed's hands. Cady had to close her mouth: Dave never let anyone else control the lift. Cady heard the lift whine as Ed punched the control button for up as Dave slammed into the driver's seat.

"Come on, come on, come on!" Dave drummed on the steering wheel.

"Christ Dave we're hurrying," said Cady. The lift reached the floor of the van.

"Wait," said Ed. "I need to strap Cady in."

"No," said Dave. "Stow the lift. And hang on."

Cady heard the crash and thud of the tail-lift and the doors behind her, then Ed swung into the side door the doors and slammed them shut. Dave screeched the van out onto the road and into the night. Ed fell on his ass and hoped Cady still had the power on, on her chair. If it rolled back, he'd be crushed.

"Dave," shouted Cady, "What the—?"

"Shut up, keep your heads down and let me drive."

"What the hell is wrong with you?" said Cady, "It was only a ticket."

"No. It wasn't," said Dave reaching into his inside pocket for the envelope with the van swerving while he did. He brandished the small white thing in the air. "It's a letter, Cady. And it's addressed to you."

He flicked the envelope down the van at them. It overshot the chair, dinged off the roof and fluttered down between the chair and the doors. She heard Ed swear as he picked it up behind her.

"Lemme see," she said.

Sure enough the small, expensive, very white envelope was written on in a very beautiful cursive script, with a fountain pen, oddly in brown ink. *For the attention of Ms Cadence Grey.*

"Shit."

Chapter 15

The three of them sat huddled in the snug of The Feathers, a particularly ratty hostelry on the edge of town that used to be frequented by market traders before the market had been closed and the site had become wasteland 'ready for development'. It was still open by dint of the fact that it was Karaoke night. In the main lounge, a drunk woman was caterwauling her way through, *Rescue Me*. Cady wished someone would. She turned her chair off.

"What are you drinking?" asked Dave.

Cady pursed her lips. Ed looked at Dave blankly.

"Look, I've already stolen a bus and participated in spying on some random guy with two students out of school who are underage with no chaperone. They can only sack me once. Do you want a drink or not?"

"JD and diet coke," said Cady.

Ed wrinkled his nose and then said, "Cider. A pint. Please."

He went to the bar. Cady reached down the side of her seat where she'd slid the envelope. Ed shuffled awkwardly on the ancient cushioning of the railway carriage style bench seat. It released a cloud of dust smelling of cigarettes, vinegar and despair. Ed was still trying to get comfortable and Cady was still staring down at the unopened envelope when Dave returned from the bar carrying four drinks in his hands and a packet of nuts in his mouth. He placed a drink in front of himself and Ed, another in front of

Cady and the last he placed in the middle of the beaten brass table top.

Ed looked at the fourth pint, "We expecting someone?"

Dave dropped the nuts onto the table from his mouth, snorted and downed the pint in front of him.

Cady sat in silence staring at the envelope.

"And the nuts?" said Ed.

"In case we get beamed up. It feels like that kind of a night." Then to Cady, "You gonna drink that?" When she didn't reply he flagged his hand in front of her eyes and she started.

"Sorry," she said, placed the envelope carefully down on the table and swigged at the JD and coke. She suspected Dave had bought her a double. She returned the glass to the table, noticing that she'd dripped on the envelope. A small bloom of brown ink was spreading out from the ts of *attention*.

"Shit, have I got to open it for you," said Dave, reaching across. Cady raised a hand and he stopped.

She picked up the envelope and gingerly unstuck the envelope flap with her finger.

"God, I bet Christmas takes ages in your house," said Dave.

Cady ignored him, eyes on the envelope. Inside was a single piece of paper, the same white, almost luminescent, expensive quality as the envelope. It was folded once, and fit the envelope exactly. She removed it just as carefully and scanned the paper. Then again. Ed and Dave leaned forward.

"Huh," said Cady.

"What does it say?" said Ed.

"'Not one of us.' "

"What now?" said Dave. Cady offered him the note. He took it, read it twice, and gave it back. "Huh."

"Can I see?" asked Ed.

Cady proffered the paper. Ed opened it and made great show of examining it in intense detail before handing it back.

Sketched in the same pen at the top of the note was a cartoony version of the set square and compass logo that they'd been looking for, this time with a 'G' in the middle. In the same hand, the text as Cady had read it, in a single line just above the fold. *Not one of us.* At the bottom it was signed with a single word: *Frog.*

"Nut?" said Dave.

"No thanks," said Cady, "I'm still full of kebab."

Back in the lounge, a male voice was doing an enthusiastic rendition of *You Give Love a Bad Name.*

"First, who sent it?" asked Cady.

"Well Frog," said Ed. "Who's obviously a Mason."

"We're being a little quick with the obviouslys there," said Dave. "It's got the logo on, sure, but does that mean the guy who sent it is a Mason? Maybe. Maybe not."

"Second who is Not one of us?" said Cady. "Us?"

"The Masons," said Ed. "And surely they're talking about Carver, aren't they?"

"That seems most likely," said Cady.

"Told you it was the Masons," said Ed into his pint.

"Hmm," said Dave. "The other possibility is that it's some kind of veiled threat aimed at us? Scare us off?"

"That gives us two pictures then. Either, Not one of us is Carver, and they've just watched you taking photos of his car or, it's referring to us and they've just watched us being shifty, don't really know what we were up to but have tried to frighten us off anyway," said Cady.

"They are a secret organisation," said Ed.

Cady rolled her eyes at that. She picked the paper up again, turning it in her hands, looking at it this way and that.

Dave went on, "Carver could've have sent it himself? Put us off? Saw us snooping round his car?"

Ed said, "That would be clever."

"Strike you as too clever though? I dunno," said Cady. "Also something bothers me about this handwriting."

Dave stood and scratched his head. He glanced from the beer mat in his left hand to the three empty glasses in his right.

"And, yes, if you're going," Cady said. "Same again. I'm going to the loo."

"Careful in here," said Ed, nursing almost a full pint. "It's out past the bar, I think. No step."

"Ta," said Cady, and drove her chair out through the lounge, where the woman in the Metallica T-shirt and long frilled leather jacket was belting out a version of *I will Survive*.

Chapter 16

Cady found the loo with the woman symbol.
There wasn't a disabled. She eased her chair forwards
to clunk into the door. It didn't open. Wasn't locked,
didn't have one, on this door, at least. She looked
either side of the chair—there was enough clearance,
just about on a standard door for this chair, so that
wasn't it. She backed away again and looked down. A
small steel lip ran across the threshold. That and the
angle of pushing at the door must have been what
stopped her. What the hell were those things ever
about? Those weird metal threshold things. It wasn't
as if they were going to have carpet in there. Perhaps
they were meant to contain floods. Cady shuddered.
She backed her chair as far as the width of the
corridor would let her, selected a high gear and
jammed her joystick forwards. The chair hit the wood
with a *thunk,* but it opened and more importantly, her
front two wheels were over the flood threshold. She
eased the joystick forward, reaching across herself
with her other hand to help push the door. Her right
hand wheel squeaked s she juddered in. Good start.

She surveyed the room, the only cubicle she'd
make it into was the one straight in front, the
bathroom was L-shaped, and she'd have to back out
the way she came. Hand washing would take some
kind of weird yoga move and she wasn't feeling all
that yogic this evening. Cady sighed and rolled the
chair forward, pushed the stall door in with her
footplate and stopped there. No way was she going to
fit a whole chair through the door. She beeped her
chair off. At least the bulk of it in the doorway was

going to provide her with some kind of privacy. She unclipped her lap strap and foot straps and stretched her legs out one at a time to get them moving. She flicked her footrests up and then went to stand. Oh, now was the time for cramp? She swore profusely and creatively. In a way she wished she didn't swear so much, but she could add that to the list of wishes she wouldn't get today, so she grabbed the toilet roll dispenser for balance, hoped it wasn't built and maintained to the shitty standard of most buildings and shifted her weight off her seat. Her phone beeped.

"Oh, for Pete's sake."

Three texts. One from Dad checking in, one from Ed's mum and dad checking in, and one from Ed demanding to know what was taking her so long. She sat again, replied in the affirmative to her dad, said Ed was staying over at hers to his parents, and told Ed to piss off. She balanced on her feet again. Although she had splints to help keep her foot angle straight to get her upright, that in no way helped with the aches in her thigh and calf muscles to get her there. She stood, unzipped and pulled at her pants to get at her pad. She hated the things. No matter what kind of hi-tech bullshit or smiley models the ads had, pads were just grown up nappies. At least the black jeans she wore to fit in with Ed's stealth uniform, were comfort fit and she'd usefully modded the tops with elastic to save arsing round with buttons, whilst still having them look like jeans. In another stroke of luck, the jeans she'd modded had sufficient pockets for girl jeans, into one of which she stuffed her phone while leaning out to get her bag for fresh pads and wipes. Which of course made it beep again.

"Really? Ed you twat." She was between leaning forward to get what she needed and turning to give herself enough room to get the pad out from between her legs. She reached her other hand round to the back pocket of her jeans, where she'd just deposited her phone. There were two messages. One from Ed, some kind of emoji. The second one read *Frog: Want to meet up?* Ed she didn't reply to. She thought quickly, her legs were getting drafty and tired. She typed *Yeah?* and pressed send. Her thumb slipped off the screen and she fumbled to catch the phone. It dinked off the plastic seat and dropped into the bowl with a *ploosh*.

"Aw, bollocks." Cady couldn't reach her grab arm when she wasn't in the chair, the holster was too far away. She finished changing her pad, put her pants back on and sat back down, knowing all the time her phone was drowning. She drew a deep breath and her grab arm and went fishing.

When she returned to the snug ten minutes later she raised her hand again, "Don't even." She pointed at the tumbler on the table. "I hope there's more JD in that."

"Yes?" Dave pushed the glass with his finger towards Cady.

"Why?" said Ed.

"Frog got in touch."

"How?" said Dave.

"On my phone."

"I think he meant, how on earth did he get your number?" said Ed.

"I don't know. But they did."

"You said 'they', you don't think it's a he?" asked Dave.

"I've been thinking about what was bothering me about that writing. I think it's a woman," said Cady.

"You can tell that just from the writing?" Ed raised one eyebrow. How did he even do that?

"Just a feeling," she said. "As opposed to your writing Ed, where it's difficult to discern anything at all."

Ed huffed.

"So what did he or she say?" said Dave.

Cady recounted.

"Just that?"

"Just that."

"Did you reply?" said Dave.

"I don't know."

"What you mean, you don't know? You either did or you didn't."

"Yeah about that," Cady deposited the pathetic dripping plastic lozenge onto the table, blank screen upwards.

"Oh shit," Ed and Dave chorused.

"I pressed send, then the phone went for a swim," she said.

"For reasons that...?" pressed Dave.

"For reasons that a gentleman wouldn't ask about," Cady said stiffly.

Ed looked at the forlorn phone, "So no way to know if the text got through, or..."

"...or anything," said Cady.

"Shit," said Ed.

Chapter 17

School the next day had an interminable lesson about accessing adult services which left Cady in a superposition of states. It was certainly stuff she was going to need to know and soon, but any time she found herself actually paying attention to any of it she found pressure building behind her eyeballs. She tried to distract herself by passing notes to Daisy to update her on the previous night's exploits at the pub. The replies from Daisy consisted of her drawing ever more elaborate cartoon doodles from the stuffed pencil case of felts she liked to do her immaculate work with. Daisy's post-its smelled of bubble gum.

By the time they'd reached break, the lesson and the smell of the post-its had given Cady a banging headache. As Daisy handed over a cup of steaming tea and Cady necked two paracetamol, she felt Charlie at her elbow.

"I thought you were tube-fed?" said Charlie.

"It depends on which part of me is shittiest today," she said. Then, "I thought you were going to private school."

"Touché."

"Don't let her be tetchy at you, Chucky," said Daisy. "It's all self-inflicted. Someone was out at the pub last night."

"Shush," said Cady, face screwed up. "Where's Ed?"

"Oh, working in the Scooby Cave," Daisy thumbed over her shoulder.

"It's H.Q!" said Ed, tersely.

"Whatevs," said Daisy, "you want tea?"

"We got any coffee left?"

"I bought new."

"Shall we go see what the boy genius is up to?" asked Cady, nudging Charlie with her elbow.

"Let's," said Charlie.

"You'd better," Ed's voice echoed from the cupboard door, "There's something here you're gonna wanna see."

Daisy moved to give them room to pass, but stopped when the common room door opened. Jenny, the youngest one of the TA team came in. She looked on the verge of tears.

"Tea?" asked Daisy.

"Love one," said Jenny.

Daisy filled the kettle and set it going before coming round the front of the counter. She waved the others on, giving them an I-got-this thumbs up.

The Scooby den was cramped with Ed, and Charlie with his chair. Charlie turned his head when Cady limped in, chair still behind the café counter, "Well, aren't you the little passel of surprises."

"Yeah, keeping people guessing, that's me. If the room wasn't totally full of your chair Sir Charlie…"

"Shall we move on?" said Ed. "There's good news and bad news."

"Oh good," said Charlie, "cliché o'clock."

Ed ignored him and carried on, "So Cady, do you wanna pick or shall I?"

"Okay," Cady sighed. "Bad news."

"Your iPhone is FUBAR."

Cady's mouth hung open. The small, thin, sad-looking phone sat on what passed for Ed's 'desk'.

She looked at Ed, slowly back to the phone and clenched her teeth.

"It's a military term—" said Charlie.

"I know what FUBAR means, asshole."

"Did you hit it as well as drown it?" asked Ed.

"It must have hit the loo seat harder than I, aw—shit," she frowned at the forlorn device.

"Sorry, Cade," said Ed. "I tried my best. It sat in the airing cupboard all last night in bags of Silica Gel but iPhones are... well, anyway, with the water and the smashed screen I couldn't save it. And if you've not got backups going on from it, you'll have lost all of that too, photos, files, music—"

"Okay, okay, I get the idea. Phone logs?"

"Text logs, yeah. Call logs, maybe, but here's where the good news comes. First, I got you a burner from the supermarket and cross-loaded numbers for everyone. Your sims in there for now, but there was a sim with it, if you're super-paranoid."

"Somehow a ten quid disposable phone is not cheering me."

"You're welcome," said Ed.

"Sorry. Thank you. You've done loads."

"What was the other thing?" asked Charlie.

"See," said Ed, "Charlie's paying attention."

"The other thing relates to information," Ed went on.

"Okay?" Cady turned the new, tiny white phone over in her hands. It felt cheap.

"Well, you know how I like it when people are spe-cif-ic."

"Yeah," Cady looked skyward. This had caused many a row.

"Well, when you told me about the texts you'd had last night, you said just that—texts."

"I think I said messages, but go on."

"Woolier still," said Ed. "One of those messages was a Gmail."

"Oh?"

"So when I downloaded your mail off the internet, there it was. And its little friend."

"Wait, what, you hacked my email?"

"You're not exactly security conscious," said Ed.

"That's not the point!"

"Well it might be, real soon."

"You hacked my mail!"

"It's not like you're peddling internet porn."

Cady had her temples between her fingers. That headache would not leave her alone. Ed drew breath to continue, but Cady held her hand up. Out in the common room she could hear the muttered conversation between Daisy and Jenny. Jen wasn't happy about something, the tone gave the game away even if Cady couldn't hear details. She thought she heard Linda and Bad Bill come in too, but he'd have gone straight to the loo anyway.

"So are you going to tell us what was in it?" said Charlie, "Or do we die of suspense."

"It'll be a cold day in Hell before I let Ed read you my emails," Cady said, coldly.

"There are one or two that warrant everyone's attention though—"

"Show me," said Cady.

"Okay. Charlie, would you mind?" said Ed.

"Oh, sure, yeah, sorry," Charlie, backed out. "So?"

"These," said Ed. "Obviously one, you've already seen."

The message Frog had sent the day before was there, no sign of Cady's reply. Then the message below. With an attachment. She stared at the screen. Ed tapped his fingers on the box. Cady continued to stare.

"I've scanned it for trojans and viruses with a fine-toothed comb," said Ed. "If that's what you're worrying about?"

"Sorry? No. Go on, open it."

The email was long but the attachment caught Cady's eye first. An elaborate wooden garden bench. A great big wooden lattice at the back, flowers growing through it. Pretty.

"Did you clock the instructions?" said Ed.

"No, precis me."

"Urrgh, I'm not your personal assistant. Today, Cady, Today. 4pm. Come alone."

She reflexively reached for her phone. On Ed's desk. In a puddle. She booted the new one. It made a perky series of start-up sounds, then demanded a whole load of information about her and where she lived. She slammed it onto the desk next to her first phone.

"Would you like me to set that up for you?" Ed asked .

"Please. I'm sorry, this is all a bit much."

"Mmm hmm," said Ed. "It's 2.15pm now. It'd take about five minutes to get there by car, or van, but we'd need to find someone to take us. Longer by chair, but yours is pretty fast."

"Slow down there, Eddie. Where?"

"Oh, the park. I looked it up on Google maps. It's where the pergolas are. Just like that."

"Right, do I even want to go?"

"I dunno, and risk being mysteriously murdered by someone you've never met? Yeah, there is that. There isn't a film I've ever seen where the whole 'and come along or I won't show' thing ever works out well."

"They?"

"Yeah, they actually said that."

"Shit," said Cady. "What do we do?"

"I think you should go."

"I think you're unlikely to get murdered, for what it's worth," said Charlie shouting from outside.

"I think we can't do anything 'till school breaks up," said Daisy, poking her head round the door. "We're stuck here till 3.15, but I think we might persuade Dave to drop us all at the park? I think Mum and Dad might meet us and pick us up."

"Then what?" said Cady. "Can I pinch your chair, Ed?"

"Oh sure." He stood, Cady sat. "Well, we need to find that pergola."

"I thought you said it was in the park," said Daisy.

"Yeah, along with another twenty of his friends, all round the park. All with different stuff growing up them."

"Okay. Can you drive my chair back in, Daze, and we'll make a plan."

"I'll print out some small copies of the park map."

"What are you two doing?" asked Daisy from behind the counter, getting the chair.

"Arm wrestling," said Charlie, struggling with two hands against Bill's one. "Damn he's… tough…"

Charlie's hand crashed to the counter top. And Bill raised his in the air in triumph.

"The clues in the 'Big' bit," said Daisy. "Now move, so I can get Cade her wheels."

Cady plonked into the chair, "Where's Jenny?" Daisy's brow furrowed. Because she spent so much of her time being her sunny self, a frown always looked worse on her. "Oh hell. Is Jasmine ok?"

Daisy shook her head, "Back in hospital. Chest infection. Bet she caught it off that supply teacher last week. Sneezing all over the place, she was."

"Poor sod," said Cady. "Jazz can't catch a break with a big net, this year." There had been a lot of hospital admissions. That and visits to the hospice had meant that Jasmine was hardly in school.

"I'll organise a whip round tomorrow and see if we can't cheer her up. There's a balloon shop on the high street that delivers," said Daisy.

"Right, maps!" said Ed.

Chapter 18

Ed had them organised into teams, the park split into areas, and Cady, Charlie, himself and Daisy each had maps and a print-out of the pergola with the particular flowers in question. After some Googling, Ed had identified the impressive mauve pom-pom flowers of Clematis "Evijohill"—a rare clematis—unusual enough to be recognisable. The teams seemed to be Ed, on his own, sporting some version of Google goggles on his phone, Charlie in his manual chair, saying he needed to get in enough miles for some upcoming race or other, leaving Cady and Daisy on the same team, since Cady's phone wasn't butch enough to manage sending pictures, even if it could take them.

The boys shot off in different directions after Dave Le Bus decided his safety threshold fell where leaving Big Bad Bill was concerned. Bill's reputation as a bit of a bolter made everyone twitchy about leaving him anywhere without a TA or a parent. The bus drove off with Bill staring out of the window at the park in the sun.

Cady looked down at the map and at her watch—3.35. If they were going to find this bench and everyone make themselves scarce, then they needed to get a shift on. She shook her head. Daisy's phone pinged, twice. Ed had found and ruled out one pergola already. Charlie had found one and was bitching about the fact that he thought all plants looked the same to him. Daisy shook her head, too and examined the map again.

"Hey wait a minute I've got an idea," said Daisy. She prodded the map. Where she pointed said *Gardeners. Private.* It wasn't far from the gate they'd come in at. Cady smiled at her.

"Genius, Daze. Hop on the back."

Daisy grinned. She loved getting a ride on the power chair, but knew what a personal thing it was to be allowed to, "Hold on kid, this might be a bumpy ride." Cady punched the chair into fast and whacked the joystick forward. The chair leaped and Daisy squealed, clinging on to the handles. They cornered and Daisy leaned, hair streaming behind her. A woman walking her dog hopped out of the way, turned and smiled at them. "Sorry!" yelled Cady over her shoulder. Then Daisy shouted something loud but unclear, Cady snapped her head to face front, and saw the barrow just in time. "Shhhhiiiii-!" She slammed the chair into reverse to stop its momentum and skidded to a stop, her knees just resting under the barrow.

The lanky young gardener with the nose piercing scowled down at them, "You wanna be careful with that thing."

"Err, Hi. Sorry," said Cady.

Daisy dismounted, "Sorry to be a pain," she said. "You wouldn't recognise this, would you?" She flashed that disarming Daisy smile and the boy's ire stopped in mid-flow. He shaded his eyes to see the picture, and shook his head.

"Sorry, I've not been on release for long enough to spot a plant from a weed yet. You want Mr. Crombie for that. Potting shed down there." He pointed. A long, single story building stained green that coincided with the *gardeners. Private* bit of the map.

Cady's phone read 3.39. Then to Daisy, "Shall we?"

"Let's. Thanks!" said Daisy, waving.

Outside was one of those small fingerposts that indicated a rough distances and directions to *home*. It reminded Cady of the one in *M.A.S.H*, one of the Grey family's guilty pleasures sometimes of a weekend. Interesting pointers on this one comprised: *Krakow 1157m*, one at the top of the post read *Pokey 3.5m,* and one painted in red and green read *Kingston 4550m* in slightly peeling yellow letters.

"Can I help you?" A kind voice made Cady look up from the sign. Was this Mr. Crombie? He was taller than the gangly youth they'd first met. Cady couldn't help wonder if that helped with pruning trees or something. Mr Crombie removed the straw trilby he was wearing, took a hanky from the pocket of his faded blue overalls and mopped his head with it. He had a faint trace of very short white hair. Cady couldn't place an age or an accent, but she reckoned he was older than Johnny B the caretaker, who was mid-fifties. He wiped his hands, carefully placed the hanky back into his pocket and reached a hand forward to shake. "I'm Darrel Crombie, what can I do for you young ladies?"

"Not sure she's a lady," said Daisy.

"Harsh," said Crombie, shaking Daisy's hand.

"But probably fair, I'm Cady, that's Daisy," said Cady shaking, too. "We wondered if you could tell us where this is."

Daisy flapped the paper in front of him, "Oh," he said and disappeared into the shed. When he came back out, he was wearing a pair of gold half-rimmed glasses. He squinted at the paper, "Ah Josephine," he said, "Beauty ain't she?"

"No, I'm Daisy…?"

"Not you, you fool," he said, gently mocking, then tapping the paper with the glasses he'd taken off. "Her!"

"I thought, it was called Emojibill or something Ed, said?"

Crombie chuckled, "And Ed will be right, mostly. Clematis 'Evojohill' is her proper name." He smiled at the paper, "but she's Josephine to her friends. Would you like to see her? I can take you."

Cady jumped, looking at her watch—3.47, "Ok this is going to sound really weird, but can you just tell us where it is? We've…I've got someone to meet there at four and I need to meet them alone."

Crombie raised an eyebrow.

"We promise that we're not looking to trash your flowers, they're beautiful and we're not gonna do drugs or anything," said Daisy.

Crombie chuckled again. Cady liked his laugh—it was warm and genuine. She wondered how she'd never noticed him before, she'd certainly been to the park loads. She guessed nobody noticed gardeners, she hadn't. One of those invisible stations in life, like chair-user, "Well I was going to assume romantic tryst and not illicit drug use," he said, still laughing.

"Can we assume that, and you tell us where Josephine is?" asked Cady.

Crombie held her gaze, "Sure. She's one of the double benches around the fountain, faces both ways so you can choose to look at the fountain or the ducks! You ladies be careful, now."

"Thank you Mr Crombie," Cady said.

"You're welcome." Crombie smiled and then went back into his shed.

Chapter 19

Cady sat on the bench in the pergola facing the ducks, her chair turned off. Somehow, staying in the wheelchair seemed like cheating, she could dash round the other side at eight mph to see who her mystery visitor was. She thought showing trust was a good start to earning it. It was what her Dad always said. It was mostly true. She noticed she was twitching her foot absently. Those Converse would need cleaning. No point in having black and white ones if the white looked the same grey as the black. Under her foot was one of the pink petals from the mad-shaped clematis, she carefully leaned over to pick it up. It seemed as if even the petals came in different types and shapes on this trippy flower. She moved the petal to where the other blooms were coming through the pergola holding it up to compare. The breeze gently stirred the fragile thing as it sat on her finger. They even smelled, the fragrance but subtle, gentle.

"Beautiful aren't they?"

Cady was too transfixed to be shocked by the woman's voice from the other side of the pergola, "Yes. They are."

"I hoped you'd like them."

"You weren't worried I wouldn't work them out?"

"Clever girl like you? No."

"Or that I just wouldn't show?"

"Oh, I think you're more determined than that. And more curious. Possibly more than a little stubborn, too."

This mystery woman knew so much about her already, but about the woman she knew nothing, next to nothing. There was another subtle smell from the other side of the pergola. Expensive cigarettes.

"Why are we here?" said Cady.

"Why indeed."

"What do I even call you?"

"Frog is fine for now."

"Why Frog?"

"It amuses me."

"Ed thinks you're a freemason. Or you're going to murder me and hide my body."

"Not exactly a freemason," she said. "And certainly not going to murder you and hide it. Whatever would I do with the chair?"

Cady smiled. For some crazy reason, she trusted this woman, straight off the bat. It wasn't the posh tones, though even they had a trace of something else, a faint Lancashire twang maybe, but Cady had inherited her Dad's natural mistrust for a posh-school voice. It seemed that too many people in the public eye told too many lies for that to ever be true anymore. But what was it? She'd known this woman for all of one minute, and something about her seemed solid.

"What then? If not…"

"I'm one of the wives." The phrase held its own quote marks.

"That sounds very Jane Austen. What does that mean?"

"That my husband—"

"Is who?"

"Is a Freemason. He speaks very highly of you, by the way."

"You're very cloak and dagger about this."

"Wouldn't you be a little disappointed if I wasn't?"

Cady snorted. She leaned forward and clasped her hands together. This time she found herself balling up the petal. When it was as best a ball as she could manage with two fingers, she flicked it towards the ducks. It was also more than a bit creepy, exactly how much Frog knew about her.

"So, charming though this is, why did you want to talk to me?" said Cady.

"I rather thought it was you who needed to talk to me."

"Oh?"

"I was going to try to save you a little time barking up the wrong tree. Or rather, barking up the right tree for the wrong reasons."

"Ok. This is about Carver?"

"Yes. Odious little man."

"So, not a fan then?"

"No, not at all, and neither are the Absdown Lodge."

"Which means, he's not—"

"A mason, no."

"But he had the ring and everything."

"Yes. Since the advent of EBay, God help us, it has become much easier as a wannabe."

"Wannabe Mason?" she asked, incredulous.

"Yes," said Frog sadly, "it's a thing."

"Wow."

"There is no way on earth that the Absdown lodge would let him join."

"Why?"

"He doesn't have sufficient moral…"

"Fibre?"

"I was going to say 'compass' but fibre would do as easily."

"What was he doing at the lodge, then?"

"Charity fundraiser. It does people's local standing good to be seen at them. And Carver is such a social pole climber."

"So if it's not Carver, who is it?"

"I never said it wasn't Carver and we never laid out the *exact what* we're discussing here."

"Okay. The whole selling the school off thing, smells funny."

"I agree."

"I think there's more to it than Carver's magic hospital wing."

"Well observed. I think so, too."

"So what do you think is going on?"

"I don't know, I haven't got a crystal ball, but as you have correctly pointed out, whatever it is, Carver is up to his neck in it."

"So now what?"

"Keep digging."

"But what are we looking for?"

"I believe at this point, I'm supposed to say follow the money."

"You're enjoying this, aren't you?"

"A little bit, yes. You're not just a pretty face, Cady Grey, I'm sure you'll figure it out."

"Err... thanks, I think."

"Oh, and be careful."

"Of Carver?"

"Unlikely, Carver is a buffoon. His wife however, is a viper. Don't follow me till the town hall clock strikes half-past. Goodbye, Cady Grey. Good luck."

Cady couldn't help look over her shoulder through the pergola, but Frog was already long gone, a faint trail of smoke in her wake. The ducks quacked in the park stream, and the low sunlight spattered on the surface as they swam. A faint breeze blew across her feet. It was too beautiful to be the setting for the weirdest conversation she'd had in her life. She shook her head as she powered her chair up and jockeyed it into position for an easy transfer from the bench. As she struggled across on aching arms, slowly, ponderously and slightly out of tune, the town hall clock struck the half hour. It had struck the hour and the next half hour before she moved.

Chapter 20

Cady raced a lazy sun going down as she made her way home. Technically speaking, her chair had no lights and therefore wasn't allowed out after dark, that and no hi-vis. What on earth had she gotten herself into? The whole Freemason thing seemed like a dream, probably from Ed's fevered imagination, but she had been there. The conversation had really happened. Every bird flapping its way to roost, every taxi running over a crisp packet made her jump. If she looked over her shoulder once, she did it ten times before she got home, which made for a jumpy journey. She'd long since learned, after a few crashes not to be driving forward while glancing behind. After about half a dozen times she stopped, pulled into a large rubbish-strewn doorway and rolled a cigarette. She licked the flap down and searched her pockets for a match.

"Need a light?"

Cady froze, her heart hammered, her hand stopped with the fag in it, not touching her lips. A flame flickered to life in front of her. The lighter was set to a long flame, so with the darkness of the doorway she could only just see the parka sleeve holding the lighter. In the flickering light it seemed the whole arm was protruding from the large pile of rubbish.

"I didn't mean to frighten you," said the voice.

"It's a bit too late for that now, arsehole."

"I said I'm sorry."

"No you didn't."

"Oh, didn't I? Sorry. Being out here makes one a little—uncertain—after a while. Look, do you want a light or not, this lighter's burning my thumb."

"Er, yeah?" The arm and its flame moved up.

"I'm John, pleased to meet you." The bundle unwrapped itself. He had the appearance of someone who'd dropped out at a festival and never dropped back in. His face was a study of heavily tattooed skin, overlaid with piercings that glittered in the lighter flame. Until it winked out.

"I'm Cady. Hey, you want me to roll you one?"

"That would be amazing."

So she got her baccy pouch out and began to roll.

"You live here?" she asked.

"Sometimes here, sometimes there."

"Must be tough."

"I usually say 'You have no idea' at this point."

"I'm not sure I do."

"Huh."

He took a drag on the ciggie that lit up his face. Now Cady looked again, he was a lot younger than she'd first thought.

"What's wrong with you, then?" John gestured at the chair.

"You mean besides cranky and irascible, with a tendency to swear too much?"

"Yeah, besides that."

"I'm a SWAN," Cady said.

"That explains the cranky, then."

"It stands for Syndromes Without a Name, it means I'm undiagnosed."

"How is that a thing these days?"

"Just is, I guess. I've got a list of symptoms, but no-one knows why. I'm in loads of genetic studies and stuff. The nerd in me would love it, if it wasn't such a pain in the arse."

"Oh. So it's not like that thing Stephen Hawking had?"

"MND? No. I've been tested for that."

"Oh."

He took another drag and blew the smoke out of the doorway. It curled off into the streetlights.

"What about you?" asked Cady.

"What d'you mean?"

"I mean what's your story?"

"Oh. Yeah. Well, I was an estate agent."

"I thought they were on good money."

"Only while they've got a job. When the arse fell out of the property market, I got laid off. I lied about it for ages while I looked for a new job, but then the girlfriend found the P45 when I was out."

He looked out into the street. A taxi went past. He shook his head.

"She went mental when she found out, threw me out. I sofa surfed for a while with mates, but everyone's got stuff going on, you know. Only so much headspace themselves. They all ran out of patience in the end."

"What about your folks?"

"Disowned me while I was with the girlfriend. We were never all gonna get on."

"Wouldn't they take you back now you…now you've left?"

"Nah, we all said some things y' know? Some stuff you can't take back."

"You tried *Big Issue*?"

"Not yet. Small town innit, no office."

"True and I'm not sure how it works."

"Me either. Can't get internet on this thing. All outta credit anyway."

He flicked the flap on his shirt pocket, showing a small phone not dissimilar to Cady's new one. The screen was monochrome with just the time and the network showing. The time was late, she should get going. She dragged on her roll-up.

"Tried the library?"

"No they're all snooty as, in there, don't like letting me in. Say I smell and it puts the other customers off."

"Might ask someone with the magazines if I can find one. Knackered today, though. Hoping I get a better sleep tonight. Got woken up yesterday by some drunk guy peeing on me."

"Eww."

"Yeah, right?"

Cady pointed at John's pocket and said, "If that's the time, man, I gotta go. Nice you meet you."

"Yeah, you too," he said. "Thanks for the cig."

"No problem."

She crushed hers between her fingers, before looking for a bin or a grid to flick it into. She couldn't just flick it into a doorway. Somehow, that felt like littering up John's house.

Chapter 21

"Frig, Cady, where have you been?" Her Dad stood blocking the doorway, arms folded.

"I did ping you," she said.

"I know, but last I heard was an hour ago, it's late."

"I know, sorry, I got sidetracked."

"Tea's on low in the oven, if it's not incinerated."

"Or in the dog?"

"Yeah, or that."

She fished the plate out of the humming oven with a tea towel. Cady had a personal hatred of oven-gloves. They were always such a pain. Driving a chair with cloth hand-cuffs was not a good look, especially if any actual manouvreing was required. The tea-towel was damp, so she ooh-ed and ah-ed her way to the kitchen table and plonked the plate hurriedly with the cloth still underneath it. Dad had already put a bottle of coke and glasses on the table. He came and sat in the kitchen chair and poured them both a glass. He placed the glass in front of her. She signed *#thank you,* since she had pasta in her mouth. He smiled. Dad was very good at what Mum would have called shovel-and-spade-cooking—everyday fare. Tonight was pasta Bolognaise. Cady had a tiny bowl with only a few pasta shapes and some sauce in. Her dad went to the fridge and brought out a plastic soup pot and a bottle of water and placed it down, with tubes and a syringe.

"The rest's in here," he said.

Although she got the majority of her food through her peg port, she still liked to taste what she was eating. Pasta wasn't that hard to eat, but her whole body was achy and tired now. She washed the remainder down with the half glass of coke.

"You okay, hun?" her dad asked.

"Yeah, bit stressed about all the stuff at school I guess?"

"Wanna talk about it?"

"Yeah, just not right now."

"You know I'm here, right?"

"Yeah. I know, Dad."

She finished squirting the last of her dinner down the tube and followed with some clean water to flush it out. She disconnected her port and turned to take her stuff to the sink. Her dad stopped her with a hand.

"'S'okay love, I'll do them."

"Thanks Dad." She handed the bundle of pipes and pots over and smiled up at him. He smiled back, but only on one side. "I'll just be outside, I need to speak to Ed."

"Okay, but do you know what time it is?"

"He'll be up."

She opened the back door, rolled out and rolled up. No rain, result. Midges circled under the cone of the garden halogen light. She removed the replacement phone and scrolled through its contacts. Under E in the list it read *EdMeister*. That, she supposed, was the downside of letting someone else sort your gear out for you. She composed a text to ascertain if he was still awake. When he pinged back straight away she thumbed the phone icon. She waited for him to pick up. She knew he was less comfortable talking than texting, but there was just too much damn stuff to impart that was too important, and she had to go to bed at some point. Cady knew to let the phone keep ringing if Ed didn't pick up straight away. He'd see it was her and if he didn't want to talk he'd just click refuse and she'd be straight through to messages. If not, he'd be pausing, closing and turning on all kinds of electronic and computerised sentries before they spoke.

"S'up Cady," Ed said finally.

The first slug of their conversation was a verbatim, or as close as Cady could manage, account of the meeting with Frog. She had to check several times during the flow of it, if he was still there. Ed didn't really do conversational redundancies, except to ask specific questions or fill in details that Cady had left out or just didn't have. Once, he'd stopped asking questions and she ran out of story, the conversation stopped abruptly. Cady waited, she could hear Ed's computer fans click into overdrive in the background. His servers were up to something, even while he wasn't.

"What do you think?" said Cady.

"About what?"

"About Frog."

"That's a very vague question, Cady."

"What do you think about what she said?"

"Hmm. Well, I think the stuff about investigating finances is really useful. I took a good long look at the whole shell companies thing but it's a total rats-nest. It's built with obfuscation in mind. But it's not my thing. Forensic accountancy is a really specialised field."

"Does that mean we're stuffed on that front?"

"No, I don't think so, I might know a guy who knows a guy."

"Oh?"

"Well the yanks are waking up now, there's a guy on 4chan I know. His stuff is all American law, but still."

"Do you think we can trust her?"

"Who, Frog? I think she has her own agenda."

"Doesn't everyone?"

"Yeah, but I think the thing that's in our favour at the moment is that hers aligns with ours."

"And against Carver and the school closure."

"It would seem so."

"What now?" said Cady.

"For now, you go to bed and I speak to our American cousins."

"And if there's no joy there?"

Ed drifted off again, literally as well. Cady could hear as he clicked in the background and a corresponding *ping* answered him. She hailed him a little louder.

"Sorry, what?"

"I said, if you don't get any help from the Americans?"

"Then, there's always Brenda, I guess."

"Who?"

"That's tomorrow's question. Go to bed."

Cady knew when she'd been dismissed. She flicked off the ash from the majority of the rolly she'd failed to smoke, dragged on the end, then pinged the stub out into the night with a sigh. She booted her chair up, turned it round and followed a pleasing smell back into the kitchen.

"Hot chocolate?"

"No. Thank you!" she said, grinning as her dad presented a steaming mug and accepted. The films of Mel Brooks had always provided a shorthand in their lives. They could quote most of them verbatim. Her phone buzzed. Mug in hand, she started texting "I'm not being ignorant, just need to let Daisy know what's going on."

"Don't any of your friends ever sleep?"

"Not this week they don't."

He pulled that one-sided smile again and took a long swig from his own mug, it was slightly chipped freebie from some kind of parts manufacturer. It was a bit faded now, so the cheery slogans proffering spark plugs or carburettors or whatever, were long since gone.

"You will tell me if there's anything- y' know—wrong?" he said.

"What, besides the school closing and getting sold off?" she said, in a brief pause from texting. "Yeah," she pressed send. "Not pregnant or on smack or joined a religious commune." She looked up into his eyes. It took him a second to look back properly. "Honest."

"Good." He put his free hand down on hers, now she'd dropped her phone into her lap. She squeezed his fingers.

"Stop stressing, Dad. We're just trying to make sure that everything's above board."

"That's my Cady. Ever the Social Justice Warrior." He smiled, "just be careful, okay?"

"Always, Dad."

She turned her chair round to face him, and beckoned him towards her. He leaned in, and she kissed him gently on a stubbly cheek. Then she drained her cocoa and made for the door.

"Oh Cady." His voice stopped her. She half turned the chair.

"Uh-huh?"

"Can you leave me your power chair at home tomorrow? There's a few tweaks it needs now that all that raft of last minute M.O.Ts is out the way."

"Sure," and she left to put it on charge and sling herself into the chairlift to get to bed.

Chapter 22

The school bus rolled in, but there was already a white van in the last disabled space in the car-park. The last space was the nearest to the grassy verge at the edge of the building, somewhere they had all started to think of as 'Area 11c'. Their usual space, where they swung in by the gate was filled by another white van, a smaller long low Mercedes, one that seemed super-shiny and sported the logo *Southern Surveying Ltd*, with the equally shiny strapline *Surveying the South*.

"Tossers," said Dave Le Bus, and proceeded to park behind the larger van, blocking it in.

Once everyone was at ground level, they headed to the door. When Cady reached the hall, she turned: no sign of Ed. Where had he gotten to now? Shouting from a disgruntled workman heralded Ed's return. Cady raised her eyebrows at him. He waggled his iPhone at her in reply, signing *wait*. They headed to the sixth-form, where Daisy had already laid out their drink mugs arrayed in a neat row across the counter. But they wouldn't get chance to drink it.

Cady had just gotten as far as looking at Ed's phone where he'd taken photos of the inside of the van where the disgruntled worker had opened the side door, since Dave Le Bus had prevented access to the back. The very ordered van seemed to contain a great deal of equipment in varying sizes and complexities. But after Ed's departure, it seemed like the fracas was only just beginning. The raised voices they now heard included Dave's, some other workers, Speakman's and now finally the Head. The sixth-formers left the building when the Head blew an ear piercing P.E whistle.

When Cady wheeled herself out there, closely followed by Charlie in his manual chair and Big Bad Bill, the argument was already in mid-flow. All the grown-ups seemed disgruntled and had huddled into two teams on the grass beyond the van. Area 11c. The quite large space, maybe an acre in total, widened as it got farther round the school. The area then would have joined the main play area behind the school itself if not for a picket fence. The workers in question had assembled themselves in a line with their leader, who wore a suit and a white hard hat and no hi-vis. He was asserting the workers' right to be laying out strings and hammering posts while the Head, with Dave leBus next to her, was apoplectic with rage at their bare-facedness to attempt this. Dave's beef seemed to be a different one, at the same time, with the driver of the larger van. Behind the front row of workers, a woman was setting up a tripod with a box at the top of it.

"I thought that's what it was," Ed was looking at his phone.

"What was?" said Daisy.

"The tripod thing. It's a theodolite."

"What's one of them, then?" asked Charlie, wheeling up to them to form a line.

"S'like a glorified spirit level," said Cady. "'Cept with lasers."

"Hmm, so these dudes are surveyors," said Charlie.

"Well done, give that man a coconut," said Ed.

The man with the suit, Cady guessed was the actual surveyor, waved a piece of paper at Miss Wintle. She went to snatch if from his hand and he pulled it away. Dave caught it instead and the two of them retreated behind the line of chairs and students to read it. The space between the front of the van and the school wall was quite narrow and Cady and Charlie's chairs effectively blocked it, with a little space to squeeze through. Dave and the Head wiggled through this. The surveyor who had a few more pounds to his midriff could not. He reached down towards Cady's chair brakes.

"Don't touch the chair!" she barked at him. Startled, he withdrew. "You're in my way."

"You're in mine," said Cady. "What's your point?"

"Well, I need you to move your chair."

"What you need, and what I'm prepared to let you do without my consent are poles apart, mate."

"I can't jump over," he said.

"No you can't," said Cady, looking him up and down.

He went to reach down to Cady's chair again. "Don't touch my chair with any part of you you're not prepared to lose." She glared at him, pleased that she'd chosen her cherry DMs to wear to school today. He narrowed his eyes and leaned in a little towards her. He clenched his fist. She slowly withdrew one foot backward from the footplate straps, while congratulating herself on being such a slack-arse at tying them in the first place. He was so close now, she could smell his sweat. Then a flash—God he moved quick for a big bloke—his hand was on her brake and had already flicked it. She twitched out her leg and stabbed her toe into his shin. He fell back howling. Cady could hear Bill cheering behind her, then Speakman swooped in.

"Children, back inside," he said in a chilly voice. Cady and Charlie reversed enough to allow Speakman past. He stepped between the two parties, a hand raised in each direction. "Now then everyone, I'm sure this can be resolved amicably, and everybody can get on with their work. Barbara, Mr. Hackburton, should we? My office."

"'Old on," they could hear Dave le Bus begin again with the parking bee in his bonnet. Cady was desperate to stay and listen it out, but they had been directly instructed to go inside, even if that sleaze-bag Speakman had called them children.

They returned to the Sixth form centre, Ed noticeably twitchy, Charlie confused and Daisy still glowing red from the embarrassment. Daisy was the first to the counter as ever, Bill was the last through the doors, "Tea!" he said.

"Spoken like a true gentleman," said Charlie.

Daisy slowly looked across the cold, full mugs of tea on the counter, and began to pour them one by one, down the sink.

Chapter 23

Cady sat in her chair in the Scooby Den observing Ed adding to the strings and pictures, muttering. Charlie offered her a mug of tea. She smiled up at him, took it gratefully and signed *thank you*. He quickly turned back to the kitchen and coughed. Cady shrugged and turned back to Ed.

"How'd you get on with your friends on the Dark Web?" asked Cady.

Ed sniggered, "Don't build his part up. He's only on 4chan. It doesn't make him the Neuromancer. Besides, he's an accountant."

"Can't accountants be hackers then? I'd've thought they'd be in pole position to be getting up to mischief."

"Oh, they do," said Ed. "But they couldn't get past a firewall for toffee. Tend not to be the same person. Different skillset. Different brain wiring."

"Hm," Cady looked skeptical.

"It's a good job too," Charlie poked his head back in. "Can you imagine the chaos?"

"I think it happens occasionally," said Ed, "But it tends to cause huge stock market wobbles."

"Never interest you?" asked Charlie.

"Why would it?" said Ed. "What would be the point?"

"Money?"

"Doesn't bother me. I've got all I need," said Ed.

"What, not even a house or a car?" Charlie looked genuinely confused.

"I could buy a car. Why would I need a house? I live at my folks."

"You might have to ask them about the why of that, Eddie," said Cady.

"Hold on a minute," said Charlie. "You could buy a car?"

"Ye-es? But why would I since I can't drive? We're getting off-topic here. You wanted to know what Black Adder had come back with."

"Is that what he's really called?" sniggered Cady.

"I know," said Ed, flatly. "Hysterical."

"I thought it was a 'she' called Brenda?"

"BRENDA is something else entirely."

"So did he come up with much?" asked Charlie.

"Well, there lies our problem."

"Oh?" said Cady.

"He came up with masses."

"That's good though, surely?" Charlie asked.

Ed's face said it all. As did the crazy multi-coloured cats-cradle that he'd made on one wall of the Scooby Den. He started several lengthy explanations of the diverse and complicated financial life of Carver and his wife. Shells within shells. Off-shores in the Isle of Man. A myriad of companies that actually appeared to do stuff, too. The complexity was mind-bending. Which was when Ed brought up Brenda again. Brenda, it seemed was some kind of AI that Ed had been developing, that spotted patterns. Cady only sketchily understood what it did, but it seemed that Ed had already set it underway, chewing on the data in his bedroom. She stared at the wooly maze and defocussed her eyes. Somehow the coloured blur was easier to tolerate. She rubbed a hand across her face.

"It looks like Spiderman sneezed," she said.

"Yeah," said Ed.

"How much further does this get us?" asked Charlie.

"Not much, if we don't know what exactly he's into here. Hence the need for BRENDA."

"You're not going to tell us, and you're dying for us to ask," said Daisy. "Who's Brenda?"

"She's not a 'who', she's a what."

"That's not very PC," Daisy pouted.

"It's an acronym!"

"What's it stand for then?" asked Cady, through clenched teeth.

"Boolean, Recognition and Noticing Algorithm."

"That spells BRANA," said Charlie.

"You don't count ands, no-one does," said Ed, affronted.

"You're still missing some though, chap," said Charlie, clearly on to something. "What do the E and D spell? Oh."

"And what does Brenda do?" Daisy asked in her best peacemaker voice.

"I'm glad you asked."

"I'm sure you are," said Cady.

Ed continued unabashed, "BRENDA is an aggregator." Everyone looked on blankly. "Okay, let's put it another way for the technically dim. It is a particularly clever piece of code, written by me, to collect and interpret massive data sets for patterns. To see what things connect. To find the fly in the web just from the vibrations if you will."

"Data sets?" Daisy asked.

"Lists of things," said Ed.

"What, like the Internet?" Charlie scratched his chin.

"You keep using that word. I don't think it means what you think it means," said Ed.

"He means the actual Web," said Cady.

"No, it can't yet, that would be too big for my server farm, but we don't need to. We've collected plenty of data ourselves, that I've already inputted."

"I guess we wait and see what Brenda chucks out, then," said Cady.

"Yep," said Ed. "Oh, there was one more thing that Black Adder spotted, a little cul-de-sac, if you like. There was a curious, brief series of transactions with a Pink Tiger Investigations, except it was only Mrs Carver's transactions, in an account registered in her maiden name of Hartland."

"Ooh," said Daisy, "Mr Carver's been a naughty boy."

"You think?" said Cady.

"Why else would she be getting him investigated?" Daisy said.

"A million reasons." said Ed. "Financial misconduct? Other non-marriage related impropriety. She may not even have been investigating him."

"Sure feels that way," said Daisy.

"Yeah, but feels don't stand up in court," said Ed.

Cady thought that had escalated quickly too. This week was having a tendency to do that. When did they start taking people to court?

Before she could say anything, there was a crash outside, shouting and more crashing. They all stood in a second. Cady and Charlie started to turn chairs around. Ed with a palm on each wall, jumped over Cady's chair and then again over Charlie's just like Spiderman. Daisy had already cleared the way behind the counter and was looking for Bill. Where was Bill? The Sixth form had no one-to-one's in it at all now Cady had emerged behind Charlie into the main room. Now she could hear where Bill was. He was one of the voices outside, screaming, howling like a wolf or a bear, maybe—an enraged, hurting, primal noise: fury and despair and bloodlust. What in the hell was happening out there? Now they'd all assembled, they headed to the doors.

They met the head coming in. She had a stray mascara streak under one eye. But her face was blank, eyes steely grey. She stood in the middle of the doorway, holding both doors.

"Students. Stay here. I'm trusting you." She swept a look over them all. Even with the noise of yelling outside and now crashing and smashing that was getting increasingly scary, she pinned them all in place. "Are we good?"

They mumbled assent. "Thank you." She swept back out.

Cady gazed over Ed, Charlie, Daisy, hoping for any kind of clue. But there were none. They piled towards the windows. Staff were rushing from the main building round the side of the sixth form to the site of the workmen and the shouting. Unfortunately, none of the windows in the sixth-form common room looked out that way. The fracas was increasing in noise with more participants, then a great smash and blood-curdling howl followed.

"Library!" Ed shouted. It was the one room with two tiny, high up, windows, pointing in the right direction. Ed and Charlie were already at the doors of the common room.

"Wait, we told Miss Wintle we'd stay!"

"Screw that," said Ed.

"Technically, we're not leaving the block," added Cady.

Ed and Charlie were gone already, Cady was at the door. She turned back. Daisy sighed and joined them. By the time they got into the library, Charlie and Ed had formed a rickety human pyramid involving Charlie's chair with its brakes on, and Ed stood on the arms. Cady wasn't sure whether to yell at them for being so idiotic or whether the act of shouting at them would be the idiotic thing, causing them to tumble. She erred on the side of silence, for what it was worth with the noise outside. It had now shifted to loud but calming voices of adults, including Miss Wintle, and Bill now shouting "Nuh! Nuh! Nuh!" at the top of his voice. Slowly the noises decreased in intensity, though the anger of the tones of the adults in some cases increased. Bill had gone quiet.

"Shit," said Ed.

"What happened?" said Cady.

"Bill. He's properly messed up their van."

"What like drawn on it? What was all the noise?"

"No," said Ed. "Like properly, violently messed it up. Like undrivable, messed up."

"With his bare hands?" Charlie shifted his grip on Ed's leg.

"No, he used that theodolite of theirs. He must have used it like a club."

"How do you know that?" Daisy's face scrunched.

"Because it's sat in the middle of the smashed-in windscreen."

"Shit," said Cady.

"Poor Bill," said Daisy. "Is he still out there?"

"No, they restrained him," Ed began climbing down again. "Took four of them, mind. With Wintle. I've not seen her do that before. Speakman's still out there calming down the surveyors. Their boss dude sounds pretty pissed off."

"But where's Bill?" asked Daisy, voice rising.

"Dunno, couldn't see. They carted him off somewhere. Sensory room maybe?"

"We should go find him," said Cady.

Chapter 24

The next couple of days felt insane, more so than the rest had felt. Bill had been suspended till the end of the week. The full story, when it transpired, was that he had found Miss Wintle trying to persuade the surveyors out of starting to work before she could examine their paperwork properly, which was unexplained but appeared official. When the senior surveyor, who seemed to be the guy in the suit, insisted they had all the authority they needed and started anyway, it appeared that Bill had taken matters into his own hands. Or the massive and sudden change had just freaked him out to the point of snapping. With Bill it was always hard to tell. Regardless, expelled he was and the students hunkered down in the sixth form centre, and the staff into form-filling for the restraint.

In a hurried Scooby Den meeting, it was agreed that Cady and Daisy should go and chase down the Pink Tiger Investigations lead and see what could be gleaned there. So, one evening after school, Cady arranged a pick-up from her dad for her and Daisy and got Dave le Bus to drop them in town.

The sign for Pink Tiger Investigations was a tiny brass plaque on a small door that hosted a masseur and an acupuncturist. It was in a part of town called The Backs, where a small maze of alleys was the remaining evidence of the town's medieval past. All now in brick and stone remodeling, of course, but Cady had always thought the shape and feel of these streets was plenty medieval enough. No-one would build streets with shops this close together nowadays. The Backs was also noteworthy for being that 'interesting' part of town—where tattoo artists and piercers nestled alongside little art galleries and hippy shops. As they stood at the bottom of the stairwell and looked up, patchouli-scented air floated past them.

"Well that buggers my conquest of the universe," Cady, frowned at the stairs.

"Let's push the buzzer and see," said Daisy.

The buzzer rattled like a squashed wasp. There was a moment of silence and then a woman's voice, "Hello?"

"Err, hi?" said Daisy.

"We're looking for Pink Tiger Investigations," Cady jumped in.

"Well you've found them." The voice on the intercom was authoritative, but busy-sounding. "Come on up."

"Err, we can't." Daisy indicated with her head where Cady was. Cady suspected that the intercom was too old school to have a camera.

"Oh?"

"Wheelchair," said Cady.

"Oh, sorry," said the voice. "I'll come down." The intercom crunched off.

They heard scuffling from upstairs, a door slam and then a tall woman, mid-forties, stood at the top of the stairs. Cady tended to assess people from the feet up. In this case the woman had a smart, polished pair of brown brogues, cream socks and a pair of deer-coloured check wool trousers, teamed with a plain white blouse. The woman stopped three steps from the top, cursed under her breath and went back up the stairs again. When she reappeared, she was sporting a short khaki jacket with numerous pockets and straps. She had a bit of a stomp in her step.

When she touched down she cocked her head, took in Cady, then Daisy, smiled, leaned her head into a doorway at the bottom of the stairs and called out, "I'm just going out for a meeting with a client, Lena. I won't be longer than an hour."

Then she gestured over their heads, indicating behind them and said, "Shall we?"

Cady rotated her chair to where the woman had pointed. In the centre of the passage, a point where it split in two, was a small building with tables outside. It seemed to be where she was pointing, but when she got to the threshold, she stopped, turned back to Cady, then went down the side of the building. The alley sloped upwards here, but levelled out again halfway down the building wall at its side door.

"I think we'll find this more comfortable," she said.

She led the way into what seemed to be the top level of a cafe. The lower level was accessed by stairs, but ahead of them was a low table, two low leather chairs and a two-seater leather sofa, all in front of a wrought iron fireplace.

"Er—" Cady said.

"Introductions in a second. Priorities. Coffee?"

"Tea here, please," said Daisy.

Cady asked for diet coke, and when the woman waved at the room in front of them she assumed that meant to sit. Daisy tried out both chairs, before deciding that the two-seater sofa was by far the more comfortable. She adjusted a rather chintzy cushion behind her.

"Nice," said Cady, gazing at the ceiling. It looked old. White, but marked out in large squares with a plaster motif at each cross where the edges met—roses, faces, eagles. She was no historian, but she'd bet that wasn't the kind of decoration found in a coffee chain store. It was lit by more modern low-voltage lights on tracks. One blinked slightly in the corner. She was still staring when the woman came back.

"Right," she said. "Introductions." When none were forthcoming she said, "I'll start. It's okay to talk in here. I use it for client meetings sometimes. Not as private as the office, but it's discreet." She twirled her finger in the air, as if Cady and Daisy would know what she meant. When blank faces were all she got in return she went on, "The wiring in here is terrible, so—" She paused, searching for a word, "—nosiness, is very difficult."

Cady and Daisy still looked uncomprehending. "Electronic listening?" They shook their heads. "Never mind," she said. "We're safe here. I'm Lena."

Cady went to shake her hand, but she had a small card in it. It had a clever logo with a pink light cutting through the darkness that faded to tiger stripes, with lettering in silver *Lena Moranti, Private Investigator*, a landline number and an email address. Cady took the card, tilted it this way and that, and passed it to Daisy. Then she offered her own hand.

"Cady Grey," and then when she was too wrapped up in admiring the card, "and this is Daisy." Daisy smiled and waved.

"So, what can I do for you?" Lena asked.

What did they want, now she was here, Cady was less sure, "Well,"

Lena cocked her head to one side and said, "You'll forgive me for thinking that you're a little, hm, young to be requiring the services of a detective. I can't imagine you've got cheating partners stashed away somewhere?"

"I wish," said Daisy.

"So what, then?" asked Lena.

The drinks arrived, Cady's coke in a long twisted glass with a paper straw, Daisy's with a tiny teapot and a flowered china cup, which the waiter who served them placed down with great ceremony, complete with a doily to protect the surface of the small table. Lena's coffee, was black and in a simple white mug. "Thanks Harry, put it on my tab please." He left and she smiled at his retreating back for a moment, then to Cady, "So what can I help you with?"

Cady began the whole tale of the school's impending closure, and the planning meeting, and the workmen, and Carver. Lena was a good listener and made notes on a small pad that she produced from a jacket pocket. Cady checked to see her reaction when she mentioned Carver, but Lena was scribbling furiously, so she gave nothing away. She omitted to mention the Masons. Somehow it seemed wrong to be spilling Frog's secrets and really, she thought, it was a bit of a side track.

"Okay," said Lena, "and what part of that can I help you with?"

"Well our friend Ed says that you've done some work for Mrs Carver and we wondered whether you had, and if you had, what it was about?" blurted Daisy.

Cady rolled her eyes.

"Oh I see," said Lena. She huffed, eyed up Cady and Daisy again, then took a long drink from her coffee. Daisy followed suit and took a long sip of tea, with her little finger stuck out.

"I'd love to help you girls, I really would," Lena said. "But you know what client confidentiality is?"

Daisy shook her head. Cady nodded once.

"Well, if I told you what I worked on for a client, or even whether I did work for a client, that would get me turned out of the A.B.I like a shot."

"'A.B.I'?" asked Cady.

"Trade association. I've not been in this game all that long after leaving the force, so they've been a massive help with my starting up. I get to put their name on my business cards. It makes a big difference to trade. If I start giving out information, it breaches trust, you see. And that's everything in this game." She smiled kindly and put her cup down.

"Can you at least confirm you worked for her?" said Daisy. "For Mrs Carver, I mean."

"No, sorry Daisy, I can't."

Damn her, but Lena had a great poker face. She held it flat and then shrugged slowly and sadly. Cady finished her drink with a slurp, took Lena's card out from Daisy and tapped it against the side of her glass, trying not to look too much like a kicked puppy. Lena, reached out, beckoning for the card, took it, wrote a mobile number on the back in biro and returned it.

"My non-work mobile. I don't often give that out. Keep it safe. Use it wisely."

"Thanks," said Cady. "For talking to us at all. And thanks for this," she waved the card and pocketed it.

"You're welcome," she said. "Best of luck, girls."

Chapter 25

Ed went AWOL.

Cady didn't worry on day one. He came in on the bus as usual, and went home on the bus. He popped his head into lessons long enough for everyone to think he was there. He just wasn't there-there. Cady made some effort to try and get a conversation out of him on the bus, but he had his head in his laptop. Being as how he was the only student ever to be entered for an A-level in maths, and he was pretty sure to get it, when he disappeared off into his laptop during school time, everyone assumed that was what he was up to. He also had a peripatetic maths teacher, Mr. Carol, come in from the technical college in town, more than twice a week, so, often he was out of class for that too.

Day two, Cady noticed that Ed's trademark black rucksack was bulkier than usual, and he wore the manner of someone acting shifty. She was trying to process the visual information, while her sensory processing was telling her that her manual chair gloves were getting too tight. That was making her feel cross at her dad for keeping her chair for another day. She undid the straps and stared at Ed's bag. He pulled it out of her eye-line, as if she might be able to see through it if he left it where it was. She couldn't even remember if the bag was full of the same stuff yesterday, she had become so distracted. The bus came to a halt and they all got out.

Cady remembered nothing about the morning except the fact that Ed wasn't in English. Not that made a hell of a lot of difference, as they all worked on different things at different speeds anyway. Bill and Jasmine, when they were in, were still at the stage of forming letters, Bill's next goal was to write his own name. Daisy was practicing writing intro letters to go with CVs, and Ed was writing a science fiction story—would have been, if he were there. Cady was writing an essay on *Pride and Prejudice*, she was about to do an AS level in English Lit. The school was excited. Cady was less thrilled. She'd liked Austen when she'd started, but she was so over it now.

She chewed thoughtfully on her pencil. *It is a truth universally acknowledged… Discuss.* She gazed out of the window, looking for a cloud to fixate on. There were none. Today was a stunning day, warm even, after such crappy weather recently. Then something caught her eye and she focused. That kind of struggling motion that spiders respond to so they don't check their webs every time the wind blows. Someone large and burly in a hard hat and Hi-vis from the surveying site had Ed by the lapels on his black denim jacket. They were achieving this with one hand as they marched him over towards the main doors, and then the Head's office. In the other hand the man dangled Ed's parents' DSLR camera by its straps. With a long lens attached to the front, it swung ponderously. Ed moved to grab it, but the surveyor snatched it out of the way.

"Give it BACK!"

"No. You were trespassing."

"Sod you, you don't own the school yet!"

They reached the school glass doors. Ed made one more desperate grab, but the worker swung the camera into mid-air and let go of the strap. In one of those slow motion moments, the camera flew towards the school gates and hit the pavement at the side of the school drive with a smash.

"You bastard!" yelled Ed.

But the man now had two hands to steer his charge with and grabbed one of Ed's flailing arms and twisted it up behind his back. Cady thought that looked way too practised, was this guy a bouncer? Ex-cop maybe. Certainly had the regulation buzz cut under the hat from what she could see of his sunburned neck. He slammed Ed into the door and too late Cady thought to fumble for her camera. Some investigator she was turning out to be. And nobody wanted to be the Daphne of a Scooby Gang. Well at least she could make herself a reliable sidekick. She signed *toilet* to Nasreen, who nodded back, and she left.

When she reached the corridor outside the Head's office, a more pleasant affair than Speakman's more utilitarian hideout, she parked herself behind a large umbrella fern. She needed to be no nearer, she could hear Mrs Wintle's voice from here.

"No," she said, "I think you'll find the thing that needs explaining is why my student has a lump the size of a goose egg on his badly bruised forehead and why is he crying?"

There was no reply. Presumably Mrs Wintle was using one of her famous glares. Clearly it worked on adults as well as students since there was no reply.

"Well? No. I thought not. If I see you or any of your colleagues manhandle any one of my students again, I will call the police and have you removed on an assault charge. Do I make myself clear?"

More silence.

"DO I?"

"Yes."

"Good. Get out of my office. I shall be forwarding a complaint on to your manager."

"But—"

"Get. Out."

Shuffling of chairs ensued, and the handle on the office door rattled. Cady leaned in as far as she could go and hoped he wouldn't look left as he left the office, but go right, straight out of the doors.

"Not you. You sit." Ed's lecture was just beginning.

He went left. Cady froze. He walked across the passage to the toilets that staff and visitors used. She was expecting him to lean down and leer at her, or at least ask her why she'd been spying, but he walked right past. Straight past her nose to the toilets. She was torn between relief at not being spotted and anger at him having gone right past her. *"Nobody notices the dude in the chair".* Someone had said that to her on a Whizz-Kids course once. And there it was, proved. Damn. She was torn between making a getaway and staying to rescue Ed. She thought discretion the better part of valor today and made a break for the doors. She banged the *door open* button and waited. She drove out across the road then stopped, before climbing the dropped kerb on the other side. Should she go back and get Ed's camera? Why was that even a question? She turned her chair round.

Then screeching and beeping filled her ears. An unmarked white van had come out of nowhere, doing at least fifty, swerved to avoid her and mounted the pavement on the school side. There was a crunch as the wheels ran over Ed's camera, once and for all.

So much for that, then. The driver wound her window down.

"Look where you're going, you retard!" the woman from the building site shouted.

In less than a minute Cady had gone from invisible to wishing she was. Still flushed, she could think of no comeback to suit the situation better than a middle finger. The woman huffed and drove off. Cady thought better of collecting the wreckage of the camera and instead returned to the Sixth Form centre. A cup of tea suddenly seemed uppermost in her mind.

It was just after the click of the kettle that she heard the anguished cry of her friend as he found the wreckage of the camera. She got out an extra mug and a sachet of the extra strong coffee he liked. It wasn't going to do his nerves any good, but it was the thought that counted. At least that was what Daisy would say.

Ed stormed in and banged the remains of the camera on the counter top. Pieces bounced and clicked left and right, some wound up in Cady's lap in the chair. She leaned forward and pushed the steaming mug towards him. He stared into it for a moment, huffed and lifted it to his lips. Cady knew better than to say anything yet. He took a swig. It had been scarcely five minutes since that water had boiled in the kettle. Cady was never sure quite how he did that. Possibly no taste buds? He took another swig and put the mug down.

"Two days' work. Wasted."

He lowered his head to the desk. Lifted it. Removed a tiny screw from his forehead then slowly lowered it again, swiping the counter with his hand before he landed.

"You think you're having a bad day. I've just nearly been run over by someone who called me a retard."

"Huh."

"What were *you* doing?" said Cady.

"Taking photographs."

Cady knew better than to be annoyed, this being Ed and all, "What of?"

"Those shifty buggers out there."

"Aren't they just surveying?"

"Yeah, you'd think that."

"And…?" Cady prompted.

"And what?" Ed said.

"What are they doing that's not, then?"

"I'd show you but…" He wafted his hand over the smashed pieces.

Cady prodded the coffee over again, till it bumped Ed's arm. He lifted his head, plonked it on the cup and drank, slurping. Cady shook her head slowly. The door to the common room opened, the edge of Ed's mug slipped and sloshed the remaining half-cup all over the counter. Cady reflexively grabbed the tech kit, but then felt foolish, trying to hold the shattered corpse of the camera. Charlie and Daisy came in.

"Aw Man!" said Daisy, watching the coffee dribble down the white melamine of the counter's front face. "You are so cleaning that up, Ed." Since Ed's face was also covered in coffee that he was wiping off with his hands, that seemed like a safe assumption.

"Give him a break, I'll do it. Eddie's had a rough day." Cady held up the camera bits to demonstrate. The back fell off.

"Yikes!" said Charlie. "I'll do it if you find me a cloth."

Cady plonked the remains of the camera onto the shelf, then rootled farther along under the counter, searching. Daisy rounded the corner and squidged past Cady, "'Scuse!" she said. "Let me grab one. You'll be forever."

"S'only 'cos you hide them," Cady, sat back, then froze. "Hold on."

"You found a cloth?" said Charlie.

"Here," Daisy tossed a rag over the counter. "Properly, please."

"Ed," said Cady, quietly.

"Whaaat?"

"What's this?"

"The smashed remains of a camera that I now need to explain?" Ed said.

"No." Cady poked at the bit of camera she was now holding. She removed a small plastic bit. She waved it triumphantly, it was black and the size of a stamp. "This!"

"What?" said Ed, looking at her. "Oh. Oh! Cady! You're a genius!"

He ran round the counter, "'Scuse". He snatched the SD Card from Cady and nearly knocked Daisy to her knees as he rounded the corner into the Scooby Den. He came back out, gave Cady a peck on the cheek saying, "Genius." Then disappeared back into the dark of the cupboard.

Chapter 26

That night at home, Cady was still chewing over the results from the Scooby den. The SD card contained hundreds of photos—mostly of miscellaneous action on the site. Ed was not the world's most fantastic photographer. One photo, he drew everyone's attention to— of yet another tripod, this one bigger and suspending a large metal corkscrew. After a heated discussion on what it might be, from some kind of archeology tool, through prospecting for oil, finally Charlie put forward looking for soil samples as the most likely scenario. Ed slunk off in disappointment. But the massive tripod made her nervous. She'd borrowed her dad's copy of the John Christopher book of the same name when she was nine and it had given her nightmares for a month. She shook her head to clear it.

"Y'okay, hun?" Dad asked.

"Yeah, I might hit the sack early," said Cady.

"No problem, nice and fresh for your birthday tomorrow."

Cady's face crinkled into a laugh. Her dad cocked his head to one side, quizzical.

"I had totally forgotten! What with school shenanigans and all. That's cheered me right up."

And she left for her bedroom, giggling.

Next morning she was woken by the smell of pancakes and coffee. She swilled her face in her bathroom sink, then began the lengthy process of getting dressed. She took a final look in the mirror and adjusted her ponytail so it was on one side and not squarely at the back. The creatively ripped black

T-shirt seemed to be working, but something was missing. She ferreted in her jewelery box and produced a sliver ankh on a chain, which she hung around her neck

"Perfect." She slid into her manual chair and wheeled herself towards the smells of breakfast. On the way through the living room, she had to maneuver carefully round a massive box nearly filling the space. It was four feet in each direction and five high. Its exterior was draped with white sheets stuck to each other with white duct tape and in the middle of the side facing her was a massive purple fabric bow. She wheeled herself closer.

"No peeking!" yelled her dad, from in the kitchen. "Come on in and eat first. We're early this morning, so you'll get plenty of chance to open pressies. There's a stack of cards here, too!"

She sidled past what would be the largest present she'd ever had into the kitchen. She rolled up to the table, took a long breath, taking in all the scents. A massive stack of pancakes, bacon and maple syrup waited for her, as well as a steaming cup of coffee. Her dad turned, frying pan in hand, with the last of the pancakes and added them to the pile. Cady smiled up at him. He waved at the spread and sat.

"Dig in."

"Cheers, Daddio."

"You're welcome kiddo. Gotta spoil you once a year," he said.

"You spoil me most of the year!"

"Pah," he said, and handed her a stack of cards which she proceeded to open, one at a time, coffee in hand.

"There's one from your Mum there." He speared some bacon and added it to his pile, stopped, thought and then went back and speared another piece.

"I've not gotten to it yet. 'Sides, it'll be a voucher," said Cady.

"Give her a break mate, she's trying her best." He looked into his coffee steam, warming his hands for dear life.

"Don't see why I should, she never gave you one. Or me, for that matter."

"She was ill."

"So am I, what's your point?"

"My point is, she's trying and sometimes, it's all you can ask of someone."

"I don't remember asking for anything. Or getting it." She got to the bottom of the card pile. Vouchers. It would join the pile of two years of unspent vouchers for Birthdays, Christmas, Easter in the bedside drawer in her room, next to the small pile of neatly piled cards.

As usual, Ed's card was weird. A gurning old bloke in black and white and a motto that didn't make sense. And Daisy's was pretty—a Monet print and a nice message in Daisy's impeccable curly script. Dad's card was massive, ironic and sported a large *17 today* badge, which she duly took off the card and pinned to a piece of her top that didn't have a hole in. The last few cards were from her cousins, and her Auntie. The two cousins were a year younger (Kayleigh) and a year older (Maxwell) than her, and she loved her slightly crazy auntie, Charlotte. For some reason lost to the mists of time, her dad called her Bobo. No present from them oddly, they normally made quite a fuss.

Perhaps they'd pitched in with Dad for whatever the huge present was next door. Cady ate the pancakes, but had no real stomach for bacon. She swilled it down with the remains of her coffee and faced her dad, wide-eyed, saying nothing. He looked back blankly. She nodded towards the living room. Dad narrowed his eyes and shrugged. Cady narrowed her eyes too and they stared at each other for a moment, like a western stand-off, neither blinking nor breathing. The clock ticked above the Welsh dresser. Then Cady's dad let loose a thin, almost musical fart. They both bulked up. Cady laughed till tears ran from her eyes.

"That's what you get for holding it all in!"

"Oh, sod off and open your present," he said, grinning.

She wheeled herself round to the side that had the bow and smiled. The first end of the duct tape wasn't far from the bow. She unwrapped the top layer of white sheet, only to find a layer of newspaper, taped together under that. She turned to her dad, who was feigning ignorance, with arms folded across his chest. She stuck her tongue out and removed the layer of paper. The cardboard encasing the whole thing underneath, caused Cady to start giggling again.

"All right," said her dad. "The suspense is killing me now, if not you, I'll give you a hand."

"Please."

The cardboard case was all a ruse to square off the shape of Cady's old power chair. Or at least it probably was? For a start, it was an amazing metallic purple, like the colour of Prince's guitar, but more sparkly, if that were possible. There were jet-black molded seat cushions. The finishing touches were awesome too. Her drive stick, that used to be topped with the fashionable chair driver's must-have of a drilled golf ball, had been totally replaced. It had a beautiful black gearstick, with leather grip, mounted on a control arm that was also completely new. It was almost too much to take in, in one go.

"Dad- I- She's beautiful."

"That she is," he smiled. "But I haven't even showed you the cool stuff yet."

"Err, okay?" Cady was so excited, she thought she might be sick.

"Sit in, I'll talk you through it."

She transferred over with an offered hand from her dad while she got her legs in order. Once she was sitting in the seat, she noticed two things straight away: firstly, she was sat slightly higher, secondly, the control arm had loads more buttons on it. She hardly knew where to start.

"So your chair now has full lift and tilt, and you've only gained an inch in floor level. The tilt and lift controls are on that button there. That one's drive."

"What's this one do?" Cady said, pushing it.

"EJECTOR!"

"Shit!"

It wasn't. But now the living room was lit by massively bright headlight beams.

"Sorry, Cade, couldn't resist."

"Hahaha."

"The lights are super-bright LEDs under lenses so they don't rag your battery too much, they go on dip and high beam too, like standard car lights. You've got indicators too."

"So now I can go on the road?"

"Yep, there's front and back reflectors, hazards—the works, but that's not the best thing."

"Wow Dad, just wow!"

"But the cool stuff—"

"Sorry Dad, show me the cool stuff."

"So, under the seat now and behind you are a totally new set of batteries. A mate was stripping down a crashed hybrid and was gonna have to pay to dispose of them, so I kinda swooped in and saved him some hassle. Mostly, it'll just give you insane long battery life but—" He wiggled his eyebrows and reached towards the control panel, "if I may?"

She raised her hands in assent and her dad flipped up a tab at the edge of the control panel. The whole control panel lifted and underneath was a single red switch. Dad pushed it. Unnervingly it lit up. Something beneath her bum hummed.

"Now all of your batteries are in parallel."

"Which means?"

"With a new coil and a drive system, your chair can go at 25mph plus."

"No. Shit."

"No shit," said Dad.

"Can I take her for a spin?"

"Before you do, two things. Once you've turned that switch on, you've only got so long and you're burning battery like crazy. I've got a percent dial there, it kinda says how long you've got, based on engine heat and battery stress. One hundred is good, less than ten is un-good."

"What's the other?"

"Well, technically you're now a road vehicle, so don't get caught speeding. The traffic cops would take a dim view of a wheelchair that can do thirty down the aisles in Asda."

Cady leaned overboard, but couldn't really see where the batteries were, due to all the purple moulded plastic that covered the underskirts of the chair. She pursed her lips. One section of the moulding was adrift on her left hand side at the bottom. Her dad clocked the look and furrowed his brow.

"Oh, yeah, that was the last bit I was tidying up before, well, now really. All the wiring looms are in there and I just need to make a little more room for them. It's only a little snagging, I'll fix it one night after school. Just try not to catch the edge of the panel before then. And steer clear of the wiring inside on that side, the cables from the coil are high power and they'll bite."

She rolled the chair out gently into the hall and trundled down the ramp on the other side of the door. Then she was free.

Chapter 27

Cady loved it when her birthday was on a Friday, and this year seemed to be revving up to be even better. Dad was letting her have a party the following weekend and more cards and pressies arrived from her cousins. She loved her cousins, and got on with all of them. Her dad even had continued their tradition of giving her something to wear, something to read as well. He'd bought her an awesome new grey skater dress and the most amazing pair of sparkly hi-top baseball boots. She matched her chair! Today was going to be so much fun. She was even ready for school early and was out on the ramp waiting for Dave.

Everyone cooed at her newly tooled-up chair, and there were more presents still! Daisy had bought her an attack alarm that attached to her bottomless canvas bag, and Ed bought her a copy of *Number Mysteries: A Mathematical Odyssey through Everyday Life* by Marcus Du Sautoy. She wasn't sure what to make of either, but she accepted them in the spirit they were meant. To improve her mood still more, Dave Le Bus had said he'd come to their party. They were all excitedly still chattering about this when they reached the keypad of the sixth-formers entrance. Before anyone could punch the code in, someone from the cleaning department, who wasn't JohnnyB pushed past them on the way out. Ed grizzled but Cady was so used to it, she almost didn't notice.

Daisy was first to the kettle as usual, busy filling it and wiping up mugs. She didn't need to ask anyone except Charlie what they were drinking, and she set to it, but shaking her head and twitching her nose. Cady saw and rolled over.

"You okay, hun?"

"Yeah, why?" Daisy sniffed. "Oh, that. Yeah, dunno, maybe a touch of hay fever." She sneezed.

"I dunno," said Cady, "I think something's getting up your nose."

"There's a very low pollen index today," Ed said. "You should be fine."

Ed took that chance to sneak round the back, desperate to get back to the ever increasing spider web. As soon as he rounded the counter, he started sniffing too. He reached the door of the Scooby den and opened it.

"Shit."

"What's up?" said Charlie, looking over the top of a newspaper.

"The Scooby Den. It's trashed."

"How can you tell?" Charlie chuckled, but no-one else laughed.

Cady whizzed round the counter, overshot and had to come back. That bigger engine her dad was talking about was going to take some getting used to. Having rounded the corner, she could smell it too. Burned synthetics, nylon maybe. Carbon, certainly but other things too a twangy, plastic, astringent smell. Ed and Daisy stood in the doorway, mouths open. Cady reached them and they parted to let her past. The Scooby Den had been wrecked, pictures torn down and walls scorched. Her heart was pounding, so hard it made her eyeballs ache. She was finding it hard to draw breath.

Ed was on his hands and knees, sifting through the wreckage to work out what was left. It didn't seem like there had been a systematic removal of everything, more a hasty wreckage. He found half a dozen random photos, a small collection of the stuff they'd put together, that he'd put together. Cady, looked down at him, and his mouth was a taut, flat line.

"How? Who?" asked Charlie.

No-one replied.

Cady's knuckles were white on the handles of her chair. She scanned the walls: thin wisps of smoke rose from some of the coloured nylon wool remnants that made the web of connections. They were all lucky none of this had caught. They could all have been in it, or at least walking straight into it when they came in. The thought of having to be part of a fire evacuation chilled her to the bone. And not half as much as it would chill their teachers when they found out. Which would be exactly thirty seconds after Linda came in with Bill. Luckily, neither she nor Bill were late.

The smell of scorching was somehow triggering something in her hind brain. It was funny how some smells just went straight into the limbic system: do not pass go. Blood, fire, salt water. She shuddered and started to back her chair out of the room. On reflection, she nosed back in again, starting to worry about how Ed was coping. If he went 'down the rabbit-hole' on this one, it could be a while, days even, before he came back. Then bang went the investigation and any chance of saving the school. But that was why this had happened, wasn't it? Not proper arson to destroy the sixth form centre: they'd have used petrol, and she'd be in a smouldering skeleton. Not an accident—too specific. So, intimidation. Someone from the building site was getting a little twitchy about how close they were getting maybe? Were these mad few days making her paranoid? Then again—

Ed was scrabbling to pick up a particular picture from the floor. It was face down, so he couldn't even tell what it was. He had both hands in on the act but the picture was too flat and the edges were too flush to the ground, and surprisingly there wasn't even any dirt on the floor to lift anything. *Cleaners have been in, then*, went through Cady's mind. Then she shook her head, drove her chair forward and flicked at the picture with one hand, propelled it towards the wall still face down and then closed in with her chair. Leaning forwards, she managed to bend the picture to a position to a position to be able to pick it up. She handed it to Ed with a smile. His face was blank.

"Now you've ruined it!" he shouted.

"Hey, it's okay," she said, backing out of the room again, slowly. "It'll all be all right."

"It WON'T! Nothing will ever be the same again."

Cady found herself reversing with some urgency. Not because of Ed, but she didn't know why. She looked up at the scorched wall again and wondered if it was some combination of the smells affecting her, but as her vision drifted, the random shapes on the wall resolved. Into words.

"Ed?" she said cautiously.

"WHAT?"

"Come here."

"What!"

"Look."

He turned from the doorway, clutching what he'd salvaged from the floor and peered back in where Cady was pointing. In an instant he forgot his anger. There were words. Burned onto the wall. They read: *LEAVE IT.*

Chapter 28

"You know we can't carry on, right?" Charlie said.

"My arse," said Cady. "We're really gonna let them beat us?"

"What can we do?" Daisy was looking about for somewhere to plug a kettle.

"We've lost all the information," Ed was pacing.

"But we haven't have we?" Cady had both hands gripping her armrests. "Most of it's still on your laptop, or your servers at home."

"Yeah, but the patterns."

"They've done their job," said Cady. "It gave us a way to frame the information, we all understand it all better now, but it's still not given us the break we need."

"Not enough data," Ed, sighed. "I've had BRENDA working overtime."

"No, just not the right piece," Cady pursed her lips.

"Arrrgh, this is hopeless!" said Daisy.

Cady drove her chair back to the counter, spun it and then went back as far as the doors to the sixth-form. She stopped, turned around and drove back again. On her next lap, she stopped, reached into her pocket and produced a black and pink business card. She trundled out of the doors, fishing her mobile out as she went.

"Back in a min," she said over her shoulder.

Outside, she texted the number on the back of the card.

Cady: We're stuck. We need a break. Running out of time to sv schl. She crossed her fingers and pressed send.

Lena: Still can't say nythng.

Cady: Can u help us work out where 2 look?

Lena: Hv you gone straight 2 horses mouth?

Cady: Tried that. Was less than helpful.

Lena: You catch more flies with honey than vinegar.

Cady: Err, ok. Thanx

Lena: Np. Good luck.

She read out the conversation back in the sixth form centre. Why couldn't anyone just say what they meant? Ed asked her to read it again. Then again, so she handed the phone over to him.

"She says 'good luck'," said Ed.

"So?" said Cady.

"She's telling us to do something. Something, tricky? Awkward?"

"Illegal?" suggested Charlie.

"No, she's an ex-cop," said Cady. "I don't think she'd do that."

"You've only just met her," said Charlie.

"Still, I get a good feeling about her."

"Hmph."

"Straight to the horse's mouth obviously means Carver," Cady said.

"Or the wife?" suggested Charlie.

"And if she's in on it? Then we give him the heads up," Cady said. "Has to be him."

"What does the whole 'honey and vinegar' thing mean?" asked Ed.

"I dunno," Cady tapped the business card against her teeth.

"I think I might," said Daisy, "but you're not going to like it."

"Okay?"

"Honey trap," she said.

"Oh one of those jar thingies you catch wasps in?" Charlie asked.

"No," Daisy put her hands on her hips.

"Hate wasps," Ed wrinkled his nose. "Hate them."

"It's not for wasps!"

"Okay," said Cady calmly, "what is it for, then?"

"People," said Daisy.

"You're gonna need a big jar," said Ed.

Daisy rolled her eyes and started to explain the concept of a honey trap. She explained slowly and carefully, having to very patiently repeat herself in parts. She got to the end. There was silence and the lingering faint smell of smoke.

"How on earth do you know all that?" asked Charlie.

"Mum watches a lot of crime drama."

"Wow, I'll bet," said Cady. "Okay, given that we now know what one is, do we even think this will work?"

"I think Mr Carver is a naughty boy," said Daisy.

"Okay," said Ed, "given, but where does that get us? What are we trying to achieve?"

"I think, with an attractive woman and a few drinks, Mr Carver might—"

"Might. What?" Cady cut Daisy off.

"Might spill some of what he's up to?"

"Oh!" said Charlie, "This might just work. I've seen it on a film where they hire a prostitute—"

"What?" Cady nearly squeaked. "We're hiring prostitutes now?"

"We are about to con somebody into releasing information," said Ed.

"Point," said Charlie.

"Where would we even hire a prostitute?" said Daisy.

"Whoa, whoa, whoa, row back there. *Nobody* is going to be hiring any prostitutes!" said Cady.

"Aw…"

"Especially you, Ed," Cady glared at him.

"So what do we do then?" Daisy had the kettle back in her hand.

"We need to get him to say some stuff he doesn't want to say," said Charlie.

"Roofies?" asked Ed.

"What?" Daisy found a socket behind a sofa. There was nowhere near to put the kettle if she could plug it in.

"Er, also no," Cady pinched the bridge of her nose.

"I think normal alcohol would work fine," said Charlie.

"Okay," said Cady, "that would work. Get him out with some mates, ply him with alcohol, get him to brag?"

"Bragging sounds about right, but he doesn't strike me as the kind of chap with many friends he'd go for a drink with," said Charlie.

"What about sending Dave Le Bus?" said Daisy.

"No, I think he's gonna be suspicious of someone he doesn't know," said Cady.

"Not necessarily," Ed unshouldered his backpack. "I may have an idea."

He opened his laptop perched on one knee. No-one could bear to go in the Scooby-den anymore. It felt spoiled. Perched like some odd kind of robot flamingo, he tapped away, head cocked to one side, muttering and hmm-ing. Everyone watched briefly, but couldn't manage to sustain that degree of tension or interest, so Daisy rounded the counter, sighed and put the kettle on the smoke-tinted counter. She took orders and dried-up mugs, then busied herself amongst the boxes that now crowded behind the counter, since the entire cupboard had been emptied.

The kettle gave a loud *click*.

"Gotcha!" said Ed. "I knew he'd be here. That's gotta be a wig, though."

"What on Earth are you looking at?" asked Charlie.

He tweaked his chair round to see the laptop, and laughed. A full-throated, deep-chested laugh, as contagious as it was loud. Before Cady could maneuver to see, Linda breezed in with Bill. From the angle they swept in, they were in the right place to see all the action. Bill had already started laughing, he didn't need much excuse for joining in.

"Aww, poor love," said Linda, over Ed's shoulder and enjoying the moment.

"When you've all finished," said Ed.

Cady rounded Ed, who was still managing to perch, with a surprising amount of grace. She stared at the screen, cocked her head to one side, cocked it back the other way. She closed her eyes, then opened them again. When she looked afresh, she recognised the person in the photo and the banner of the website it was on.

"What?" she said to Ed.

"Well I knew he'd be on one dating site or another, if Daisy was right. And here he is."

"It would be a great way to get him to talk," said Daisy.

"Ok," said Cady. "So assuming that this crazy trap would even work, who's our bait?"

She looked round at her friends, who were all looking at her. Without exception.

"No. No, no. In no way. No chance in hell. You're out of your tiny minds." They stared on, "Just no!"

Chapter 29

Saturday night, Cady found herself sat on a bar-stool, in Zapparelli's. Absdowne's newest wine bar was chosen by the Scoobys as an ideal site for their sting operation, due to its on-the-edge-of-town location and the newness, hopefully making the bar staff slightly more willing to undertake some of the evening's odder goings on. Its combination of 70's rock memorabilia and 60's Italian film posters hung in odd juxtaposition on the walls. She fiddled with the Bluetooth ear buds that Ed had insisted on acquiring off eBay—*"If it's going to be a proper sting we'll need to be able to talk to you."* She was pretty sure everyone was enjoying this hugely, except her. She had an extraction code word in case of emergency and everything. The rest of the team were sat outside in the back of Dave Le Bus's beat-up white van with all of Ed's improvised listening and recording gear. He'd even gone to the extent of sticking a wireless helmet cam up on the large plaster head of Frank Zappa up on the wall that provided a feed to his laptop screen.

"You okay, hun?" asked Daisy from the van. She had been overjoyed at the fun of taking Cady shopping for the ideal date outfit. It was a deep peach-coloured monstrosity. It was too short, too sparkly, where it wasn't frilly, and the need to wear it with tights was making her itchy. There were even peach-coloured heels to go with it. Luckily, she thought, she couldn't walk anywhere in them, whatever the circumstances. Even with her feet perched on the bar stool, they still hurt.

"No, no I'm not okay. I feel like a duck in a frock."

"Stop worrying," said Dave le Bus, "I told you, you look great."

"You look," said Ed, "all like a girl."

Cady pulled at the hem of her skirt. There was a thud as the Vida Rock-a cocktail she'd ordered arrived on the bar. She looked up and thanked Marco the bartender—she suspected more likely he was a Mike-o or a Wayne-o, but she noted the effort of the accent and genuinely appreciated the cocktail. She stopped pulling on her dress and took a pull on the drink instead. God only knew what was in it, but she could taste vermouth and some sweet something or other. At least it seemed to also contain Bourbon.

"First date nerves?" the bartender asked.

"Something like that," said Cady.

"Remember the code word in case we need to extract you?" said Ed.

"Yes. Coconut," said Cady.

"Sorry?" Marco frowned.

"Is definitely, one of the ingredients in this drink," she recovered.

Marco laughed nervously, "Nope. Guess again."

"T-minus ten minutes," piped Ed, as if Cady wasn't nervous enough. She tapped her glass twice on the rim in the sign they'd chosen to acknowledge she'd heard.

She sneezed, then opened the clutch bag carrying the main microphone that was supposed to be picking up the proceedings. She fished out a tissue, but before she could get it near her nose Daisy shouted in her ear.

"Don't you dare! That make-up took ages! Smudge and die."

"Well?" asked Marco.

"Keep your hair on!" Cady, put the tissue back into her bag.

"No need to be rude," said Marco, "Just passing the time."

"Oh, not you," she said. "This is going to take some getting used to."

"Pardon?" asked the increasingly bemused bartender.

"Oh, er, being out on my own, is going to take some getting used to."

"I thought you were on a date?"

"Yeah, but I haven't been on one in ages." That at least was true.

"Incoming," said Ed in her ear.

"Here goes nothing," said Cady.

"You want another?" asked Marco.

"Christ, no," said Cady.

"Oh, sorry," said Marco, "I thought you'd downed it."

"No. Not yet," Cady craned her neck nervously to see if she could take in the door, but if she turned round any farther, she'd fall off the stool. Then she'd really be in trouble.

"He's coming in," said Dave le Bus.

"Try to smile when you see him," said Daisy.

Cady took another long sip of her drink, through the glass straw. She felt a hand on her back and coughed, then started choking. The hand behind her started patting, a bit too firmly.

"Gosh, sorry," she gasped. Marco had already put water on the counter. She smiled at him, through another barrage of coughs.

"Betty, I presume," said the voice attached to the hand behind her. Daisy had decided she was a Betty in her dating profile picture. "I'm David," said Councilor Anthony Carver, craning round her in a cloud of aftershave.

"Hiya," said Cady, "sorry to choke all over you."

He laughed, but it never reached his eyes. "May I get you another drink?" he asked, proffering a handkerchief.

She took it, gratefully. It was white, expensive and monogrammed in cream on the corner *ADC*. David was his middle name, then. Not a great deal of imagination. She was feeling a better Betty.

"Sure," she said.

Marco nodded before anyone spoke to him and started making another cocktail. Carver ordered a scotch and lemonade. Cady resisted the temptation to grimace. Marco presented both drinks with a coaster and a flourish. He was so angling for a tip.

Carver stared at Cady, taking a swig of the drink, "Don't I know you from somewhere?"

Cady dropped her head to her drink, "Worst chat up line, ever."

"Not likely he'd recognise her in that face of make-up," said Ed in her ear from the van.

"Are you criticising my beautiful handiwork?" asked Daisy.

Cady stirred her drink. Carver laughed again, belatedly.

"Sorry, I'm a bit out of practice at this," he said.

She lifted her head again and smiled, "Why are you here?"

"Hell, way to go Mata Hari," said Dave in her ear. "Take it easy, he's already spooked."

Behind her back, but in view of the camera, she flicked a 'V' sign at the van crew.

"You're very direct," Carver said.

"I prefer it that way. Life's too short."

"Huh," Carver sounded surprised. "Really want to know?"

"Yeah," Cady said. "I don't do that 'just asking' thing. Can't be bothered."

"Okay. My, marriage since—"

Cady held his gaze. He seemed on the verge of tears. He'd stopped talking, aware she was paying attention, "Since what?"

"She died. Since Eva died."

"God. I'm sorry. Your daughter?"

"Uh-huh."

"How old was she?"

"She'd be seven now. She was five when she died."

"Shit. No-one should die that young." She went back to stirring her cocktail.

"No. No-one should."

"What was it? Do you mind me asking?"

"No, I like talking about her. Leukemia."

"Awful."

"Yes it was. It's why…"

Cady looked up again, "Why you're here?"

"No. Why I'm— never mind."

"No, tell me, I'm interested."

"The hospital."

"The County?"

"Yes. I'm building a new wing. Well, I'm not building it, but I'm, influencing-"

"Oh you in building then?"

"No. Council. I'm on the Planning Committee. I want to get it named after her."

"That'd be nice," said Cady.

Carver swirled the ice in his empty glass. Cady leaned towards Carver, placed a hand on his. He gazed over the top of his glass. The corner of his mouth tweaked up. He clearly wasn't used to smiling. Cady noticed he did have a crease at the side of his lip where he did whatever this was that passed for a smile.

"You're kind," he said.

"Hmm," Cady reached for a peanut from the glass on the bar. Despite what she knew about the perils of peanuts in a bar environment.

There was rustling in her ear from the van, "God, this is getting us nowhere," someone said quietly, probably Ed.

"You seem distracted," Cady realised she was still looking at Carver, but hadn't been paying attention.

"Oh god, sorry. I'm miles away."

"Why are you here?" he asked, tone blank.

Cady's throat dried. The peanut she was half-way through chewing, was already dry. Coughing became choking. This was bad, this was *really* bad. Marco at the bar was wide eyed. Carver patted her firmly and then vigorously on the back. She was gasping now. Carver gave one more whack, the peanut shifted but she felt herself shift on the stool. If she fell off she'd have real bother getting off the floor again. Tears were now running down her cheeks. Great, smudged make-up too. She was waiting for the van team to chirp up with something sarcastic, but nothing came. Perhaps they were feeling sorry for her.

Carver was checking his phone. Cady began to panic again, "It's okay there's no need to call—"

"I know," Carver said. "It was just a friend."

"Oh."

"I should get you a paper towel though," he said.

Oh, god what must she look like? Unlike Ed not to say something sarcastic at that point. Maybe they were waiting till Carver went. He trotted off to the gents, which was surprisingly close to the bar. Then the door behind her went and someone came in, clicking across the shiny wooden floor. Over her shoulder she saw it was a bloke on his way to the bathroom, without even having stopped to buy a drink. Cheeky sod. She leaned over her drink and touched her finger to her ear to check that the talk button was activated. It wasn't there. All of a sudden the bar felt really quiet.

Chapter 30

"Hey, keep your heads down: incoming!" said Dave le Bus.

"Where?" said Ed.

"Over there," Daisy pointed, "That weird bloke in the suit. He's been hanging around for ages."

"Keep your heads down, I think he's suspicious," hissed Dave.

"Of what?" said Ed.

"Of us, you pillock," Daisy, pushed Ed's head down below the level of the windows.

"Owww!" said Ed. "Get off me."

"Shush, you'd think I was murdering you."

"Both of you be quiet," said Dave, "He's looking over."

And he was. The man in the suit had a weird feline grace to him. All of his movements were sparing, and now he'd turned his head to face the van, he stood stock-still.

"Shit." Dave crouched, staring at the massive bus wing mirror. The man was moving, almost in slow motion, towards the van. "Shut that laptop lid!" whispered Dave, "He's coming over."

The man moved like a panther: fluid motion and silent poise. Not silent motion, Dave noticed, now everyone on the bus was holding their collective breath: the man clicked across the pavement as he walked. Dave tried to measure his approach in steps, what he'd do then, he had no clue. While Dave was lost in that thought, the clicking stopped. Was he staring in at the bus windows? Dave shuffled on his bum to get a better angle to stare up, without giving himself away. He could just see the bus wing mirror from where he'd wedged himself, but where he was, made looking at anything but the sky impossible. Something caught his eye in that weird fish-eye bubble reflector at the bottom of the main wing mirror. A blue glow. It was all too small to see anything, but he recognised that colour—the guy was on his phone. He was too quiet to hear, but the conversation was important enough to freeze him in his tracks.

Then the tiny blue light went out and the clicks of the man's shoes retreated across the road. Towards the bar.

"Quick," said Dave, "heads up. Get that pute back up, Ed. I think he's headed into the bar."

Ed banged frantically on the laptop till it came out of sleep mode and found the correct window. Cady was sat at the bar alone. The camera feed updated in time for Ed to see the man in the suit enter the bar. Cady clocked his back as he passed. Her mouth was moving and she was talking.

"Is this headset working Ed?" asked Daisy.

"Huh?" Ed, was still trying to take in the action happening in the tiny window. Cady was scratching her ear?

"I can't hear Cady!"

"Shit. Mute the mic," Dave, put a hand on Ed's shoulder.

"Then we won't hear anything," said Ed.

"Not Cady's mic, Daisy's."

"'Kay," Ed stabbed at the touch screen.

"What's going on?" said Daisy.

"I think she's lost the in-ear," said Dave. "It could be anywhere and Mr Burly and ex-military there has just gone in to talk to Carver. We need to get her the hell out now!"

"We'll need to take her chair in," said Daisy.

"No time," Dave was already on his way, the van door open in his wake.

"What do we do?" yelled Ed.

"Can you drive?" Dave shouted back.

"Yeah," said Ed.

"Then start her up!"

Dave disappeared into the bar.

Cady's head snapped round when Dave entered, "What?"

"No time," said Dave, closing on the stool.

"How are we—?"

"Need to carry you, okay?"

"I guess," said Cady.

Dave reached round her back with one arm and under her legs with the other and lifted her off the stool. The toilet door crashed open behind them. Dave broke into a run. Cady adjusted her arm round his neck, one shoe fell off: she shook off the other. The tall suit guy's shoes clicked across the fake wood floor after them, and he was reaching into his pocket. Dave kicked the bar door open. The van was revving outside. Daisy slid the side door open, "Get in!"

They bundled Cady and Dave into the van. Cady clung to the seat she'd been plonked on, Dave sprawled on the van floor. "Drive," he said, through the grit on the rubber mats. Ed glanced over his shoulder, then gunned the accelerator and sped off. Dave managed to struggle up to his hands and knees while the van leapt and swung, obviously Ed hadn't driven that much. Dave looked up at Cady over the laddered knee of her tights, "You okay, kid?"

"Yeah," said Cady, "I think so. Just feel a bit like that was a total waste of time."

Daisy peered into the dark behind them, she glanced at Ed and then down at Dave.

"Are they following us?" Dave asked.

"I think?" said Daisy. "Some kind of soft-top thing."

"Speakman," said Ed, between his teeth.

"It's not Speakman I'm worried about, it's his minder," said Dave. "D' you know where the rugby club is?"

"Yeah," said Ed.

"Get us there and we can swap over, my biggest worry is us getting pulled over while you're driving."

"What are you saying?"

"That you're under age?" said Cady.

"No license?" said Daisy.

"Not great under stress—"

"All right," said Ed. "You hate my driving."

"Concentrate on getting us there." said Dave.

"Shit. Upgrade waste of time to, dangerous mistake," said Cady.

"If they've noticed us, it means we were shaking the right tree," said Dave.

"If it doesn't fall on us," said Daisy.

"Hang on!" Ed shouted.

The van cornered sharply. A massive bump went through the frame nearly tipping Cady onto the floor and knocking Dave back onto his knees. Daisy was hiding behind her hands, whimpering. Then Ed put his foot down again and the van shot forward.

"Right here," said Dave.

The van slewed again. Cady looked across out of the window, the soft-top sports car, was one corner behind them and trying to keep pace to keep them in view. There were two of them in it, Carver's henchman was driving. He'd clearly done this before.

"'Kay," said Dave, "swing in to the car park here, turn it round, turn the lights off, leave it running, hop out the driving seat and come back here."

Ed did as he was instructed. He cranked the handbrake on and squeezed himself through the gap between the front seats, caught his foot on the brake lever and fell full stretch into the back. Cady caught him, or at least the top half of him.

"Steady there fella," she said. He stuttered an apology and Cady held on to him while he shook his foot free. "Hey, you did good there." His face flushed so scarlet that Cady could even see it in the sodium lights of the rugby ground car park. Tyres screeched behind them and blinding headlights hit the van.

"Strap in!" said Dave.

Ed just had time as Dave accelerated away in a spray of gravel. He aimed past the side of the oncoming car and sped up as he went. Cady could see the shocked face of Carver in the passenger seat as they hammered past and lurched left out of the gate. Dave properly floored it, pointing the van towards one of the range of hills that flanked the town. Dave gripped the steering wheel, looking into the night and flicked the headlights on low beam, scanning the mirrors and muttering under his breath.

"Where are we going?" said Daisy.

"Up on the hill," said Dave. "They'll never find us up there."

Chapter 31

"Happy Birthday to you,
You belong in a zoo.
Get plastered you bastard,
And you look like one too."

****

Her dad brought her cake through from the kitchen with great ceremony, seventeen candles curling smoke behind them. Parties in the Grey household had always been legendary, even before her mum left, when things were, well different. Cady couldn't help wondering whether her dad was overcompensating, but it would be rude to look a gift cake in the mouth, even if she didn't feel like being seventeen. She wasn't even seventeen until Sunday, but Friday night was a way better night for a party, so she was gonna be seventeen tonight, tomorrow and Sunday too. The reason the parties had legendary status among her friends was, the underage kids were allowed to drink. There was always a bar—a plank in the kitchen and a trestle table—and the rule was, surrender all ale at the door and prepare to be rationed or cut off if the signs of inebriation showed too strongly. The music was loud and the decoration was garish, usually needing no excuse for at least twinkling lights, if not full-on strobe effects. Dad's brother George tended to work the bar, with the added fun of him bringing Cady's three cousins. If Auntie Char came too, that'd be two cousins more. With the added coterie of other mates and plus ones, it made for a riotous time. Her eldest cousin, Max, had just got into being a D.J. so with his laptop and the large PA system that Dave Le Bus seemed to have filled the garage with, this party stood a good chance of being more of a riot than usual.

Cady blew at the candles. In the fuss it took her three goes to get them all out. Everyone cheered.

"Speech!"

Cady found someone had pressed a microphone in her hand. It was probably a good thing, with so many people there.

"Thanks for coming, everyone. I'm very lucky to have so many people around me with nothing better to do on a Friday than help me commiserate my old age. Err, that's it? Everyone party!"

The music kicked back in, some godawful chirpy Ed Sheeran thing or other. At least Daisy seemed to be enjoying herself and she seemed to have kidnapped Cady's cousin Henry, to do some frantic impression of Irish dancing. Cady drove back into the kitchen, grabbed a can of cider on the way past and went out of the back kitchen door to have a smoke where the littles wouldn't see her.

Two more cans of cider and another cigarette, found her at the side door of the garage. It had been propped open as the dancing in there was sufficiently frantic to make sweat drip off the metal girders of the garage door. For some reason Max had started playing slowies already. Cady glanced at her watch. Gone eleven, she guessed slow-dancing was permissible at that point. Kayleigh, Max's sister, seemed to have pulled one of Henry's friends, who looked extremely pleased with himself, when he could be seen at all, and Dana, Cady's favourite cousin, was dancing with her long-time boyfriend. She was thirteen—who had longtime boyfriends at thirteen? Where the hell had Dave managed to find a mirrorball? Then he was there. In front of her.

"You dancin'?"

"What?"

"I said, you dancin'?" said Dave. "The traditional reply is 'you askin'? But yes or no is okay too."

"Err..." said Cady and indicated the chair.

"That a yes-err or a no-err?"

"Yes-err?"

Dave held both hands out. She felt her face flush. Cady had chosen what she thought of as her most festive skirt—a short black number with big blue and green flowers on it, but the critical thing was that she could wear leggings under it and her black Converse that would hide her leg splints. Why was he? What was—? But then Dave had gently pulled her up to standing, then slowly shuffled towards the other dancers with her and was carefully holding her lower back. Could he feel that this was an effort for her? That, if she didn't concentrate on tensing all the muscles in the top of her thighs that her bum would stick out and she'd likely buckle at the knees.

Dave leaned in close and said, "Y' okay?"

"Uh, why?" she choked out, hating herself immediately.

"You looked like someone who wanted to dance?"

"My hero," she said, as ironically as she could manage.

He said something that may have been "Huh" but she found it hard to hear with the blood pounding in her ears. She let her head go and rested her forehead on Dave's shoulder. That was gonna leave a make-up mark that'd need explaining. This year, her seventeenth year, was working out as weird as it was possible for her to imagine. She let him lead her round in a small shuffling circle, chasing the tiny bright chips of light on the floor at about half their speed. He held her closer, she could smell soap, not aftershave like the sixth-form lot wore.

She looked up, following the lights onto the walls, round and round. Was that Ed in the kitchen doorway? She thought about waving, but didn't want to lose her grip and fall. She smiled. His expression was blank. Then as the next song started, it was too early for Christmas music surely, even allowing Wham. She found herself humming into Dave's ear. He smiled at her. She couldn't not return his gaze. Her face felt frozen in a smile as a smashing noise came from the main house, followed by screaming. Someone shouted, her dad? Rushing about, Dave deposited her back in her chair and ran to the door. Late as ever, the DJ stopped the music. There was plenty of noise in the house as it was. The screaming came from Daisy. Cady jammed the chair into drive and sped to find the source of the chaos.

When her chair rounded the corner into the massive living room, everyone stood in an arc facing the big bay windows, which had the curtains billowing in. Her wheels crunched on something on the floor. Ahead was Daisy, a small trickle of something dark was running down the side of her face. Cady mouthed "Okay?" to her, but Daisy just pointed across to where her dad was cradling something: unwrapping it? She wove her way carefully round the back of the crowd.

"What the hell?" Now she was closer, she could see what it was—a large concrete cinder block wrapped loosely with brown paper. She raised her eyebrows, about as high as they'd go at her dad. In response, he unwrapped the paper and turned it to face her. The words, scrawled across the paper with a thick black marker were stark and clear: *LEAVE IT!*

Chapter 32

The bus drew up outside the door in a flurry of leaves. Two women Cady didn't recognise got off and started bustling with her bags. One was half a head shorter than Cady at full stretch—hand-knitted V-neck jumper and matching ankhs as a necklace and earrings. Her oppo, the woman nearest her, tall, tied-back blonde hair, baggy jeans and a sweatshirt, was clearly the driver. She took a last drag on her cigarette and flicked it into the pot.

"No smoking on the bus dear," said Driver Lady.

"Where's Dave?"

The woman wouldn't meet her gaze, then spoke over her shoulder on the way to the driver's door, "Not in today dear. Get on the bus please."

As the tail lift crawled up to deck height, Cady caught Daisy's eye. She had a plaster on her face. Cady pantomimed a what-the-hell twitch and face-scrunch combo, with an added head bob towards one of the new bus-driving team. Daisy shrugged back. Ankh Earrings coughed politely, indicating Cady should drive off the ramp. She smiled a sorry back and drove on.

On board, Cady leaned over to Daisy and hissed, "Where the hell is Dave?"

"I dunno," said Daisy, "I thought you would?"

"What's that supposed to mean?"

"I just thought after the party and you two and everything."

"It was just a dance."

"You like him."

"Well yeah, but—"

Earrings butted in and said, "No leaning forwards in your seat please, if we stop suddenly, you'll get hurt."

"Ok-ayy!" said Cady.

"Hey, we don't have to take any backchat from lippy teenagers," snapped Earrings.

Cady opened her mouth, then closed it. She signed #*sorry* on her chest.

"And none of that kind of language either," she said.

Cady couldn't bring herself to reply, got out her earbuds and put them in. The woman stopped glowering over her, shook her head and sat down half-way down the aisle across from Daisy.

Cady texted Dave. No sign of a reply. Even a blast of Vampire Weekend didn't cheer her up. She texted Daisy instead:

Cady: Where's Ed for that matter

Daisydoo: We didn't stop at his this morning

When Cady disembarked the bus, Daisy had gone ahead as usual to deploy the kettle. Cady broke out a stick of gum in lieu of a cigarette. Her jaw cracked as she put the gum in. The smell of smoke draped everywhere, like a damp campfire blanket. A large arrow made of pink post-its pointed to the library. A last post it below read *6th Form*.

"Huh", she said and turned right, not left and went in through the doors to the library. Inside seemed to be a very cheerful full house. Even Bad Bill and Jazz were in today, so the library was packed around its central wooden table, and it was the noisiest it had ever been. There was still no sign of Ed, so Cady went to search for what passed for their stacks, while Daisy bustled in and out taking drinks orders.

When Daisy returned with a black coffee for Cady, they both stared, impressed at the temporary control centre Ed had made. There were even cables snaking off God-knew-where up and into the tops of the stacks. Daisy silently presented him with his black, insulated metal mug, with a simple font saying *geek* on it. He took it and nodded his thanks. He was absorbed with several bars uploading several things at once, and was muttering about the school's internet speed.

"S'up," said Cady.

"Everything," said Ed, "You want me to make a list?"

"Precis me."

"Well, I'm uploading all the audio from your bug, which was pretty much a waste of time. But at least once it's on the secure cloud I'll be able to analyse it."

"Why didn't you do that last night?"

"At your party, slave driver," Ed returned his nose to his coffee.

"What's that bar there, then?" Daisy poked at the screen.

"That's the footage from the hidden camera that overlooks the building site. For some reason, its gone wonky and it's pointing at the sky. All you can see are birds and stars now it's moved, but it moved at dusk and there's a brilliant cloud of bats. I'll have to get back up the bookshelves and fix it."

"Don't do it with the library full," said Cady.

"I'm not stupid," said Ed.

"No, you aren't. Jeez, what's that noise?"

"That's a super-fast forward version of last night's recording, now it's uploaded," said Ed.

"I meant what's that specific noise?" she said.

"Oh." Ed hit an icon on the screen and the recording slowed down to play the sound of muffled running water and faint singing.

"What the hell is that?" said Cady.

Daisy had her face screwed up so hard, it looked as if it might implode, "I think I might know—"

"What is it?" Ed asked.

"I think he's spending a penny-"

"Carver? Eugh," said Cady, frowning.

Charlie cheered at that point from across the room. He was refereeing a loud match of blow football on the table between Jazz and Bill, with TAs cheerleading their charges. In a brief lull in the action, Charlie yelled over his shoulder into the stacks, "You're recording people peeing now?"

"Eeewww!" cried Bill.

"Shut up!" yelled Ed. "I'm trying to listen."

He had headphones back on now and was rolling the recording back and forward across some point in time.

"Don't be an arsehole Ed, just because someone wrecked the Scooby den!" shouted Cady.

"No, you're being an arsehole, just because Dave wasn't on the bus!" Ed shouted back.

He yanked the headphones out of the laptop, with the volume blaring. Ed had tweaked the sound already so the bathroom noise was now background and blaring out, with a good deal of distortion was a small ditty that Carver was singing to himself. *Hmm-hmm-hmm-hmmm, doo-doo-doo-doo, hmm-hmm-hmm-hmmm.*

"What *is* that tune?" asked Ed.

"Baby Shark?" suggested Charlie from across the room. But he was the only one paying attention to the music. Every other eye rested on Cady, who'd stood from her chair and was staring at Ed. Ed was staring at the computer and looped the music again.

"Turn it off," she said.

"Eh?" said Ed.

"Turn it off!" Cady banged her hand on the bookshelf beside her and the coffee that she'd perched there leapt, and fell, slowly in silence. Cady, Daisy and Ed watched it fall, arcing coffee over Cady's new boots. Daisy's mouth was open, but no sound came out. The whole library was frozen.

Crash. The coffee pooled out. Daisy closed her mouth, then, "Mop. I'll get the…"

"How did you know Dave wasn't on the bus?" asked Cady.

"I, er…"

"Don't lie to me Ed, you're a shitty liar."

"I—"

"What, Ed? What did you do?"

Ed was reaching for his headphones, but then didn't and allowed himself to rock back, then forward.

"I told them."

"Told who?"

"Bus people."

"Told them what?"

"'Bout the party."

"What?!"

"You and D-dave, at the—"

"Nothing happened!"

"I just told them what I saw and they said I was right to report it and that it was inappropriate behavior for one of their drivers, and that they would suspend him pending an investigation and that— It's not right, Cady,"

"Christ, Ed!"

"Don't shout, Cady, you know I don't like it when you shout."

"You're meant to be my friend."

"Not right…not right,"

"For once, someone wanted me, for me. I felt special. He saw a girl not a chair! Is that so wrong?"

Ed was muttering under his breath and rocking. Cady turned her chair and aimed it for the door, "Screw you Ed Buckmaster! Screw you!"

Chapter 33

Cady drove her chair flat out, not caring what direction she went in. She drove with her left hand so she could wipe her face with her right. The chair frame shook as it battered over the badly made pavements of Parkfields. It rattled her jaws, but she just clenched them tighter.

She nearly ran into the traffic light at the crossing before she noticed it. She turned and headed across, only sketchily aware that the lights were in her favour. The chair banged up the other ramp and buzzed over the textured pavement. She jinked right and the chair lurched and then ran alongside the blur of park railings near the school.

"Hey, steady lady!" Came a woman's voice in front of her.

Cady looked up. By reflex her hand was off the controller. She was nose to nose with the woman's pram which had some kind of tightly wrapped bundle in pink inside. She muttered a sorry and jammed her controller left through the park gates.

Head down, she followed the path. The tarmac was grey, the edges needed attention as they gave way to those fierce sprouts of grass, unique to public spaces. Over her shoulder she could hear wild laughing. She knew it was the kids on the play equipment, but that didn't stop her needing to get away from it. Away from the noise. Away from everyone. She needed to make sure she was far enough away that no-one would come after her.

She pushed her controller harder forwards, the golf ball digging in her hand. She glanced down at the new switch on her control panel, then nearly drove off the path while she wasn't watching and the path curved away. She corrected the swerve as the path disappeared into some trees. Was that ticking she could hear? Dad would be so pissed off if she'd trashed her chair on day two. She took her hand off the controller again and the chair stopped. No, the ticking was coming from behind her. She craned her neck as best she could, then turned the chair too. There was a man on the path, the ticking coming from his crisp march. She recognised the shape of him. The awkward shape in the suit, matched with oddly graceful motion. And he was walking. Quickly. Towards her.

She slammed the stick forward again and sped farther into the wood, leaves now crunching under her wheels. She didn't dare go off-track in case she got bedded down, but the tic-tac, tic-tac was getting closer. He wasn't running, this chair had done eight mph even before her dad had fiddled with it. It didn't even sound like he'd quickened his pace at all. But the steady click was nearer by the second. Where could she flick her new overdrive switch? If she took a chance and went right at the end of the path through the trees, there was an underpass below the main road into town, it was a good straight stretch, with more garden on the other side of it, she could pick up some distance and maybe some passers-by.

'Caaa-dy!' He had a thick, greasy, Estuary accent. Somewhere not quite London, Essex maybe? He was close now, she turned the chair and saw him cut across the last of the woods to meet her. *Shit*. She flicked the switch. It was one of those switches that lit up when it was on. It was hard to see in the daylight.

She guessed it was on. Nothing else had happened. *It better had be on.* A breeze blew from behind the man, wafting the scent of some god-awful aftershave. She looked across her shoulder and he was ten strides away and holding his arm in an odd stuck-out fashion. Shit, was that a gun? She pushed the chair into drive and it sprang to life, tyres squealing. Hell, she'd better be careful she didn't crash the thing, if it was going to go that fast. She eased of the control while she cornered to face the underpass, then pushed the stick again. This time she was facing in a straight line and she could let it rip. The chair leapt down the tunnel, flashing past sickly flourescents glowing through dirty plastic.

"Cay-dee! You can't run!" But that was exactly what she was planning. There were twenty strides to the end of the tunnel, and she was racing. Her overdriven electric engine whined. The bastard would never catch her.

Then her world exploded. Something smashed over her head, she felt the loudest *smack* she'd ever heard, like a slap round the head on both sides at the same time. Plastic shards rained from above. God, he was shooting at her. For real. A shrieking echoed round the tunnel. That must've been her. Her own voice. She felt out of herself. The chair was still in drive, and she snapped to in time to choose jinking right and losing some ground in favour of not giving him a straight shot. A massive *whang* ricocheted from the tunnel and then *tic-tac-tic-tac-tic* as the shooter broke into a run.

Surely, there must be someone in this garden somewhere? It was one of those council interstitial spaces that didn't have enough space to have a proper planner consider it a park, so it had paths and streetlights and sad-drooping flowerbeds behind ornamental edging, and had to be happy with that. But there was no-one there. Not a dog-walker or a jogger. No-one. Cady risked a look upwards. Though it had been dry for ages, the sky loomed battleship grey and heavy. Was the threat of a bit of rain keeping people indoors? She didn't know what people thought anymore. Didn't they know what was going on? Didn't they—?

Crack!

It was a really odd noise. Not a bang as such, but a massive, loud mechanical crunch, just behind the *whack* from where the round hit. That one dug up a foot of turf in front of the flower bed on her left. Was he using a silencer? It wasn't all that silent. Should she swerve like they did in the movies? Her chair lurched left and she fought to right it. Another *crack* followed. Had she been hit? The chair was still moving, but the covers on the wheels on the right were in shreds. Luckily, her wheels were solid. Was she veering now? There was a definite lean to the right. Shit, had he hit her motor? At least trying to correct for straight at the speed she was now at made her swerve anyway.

Thud, thud, crack, crack.

The chair lurched again. Cady felt as if she'd been kicked in the back, hard. The slam made her fumble her controller, and the chair lurched. She tried to correct, but switching the direction of the chair made a wobble into a rock, and the chair pitched past its point of balance. The world and time turned to treacle as the chair toppled and Cady tried not to black out. *tic- tac- tic-.*

Chapter 34

The library was in chaos. Books were flying. There was screaming and laughing. Daisy had gone out to find Ed, leaving the two TAs and Nasreen trying to restrain Bill from throwing anything else. Everyone seemed to be at it though, even the normally charming and compliant Charlie. Some kind of send-help alarm was beeping semi-discreetly. When Daisy found him she was sorry that she had.

Ed was sat on the kerb, feet over into the road, head in hands, rocking backwards and keening. If any of what Ed was saying was speech, Daisy couldn't make it out. She sat next to him and put her arm round him. He froze, then shrugged her off, resumed rocking but now moaned "No-no-no-no-no", stopping only to catch his breath every minute or so. He'd started scratching the sides of his face. The sight of welts rising on Ed's cheeks made Daisy want to cry.

"It'll be okay," she said.

"No it WON'T! Nothing will be okay. S'all broken. Cady hates me, the school's done and it's all my fault!"

"It's not all your fault."

"Yes it IS." Ed stopped to wipe his nose on his sleeve, ignoring Daisy's proffered tissue, "I'm the smart one. I should have worked this all out. It should be easy. It's what I do. But I couldn't and now I can't and it's all screwed."

He stared at the tissue, took it, blew his nose and then let the tissue fall to the ground. Daisy rolled her eyes, picked up the tissue, using a plastic bag, and stuffed the lot back into her pocket.

"Litter-bug."

The doors from the main building crashed open and a crack team of TAs ran to the rescue, lanyards with security tags trailing behind them. They flew into the doors to the sixth-form block and the alarm stopped. Loud shouting ensued. Daisy turned back to look at Ed. Ed looked at his feet.

"It will, you know," said Daisy, "be okay, I mean."

Ed made a non-committal grunt.

"Cady needs us. We're the Scooby team to her, y' know."

"Scooby Doo?"

"Yeah, her."

"It was a him."

"Oh, was he? I thought it looked like a she. You're gonna tell me the puppy was too, now."

"Yes. The puppy was called Scrappy, yes it was a boy and yes, they were shit. At least after 1975."

"I'm scared, you know that."

"Yeah, me too."

The window in the library slid open, distracting their attention. Daisy turned in time to see Bill trying to climb out of the window, Ed returned to examining at his feet. Daisy sighed, clocked Ed, then stood slowly. By the time she'd gotten as far as the window, Bill was nearly out of it. All thought of safe restraint or team teach had been abandoned, they were trying to stop Bill hurting himself, though one of the TAs on the inside of the library still had a hold of a corner of his jumper. Daisy met him at the window, sizing up the location and size of the baldy rose bushes in his way. Huge raindrops began to fall.

"Want a hand out there, honey?" she asked.

"Huh," said Bill.

"Come on then, careful." She held a hand out. Bill grasped it, then pulled himself onto the ledge and perched like some kind of ungainly bird.

"Whoa there!" said somebody from inside, still holding his jersey. He rocked gently, grinned and then in one smooth move shucked himself out of the pullover and jumped. Everyone inside rushed to the window, seemingly in slow motion. A TA appeared at the window and cried, "Billy nooo!"

Bill turned his head from his new position in the flower bed and said, "Wot?"

Daisy helped him to his feet, and in return he gave her a massive hug. She grinned. If it had've been Ed on the receiving end, he'd have freaked the hell out. She looked over her shoulder. There was a dry heart-shaped patch on the kerb where Ed had been. She squinted down the road towards the gates, then quickly up to the main building. No Ed.

The doors behind her opened and Linda and one of the Jennys came out to retrieve Bill. They unwrapped him from Daisy and gently led him inside, shepherding Daisy as they went. She protested about Ed, but since he was one of Absdowne's more independent pupils, the staff didn't seem overly concerned, or were way more concerned with the chaos that had ensued over the last hour. She crept in, looking over her shoulder at the rain falling, filling in the shape on the pavement.

Inside, the world was returning to whatever passed for normal on a weekday. But even as the books were put back on the shelves and Daisy went to retrieve the hoover, no-one had noticed Ed's laptop, slid off its stack of books, face forward into the shelves, screen still on, chiming an alert quietly.

Chapter 35

The metal of the gun muzzle made a cold 'O' on Cady's forehead. Her jaw ached where she'd been clenching her teeth. This bastard was really wringing every second out of it. Cady had imagined what it would be like to die. Of course she had, she had a slowly degenerative genetic condition, though no-one quite knew what, but she'd always imagined getting caught by some maddening chest infection, not some arsehole with a gun. She thought, faced with the threat of death, she'd feel that watery-guts desperation, but no. She just felt very pissed off. She struggled again against the chair pinning her and the ragged edges of the chair's bullet-shredded plastic casing.

"Any last missives?" The words were marinated in halitosis and aftershave.

She couldn't think of anything. Then under her fingers, inside the wounded skin of the chair was a small plastic-covered breath of hope.

"Yeah," she whispered, "I need you to—" She coughed, her hand coiled under the chair. He leaned over her, all stale breath and eagerness. She tugged as she leaned up to whisper in his ear, "I need you to—". Then with the speed of a viper she tugged the cable and jammed it into the assassin's leg. The bare ends where the right-hand motor had been shot, stuck into the fabric of the man's trousers, right near his groin, "Bite me, you asshole."

There was a crack and a flash, she felt herself jerk as the high-tension motor cable gave all its stored charge in one go. As her vision sparkled out, she hoped she'd got him as well.

Chapter 36

Daisy jogged from the school gate facing towards town. It was the only thing she could think to do. If Cady had fled in a straight line she'd have gone through the park. Daisy loathed jogging, or any sport for that matter. It made her tired and cross. She instinctively patted her jeans pocket where her asthma inhaler was. She knew it would be there, but it never hurt to double-check.

She stopped and scanned the scrubby park for clues. Since the rain had started falling there was really no clue as to which way Cady might have gone. The way the park was laid out, a huge stand of trees occupied most of her eye line. It was unlikely Cady had gone through there, what with the amount she complained whenever she had to go more than twenty yards to find a dropped kerb to drive her wheelchair up. So she must have gone one way or the other around the trees. There was no-one to ask. The sight of Cady in her chair and hoodie would have stuck out in someone's mind. But there were no minds to stick out in. Weird. Why was there no-one out today? Okay, it was raining, but still. Daisy's Grandma, always good for a quote, would always say "You're not sugar, you won't melt."

"Come on Daisy, think," she said out loud, as if the trees might give her an opinion she could act on. The rain patting the leaves was the only reply she got.

The howling of sirens broke her indecision. Across the road that cut the park off abruptly, shot a white car with flashing lights all over the roof. Daisy jogged down the path towards where the tunnel that led to town scooped under the carriageway. As she passed the trees, the howl of the police car started again, echoing out of the throat of the underpass, as if it was a wounded animal. Surely, the sirens couldn't be—

Daisy ran.

It seemed like one of those dreams where she ran and ran and didn't get any closer. In the distance Daisy could see the pathetic form of Cady's wheelchair, on its side, powerless. From her vantage point, she couldn't see where Cady was at all. She barreled on. Her senses seemed full, face wet, legs full of pounding, ears full of her own voice yelling, "CadyCadyCadyCady". She followed the path, it was a good job it was straight. The chair had tipped to its right, off the path and was in the grass. Was the back of it off too? There were plastic panels missing, she was sure. Someone shouted. She ran on. The shouting got louder. Louder than the police siren. The shout was aimed at her. So was a gun.

"STOP! Armed police! Tazer! On your knees, now or I will shoot!"

Shit, how many times had she shouted that already? That was the voice of someone who did not like to be ignored. Daisy stopped.

"Knees! Now!"

Daisy slowly kneeled. These pink leggings were never going to be the same again. She had somehow wound up on the grass. She was about two Daisy lengths to Cady's chair. Was that a hand she could see? Was there blood? Ow. There was something under her left knee. Had she kneeled on those clay edging tiles? No, too far over. She moved her arm down to see.

"Hands behind your head!" The woman's voice was a lot closer now, but over Daisy's right shoulder and she daren't look. Daisy put her hands behind her head. When they were in place, the woman in the police uniform came into view, she seemed to be simultaneously trying to hold Daisy and the crashed chair in view at once. In one hand she held what appeared to be a child's plastic gun. In the other she was trying to lean part of her walkie-talkie to her mouth. The hand with the gun shook.

"Where's that back-up, Noah?" she shouted into the microphone. "And we're gonna need an ambulance."

"No!" The words were out of Daisy's mouth before she could take them back.

"You!" The woman gestured with her eyes, not the gun, but it still shook slightly in her hand. "Quiet."

The woman looked at the chair again, then Daisy. She walked forward to where Daisy was and moved behind her, using the hand that had finished with the walkie-talkie to remove handcuffs and clicked one round Daisy's right wrist. In a deft motion she swept up hand and cuff and collected the other arm. Now Daisy properly felt in trouble.

"Shit," said the PC quietly. "Stand up, slowly." The woman helped her to her feet. At least her left knee could get a break. Whatever had been digging into her was pointy. The PC still stood behind her.

"What's this?" the officer said. When Daisy didn't reply, she found herself jerked ninety degrees and her head prodded down to where she'd just been kneeling. In the dirt was the black shape of a gun.

"I d-d. I don't know," Daisy said.

"I think you've got some explaining to do."

Chapter 37

"Where's Cady?"

Daisy sat in an interview room. She looked over the rim of the paper tea cup she'd been presented. The tea smelled faintly of soup. She was shouting alone into the void. There was no glass two-way mirror like on the telly. Just four white walls a horrible polystyrene ceiling, and a grey band round the room full of sockets that seemed to have an old-school cassette player plugged into it. The chair was making her bum numb.

"Where's my friend? I want to see her!"

The door opened and someone new came in. The tea had been provided by a kindly older man in a proper police uniform. He reminded her of her dad. The woman was dressed in a grey trouser suit and a white blouse. She wore a pair of black Doc Marten shoes. The kind of shoes to run and kick and climb in. In another time and place Daisy would have had shoe envy. The woman had a similar paper cup in one hand and a sheaf of papers in a grey card folder in the other, which she placed squarely on the table putting the cup down at the bottom right of it, like a full stop. She pulled out the chair, sat carefully, and stared at Daisy. She had a round face with grey eyes and a quite big nose that been broken and reset at some point, a slight kink in it. Her brown hair was pulled back into a pony-tail from which not a single hair escaped. She reached down for her cup, drank from it and replaced it, all without breaking Daisy's gaze.

"You're in a lot of trouble young lady." She had a slight accent, Scottish maybe? "You do not have

to say anything. But it may harm your defence—"
There was a knock at the interview room door: "If
you do not mention when—" Then another knock.
"What? It can't be that urgent!" The door creaked
open. "Gah, where was I?"

"Defence?" said Daisy helpfully. The door-
opening person, the constable who'd handcuffed
Daisy earlier, stood behind the suited detective, trying
to catch her eye.

"Thank you. It may harm your defence—"
She paused and snapped her head round. "What!
You've stopped me now Stone, *what* do you *want*."

"Sarge sent me in."

"That, Stone, was not what I asked."

"Well, Sarge said that…" Stone flicked her
eyes towards Daisy and then back again. A pregnant
pause hung in the air. Stone flicked her eyes to Daisy
again, with more desperation. Daisy waved.

"No. The panto's gonna kill me," said the
suited detective. "Just tell me, in words."

"The sarge said that the suspect was special
and if she was special that we should sort out
someone to accompany her and we should bloody
well sort out a duty solicitor or the chief would be all
over us. Ma'am."

The detective looked skywards and through
gritted teeth said, "Would you like us to call your
parents?"

"Hell no," said Daisy.

"Thought not."

"Do you have a solicitor?"

"No."

"Okay. We will provide one for you." She rubbed her eyes, in a way that Daisy thought was a bit theatrical.

"Where's Cady?"

"Hospital," said Stone. The detective sliced a look at her. "Sorry."

"You will be," the detective sighed.

The woman stood slowly, collected her notes, as carefully as she'd placed them, drained her coffee cup, screwed it up and dropped it into the basket under the table, before stalking out of the room. The constable held the door open, when the detective had gone, she looked back at Daisy, "Do want something to eat love? You might be here a while."

Daisy couldn't concentrate to answer. The constable withdrew then returned with a bar of chocolate from the vending machine. Daisy hands were shaking too much to unwrap it. After three failed attempts, she let out a howl and swept her arm across the table. Tea, paper-cup and chocolate flew onto the floor. Daisy burst into tears.

Chapter 38

Cady was conscious. Her eyes were still shut, though. She wondered whether Daisy could tell she was faking. She'd been at her bedside for at least an hour that Cady had been awake. And she'd talked without interruption. So far, Cady knew about Ed's newest research—he was convinced Carver was guilty, but still hadn't found a motive, but Cady was still too cross to listen, she knew about the whole crime scene and Daisy's subsequent arrest and release for something to do with firearms, but sadly no news of the arrest of the dude whose gun it was. There had been no mention of him at all. Vanished. She couldn't help thinking of him as Tic-Tac. She couldn't help hearing that noise, every time she nodded off, which was why she had been trying not to for twenty-four hours. She felt like hell. No doubt she looked like it too.

I Should Be So Lucky by Kylie broke the flow of Daisy's chatter. It was her text notification noise. She rummaged in her canvas shoulder bag.

"It's from Ed," said Daisy, looking up at the lump of covers. She looked down again, "It's about Carver."

"Wanker," said Cady from under the covers.

Daisy flew across the room and enfolded Cady, in a huge hug.

"Lay off," said Cady. "I've been shot. And electrocuted."

"To be fair," said Daisy, "you did that to yourself."

Cady grunted and rolled over slowly, grunting more as she did so. She signed for Daisy to help her with a plastic water beaker with a straw in it. It was impossible to drink from the angle she was sitting at, so she spent some time fumbling with the bed controls to get the head of the bed to a better position. Cady got her to help by adjusting the pillows and then being water bearer again. The hospital gown gaped at Cady's side. Somehow, it had gotten all twisted round. There was a massive bulge of gauze taped to Cady's side above her hip that showed through the gap in her gown. The gauze was pink in places. Cady caught Daisy staring at it.

"Does it hurt?"

"Uncomfortable, but yay for NHS painkillers."

"They really shot you, then?"

"Doesn't seem real. The docs said I was lucky, straight through me and not any major organs. Missed my liver by a coupla centimetres. I didn't even bleed that much."

"Your chair's pretty banged-up."

"Yeah, Dad brought the manual in. I've not been in it yet."

Daisy was still holding her phone. She fumbled to put it back in her bag. Cady interrupted, mid-fumble, "What does the text say? You're dying to tell me."

"Oh," said Daisy, "It says Re: Carver. Fracking.'"

"Eddie's laconic as ever."

"He's really upset."

"Yeah. Well so am I."

Cady drew a deep breath and Daisy's shoulders hunched. The door opened and a cheerful long-haired brunette in a white coat, weird blue trousers and trainers came in. "Hiya! I'm Katy, your physio. Shall we try and get you back up and about, eh?"

"I'd better be going, then."

"S'okay, you can stay if you like," said Cady.

The physio and Daisy exchanged a glance, "I'll be back later."

"'Kay."

And Daisy left. Despite not being alone, in fact being in a whole hospital filled with staff, security and even the occasional couple of police, Cady had never felt more vulnerable. Tic-Tac was still out there and presumably still wanted to kill her. More so now she knew what he looked like. Why the hell would anyone decide to have anyone killed? Was she that much of a threat? They must be closer than they thought. Fracking. Christ, what did she know about that? Not much. Stuff on the telly about OAPs and hippies protesting up north? Was there some stuff from the States, too?

Once the physio was over, she grabbed her phone. Despite her dad taking her laptop home, her phone was still here and the Wi-Fi in the hospital was free. When she smelled the arrival of the catering trolley in the ward somewhere, she realised how long she'd been glued to her browser for, and how hungry she was. She was still eating with one hand, phone in the other when Daisy arrived. Cady waved her to sit with a fork.

"Have you read this shit?"

"Which in particular?" Daisy could never really bring herself to swear. God, if this week didn't make anyone swear. *Old habits die hard, I guess.*

"The fracking stuff."

"Oh, Ed showed me."

"Did he show you the crazy YouTube with the dude with his tap water on fire?"

"Yep."

"What the actual—? The colour of it."

"Yeah," Daisy sighed. Cady's fork was still mid-air, "You gonna finish that?"

"Oh no," said Cady. "Knock yourself out."

Daisy sat on the covers and gathered the bowl off the over-bed table, that peculiar fixture of hospital rooms. Cady leaned back on her large mound of pillows still transfixed by the flaming water on repeat. She shuffled her bum, bashed the pillows and shuffled again.

"What do we do about it?" mumbled Daisy from around a mouthful of sponge pudding and congealed custard.

"Why do *we* have to do anything?"

"'Cos no-one else is gonna?"

Cady returned to pillow punching.

"I hate it when you're right."

Daisy shrugged and finished the sponge pudding. "He was right too y' know," she said when she'd finished.

"Who?"

"Ed."

Cady sat up against the head of the hospital bed and clutched one of the pillows to her—half teddy bear hug, half like she was trying to wring it out. "I thought you were on my side."

"I am," said Daisy, "That doesn't stop him being right."

"Fuck Daze, you're always so fucking sensible."

"Sorry."

"I just wanted something, someone for me y' know?"

"Yeah, I know. He's way older than you, though."

"I'm old enough, he's old enough. Besides, what the fuck difference does that make when I don't know how long I'm ever going to live? Huh?"

Daisy looked at her feet.

"If I die when I'm twenny-one, I'm seventeen now, that's the equivalent of most of my life! I'm a fucking mayfly. And at least they get to do it before they go. What's wrong with me having a little fun? Hey?"

"No-one said you can't have fun. It's just—"

"What? Just what Daze?"

"Dave. He shouldn't have. He was meant to look after you."

"I kinda hoped he would."

"What would Barb say? 'Inappropriate!'"

"Screw Barb," Cady muttered into her pillow.

A thin version of *The Macarena* burst from Daisy's bag. She rustled. "It's Ed."

Cady pulled her head under the covers, just the middle finger of one hand showing.

"S'up Eddy?" Daisy asked.

He told them.

Chapter 39

"You can't go," said Daisy.

"The hell I can't," said Cady.

"They'll never let you out. You've just been shot."

"I'll discharge myself."

"For you to get shot all over again?" Daisy whirled round and folded her arms. "It's a trap!"

Daisy had relayed, via Ed, that Councilor Carver had sent a message to Cady. He'd left it in a folder that Ed was snooping in on Carver's council server looking for evidence. Cady couldn't decide whether she thought that he'd been rumbled, or what the message said was more disturbing.

****

To: Ms Cadence Grey. We need to talk. Meet me. Council chambers. Midnight. Come alone. A.D.Carver.

****

Cady stared at the copy of the message on her screen one more time, as if her eyes could wring more meaning out of the sixteen words displayed there. She threw her phone onto the bed. The clock at the end of the bay she was in read 9.15 a.m. She drummed her fingernails on the bed rails, thankful that there was no-one else in this bay today, though that could change in a minute. She was still just old enough to be in the children's ward, which meant she didn't have to spend hospital time with loads of wheezy old men.

"I know charging in there without a plan isn't like you at all Cady, but seriously?" Daisy stared at her.

"All right, Ms Sarcasm, what kind of a plan?"

"Police? Let them deal with it."

"And let that slippery bastard off the hook? I'd rather get shot again. We don't know enough yet, if we fold now, he'll walk. Rich folk always do."

"Ok, what about—?"

"No Ed." Cady said.

"But—"

"No."

Cady folded her arms. Daisy sighed and turned her back, looking up at the clock herself. Then she checked her watch, as if that was going to be any different. A nurse came in to do Cady's obs. Her cheerful bustling seemed out of context across the skein of tension in the room. When she'd finished, parked the blood pressure machine and delivered cheery goodbyes, Daisy turned back to Cady, "At least let me come with you."

"It says alone."

"I know it does, but no-one's gonna count me, are they?"

Cady shrugged and picked her phone up again. It would give her time to read the rest of the stuff Ed had compiled, even if she didn't want to see him. No point walking in totally unprepared. Sat on the bed and then leaned to the bedside cabinet. Once she'd struggled the door open and pulled out the plastic bag it contained, she righted herself and presented the whole thing to Daisy.

"Take this home then and bring me all my clothes you can find that are black. There should be leggings and a hoodie, at least. Oh, and clean pants."

"Do they need to be black as well?"

"Har, har."

"Won't your dad think it's weird, me bringing stuff in for you not him?"

"Meh, bring me some towels in too and tell him I'm on my period. He won't ask after that."

"Oh sorry, I didn't know I'd have brought some," said Daisy, then realised. "Oh."

"Meet me back here at visiting time tonight and we'll play it from there."

"That's our plan?" said Daisy.

"Pretty much, yeah."

"How are we going to get you there?"

"Manual chair? Oh, bring my leather gloves in, too."

Her power chair, released from the police now the SOCO team had measured and photographed all the bullet damage they could find, was languishing, wounded, in her dad's garage, waiting for the completion of a late engine strip-down that trumped even her.

"But we haven't got a van, now Dave—"

"Yeah, I know," Cady gazed out of the window. "But it's only a walk from here."

"It's the other side of town!"

"It'll only take ten minutes. What? It'll be fine."

Now it was Daisy's turn to shrug. Cady watched her go over to the window and look through the drizzle to the street outside, hands on the windowsill. She recoiled, when she found the large patch of damp that was pooling to one side of the ledge. She wiped her hands on her trousers, tutted and took the plastic bag from Cady.

"When's visiting?"

"Attagirl," said Cady.

Daisy rolled her eyes and left the room. Cady went back to her phone and started going back through all of Ed's information that she'd kept on it. Every file, every video, every photograph. She asked her favourite nurse as she passed if she could get a coffee. On balance, she was going to need it.

****

"What took you?" said Cady, sitting on the side of the bed.

"Oh, my Mum and Dad were a nightmare." Cady quirked an eyebrow in response. "They were getting ready to go out to one of their BCT meetings."

"Get you with the acronyms."

Daisy mimed flapping in response. Cady looked blank, "Bats," said Daisy.

Cady smiled. "It keeps them out of trouble, I guess."

"We can talk."

"Point," said Cady, "Close those curtains round the bed, then keep an eye out for me while I get changed. They'll be chucking people out in about half an hour. At which point, you need to be going to the loo."

"I don't need to—"

"No, I wouldn't think you do. You've went on the way in didn't you?"

"Yes? How—?"

"You're nothing if not a creature of habit, honey. You need to hide in the loo while they think they're kicking everyone out," whispered Cady.

"Oh, hah, yeah."

Cady always found closed bed-curtains oppressive. It didn't matter which hospital and she'd been in quite a few, they always felt too close and the crush of doctors and equipment that made the bottoms billow out like a badly worn skirt. She always wondered if it must drive the doctors mad. Always having that fabric shroud round them when they were trying to work. And when the curtains were closed it meant two things: bad news or intimate examination. She shuddered, then pulled her black turtleneck over her head.

"You okay in there?" whispered Daisy. "They're starting to come round."

"Nearly done."

She struggled on with her leggings, tugging them over reluctant legs, then rustled in the bag for socks. She was in luck, Daisy had packed her favourite wooly black pair. If she was going into the belly of the beast at least she'd have warm feet. She swung her legs back over the side of the bed and swept the curtain aside as best she could.

"You look very… stealth," Daisy said.

Daisy had her favorite black and white stripy jumper on and a leggings and skirt combo in purple. She noticed Cady staring, "What? They're the darkest things I own." They clashed alarmingly with Daisy's bright pink converse.

"You look great," said Cady, with a smile that caught on. "We look great."

"You want helping into your chair?"

"No, we wanna leave all that until they think everybody's gone."

"How exactly are we going to get out past the nurse's station?"

"One bridge at a time," Cady said. She looked up the ward and then down. "Right. Go!" Then, when Daisy was about to go straight up the main ward corridor past the nurses' desk to the public toilets, "Not that way! Behind you, that door's patient toilets. Go in there. I'll knock when it's all clear. One long, two short, one long. Okay?"

"How long?" asked Daisy.

"I don't know," said Cady, "when they've all settled down. Could be a while. Here, take this."

Cady proffered a copy of *Hello* magazine. It wasn't something she'd read herself, but the school nurses had brought it round earlier. She'd have preferred a *What Car?* or an old *NME* but you couldn't have everything.

"Thanks," said Daisy, biting her lip.

Cady held her hand briefly as she handed the magazine over, then used the other hand to waft her in the direction of the patient loo. Daisy went in, peered round the door, went the other side of it and took one last glance back at Cady. She gave a thumbs up in return. Now they just had to wait.

Chapter 40

Knock – knock knock - knock.
Silence.
Knock - knock knock - knock.
Silence.

Cady looked down the ward again. There was only one nurse at the nurses' station and she was answering the phone. Cady knocked again, randomly this time and hissed through the door. "Daze, come on kid, we need to scoot." There was a clunking of bathroom lock and Daisy's usually smiling face poked round the door. Her eyes were red.

"You okay, hon?" said Cady. Daisy nodded. It was very dark in the bathroom. "Why didn't you turn the light on?"

"They would have found me."

Fair point. Cady beckoned Daisy out, hoping that her friend wouldn't panic too much if she realised that this, really was as far as her plan had been, well planned to. But "one bridge at a time" as her dad would say. Get past the nurses station, then… Well that was the next bridge.

The phone at the nurses' station rang. Cady jumped. The nurse seemed oblivious to them, and was fifty metres down the main ward to their right. She was staring into the distance, round the corner relative to Cady and Daisy—the direction Cady and Daisy needed to go if they were to get out, up the ward to the main doors. She signed *shush* to Daisy. The conversation at the nurses' station seemed to be about admitting an emergency patient, right then.

"Jenny!" the nurse called out, in the direction away from them, "We've got a bed to make up. Incoming."

Jenny, replying with the tone of a superior said, "Put her in bay three."

Shit, that was Cady's bay. They were coming towards them, right now. They were trapped. She looked both ways—back behind them, the HDU beds, where the beeps of diverse alarms had kept her awake much of the night; ahead the nurses station and the school day room. The day room—that might just be enough. She wheeled herself forwards with a firm forward spin, Daisy followed. As the door loomed on their left, she heard the squeak of plastic footwear.

"Quick! Door!" said Cady. "Push me in!"

Daisy's face was a mask of confusion: Cady never let anyone push her, hardly ever.

"Just do it." Daisy did as she was instructed, then: "Now spin me to face the door," The footsteps were nearly upon them, they'd get discovered for sure. "Duck!" said Cady.

Daisy dropped from the knees and fell to a crouch behind the chair. The chair now faced back into the ward, but sat within the playroom. The nurse, caught sight of Cady as she rounded the corner with an armful of bedding.

"You okay, lovely?" The nurse was one of the night staff and had a slight accent.

"Yeah, I'm just looking for some grown-up books in here," she said hastily.

"Okay, want me to come look for you?"
"No!"

"Okay, just askin'. Here if you need me." She turned her fixed smile to the bay and strode off to make the bed.

"Sorry," Cady said to her back.

The nurse waved in acknowledgement.

Cady reached out and swung the door over. It banged shut. God, the nurse was already going to hate her. She felt a touch on her hand and flinched. Cady looked down. Daisy was trying to proffer a piece of paper that she'd written on in crayon in her big round writing: *What now?* Cady turned her head and Daisy flipped the paper and gave her the crayon to boot. She wrote back. *Let's go.* Cady edged the chair forward and reached for the doorknob. She looked to see what was going on. The nurse in bay three had her back to them. She whipped her head round to see the nurses' station. No-one there either, but no sign of the nurse in charge. Cady flicked a hand behind her to Daisy and they edged out of the door. Cady checked again and waved quickly twice, then rolled herself to the nurses' station. The staff nurse, Jenny was looming down on them from the exit to the ward, Cady spun her chair to face her and hoped Daisy had the sense to keep crouched behind the chair.

"Out of bed?" Jenny said. One side of her mouth seemed higher than the other.

"Can't sleep, looking for a book," said Cady. Jenny raised an eyebrow in response. "Thought there might be some on the bookshelf in here," Cady waved vaguely in the direction of the play area in the part of the ward, with the piles of plastic toys with no battery and the barely dressed babies in threadbare prams.

"Only if you're happy reading *Bob the Builder*."

"Ha. I might have to settle for *Bob the Builder*, but there was nothing in the classroom."

Jenny cracked a smile, "I'd help you look but we've got patients on the way in." Then she looked up over Cady's shoulder, "You done in bay three, Bets?"

Cady froze. If the nurse from bay three was behind them, she must be able to see Daisy.

"Yeah, easy peasy," Bets said.

"Good," said Jenny. "Let's get some oxygen sorted in there, we're not sure what we'll need. Ortho have been bleeped too."

Bets crossed in front of Cady. She returned the smile uneasily. Where the hell was Daisy? Cady craned her head round. Not behind her. She wheeled back, then caught a flash of movement out of the corner of her eye. Daisy was crouched in the kitchen, head poking round the door, finger to her lips. Cady nodded once slowly. Then it was Daisy's turn to wave her on. Cady hoped she knew what she was doing. She turned the chair to face the exit again, Jenny was back behind the nurses' station. Cady rolled towards her, "Mind if I go up the other end and stretch my wheels?"

"No, please yourself. You're old enough to stay out of trouble."

Oh, if only you knew. She pointed the chair uphill towards the exit door and leaned forward to push. She was halfway up the wide passage when the outside doors crashed open and a team with two nurses and an orderly shot through, pushing a bed. The demeanour of the team alone told Cady that this lot were from A&E. She gripped her wheel rims, if she was quick enough, she could get out behind them before the door closed. The corridor chose exactly that point to be steeper. Cady puffed and put her head down. The bed was in, along with all the nurses.

"'Scuse'!" said the orderly, brusquely.

Cady had to stop and pull into a doorway. And there was Daisy. How had she done that? Cady hadn't seen her, heard her. And the smug cow was smiling. And *so* expecting Cady to say something. They locked eyes. The exit door up the corridor shut with a loud *click*.

"Bugger," said Cady wheeling towards the keypad guarding the door. "Come on ninja-pants, help me get this open."

"Don't we need a bag of flour or something?"

"We're getting out of a jam, not putting it in a cake."

"No, don't you blow it on the pad to work out what keys people press?"

Cady squinted at the key pad. The keys were metallic, dark and concave. That plan was a duck that was never gonna fly. She stared at the door. It remained firmly shut. She cocked her head to one side and squinted with one eye. Turning her head back to the corridor, she looked back up to a second panel with only one button and a speaker and pushed it.

"Hello?" said the disembodied voice.

"Hiya, it's Cady. Can you buzz me out? I could murder a cig."

"Sure." The crappy quality of the intercom hid the sigh but Cady could hear it in the nurse's voice. Hypocrites. She knew both the nurses on duty indulged. Not that she begrudged them a smoke, nursing had to be a shitty job at the best of times but she could well do without the holier-than-thou act. The door buzzed, she stretched up to grab the handle, opening the door and wiggling her eyebrows at Daisy as she did. They were out. Now to meet the bad guy.

Chapter 41

They could see the four-sided clock on the town hall from the hospital, it was clear to see from most of the town, its insipid yellow eyes staring out at night, more insomnia than vigil. The road down to it was curved but, downhill and level, at least as far as a wheelchair was concerned. The sickly sodium lights cast a dim rotten lemon wash on the whole street, shining up from the wet pavement, despite the rain now having stopped. As the curve unwound, the edge of the massive town hall slunk into view round the modern, orange brick curve of offices hugging the main road. It was an imposing sight, a massive, dark, gothic pile, incongruous with the smallish modern town it squatted in. And when they, whoever had built it, had decided to do gothic, they had gone ballistic. Every surface had a scroll, every corner a pinnacle, every face was pocked with niches and arcades. Pity the poor bastards who had to do the cleaning. Cady knew the inside was as bad, or good depending on prevailing opinion, but whereas the outside was sculpted in dark stone, the inside was all rosewood, thick with the smell of ten thousand meetings. That the inside so exactly matched the outside in form and each of those forms themselves spiraled off into more complexity, made Cady think of fractals. The whole building twisting in on itself, like some kind of nightmarish Mobius strip. Except, instead of ants, tiny and ignorant of the path ahead of them, it was just her and Daisy. And maybe they weren't so ignorant any more. Would that make it any better for the ants? She doubted that very much.

"How are we gonna get in?" said Daisy.

"There's a wheelchair ramp at the side."

"But there's no-one here?"

"He's here all right, come on. If he wants me to come, then he'll let me in won't he?"

"We're walking—"

"Straight into a trap? I know, but I'm sick of all of this, I just want it over."

Daisy cocked her head to one side, furrowed her brow, then followed Cady, slowly shaking her head. The wheelchair ramp was around to the side, as decorated as the rest of the building. The builder must have felt that whoever would see this side entrance, was at least worthy of as much effort. Cady was in no way convinced it had always been a disabled entrance. Twisted gothic plants and dragons followed her route in.

At the top of the ramp was the standard glass door and square chair logo button reading *Push to Open*. Her friend was nearest the button, Cady nodded assent but Daisy was otherwise occupied with unwrapping a stick of chewing gum. Cady looked, waited, eyebrow raised. Daisy carefully put the gum in her mouth and the wrapper into her pocket, then chewing, turned to the button and pressed it. The door swung open. Cady grabbed her wheel rims and forced the chair over the metalwork.

The council building was cool, and lit mostly by low-level lighting. Nobody was spending too much money, save that to prevent law suits from tripping night-time miscreants. Cady quite liked driving in here, the exquisite mosaic tiled floor was flat enough to play marbles on and shiny enough for her to skid to a stop if she wanted. Perhaps not in the manual, that would tip way easier than her power chair. She gave herself a good spin of speed regardless and left Daisy trotting to keep up.

"Where's the lift?" Daisy asked, from round her gum.

"Other side from here," said Cady, "and keep your voice down."

They turned the massive corner of the building, where a trolley with a stack of folding tables, and another with chairs was parked waiting for some public assembly or other. Cady couldn't help wonder if they were all such an enormous waste of time as theirs had been. Was all council maneuvering done in secret meetings, decided by the powerful or rich with a thin veneer of people's approval? The only democratic impact voters had being the actor they chose to play that out on the local stage? Cady shook her head. This whole thing was making her cynical. More cynical.

At the next corner they passed massive doors to a huge pillared banqueting hall complete with stage and a pipe organ. "Nice," said Daisy.

"Yeah, if you get an invite. Lifts are here if I remember right."

In a corner, opposite where they'd entered the building, was the small cubbyhole that the lifts lived in. There was enough room for two chairs abreast, and for some reason there were three lifts, one on the left side of the cubby hole, two to their right. Cady rolled into the cubby hole and punched the button on every lift as they passed.

"Patient much?" said Daisy.

Cady turned and stuck her tongue out. Daisy didn't reciprocate. There seemed to be three floors above them and one below, the council chambers were on floor two. The lights above the lifts counted down, then as the lifts reached them in staggered order, there was one muted *ding* and three sets of doors opened.

"Do me a favour and punch floor two in that lift, Daze, I'll do this one then we'll get in the third."

"Why?"

"Tell you on the way up."

Cady turned her chair and entered the last lift, she stayed in the doorway on the sensors until she heard Daisy behind her, then rolled in the last of the way and turned back to face the doors. Daisy pressed the *2* button. The car slowly lifted. Cady's explanation of giving them better odds where they to come face to face with her would-be assassin was meant to be reassuring. From the rather scrunched expression on Daisy's face, and the increased rate of chewing, Cady assumed it wasn't. Couldn't have everything. Cady patted her friend's hand. Daisy grasped it and held on tight. It felt cool and clammy. The lift stopped with a bounce and its doors *dinged* open.

"That's our cue." Cady looked up into Daisy's eyes. "You okay?"

Daisy nodded. She had to let go of Cady's hand to get out of the lift first. The doors closed behind them. When the noise of the lift had gone, Daisy had turned, head cocked, listening. She motioned for quiet, then pointed toward where she was listening. Raised voices echoed down the hall. Cady pointed to a bin on the corner of the tiny cul-de-sac passage that held the lifts. Daisy turned, bemused. Cady pointed at her mouth and then the bin. Eventually Daisy twigged and retrieved the wrapper from her pocket, placed the chewed gum in and then leaned over to bin it. Then creeping and wheeling, they edged out onto the main grand passage and closer to the noise.

"What the hell where you thinking?" A man with a nasal voice shouted.

"I try not to think, clouds your responses," The reply was delivered in a quiet, familiar voice with a south-east, Greater London twang. Cady flinched. He was here then. "'Sides, I was following your instructions."

"I said 'scare her off'!" The other voice was Carver, but so whiny she hardly recognized him.

"I thought I was quite frightening. I pride myself in being frightening."

"You shot her, for God's sake. With a gun. No-one mentioned guns."

"I find them to be extremely scary. And she's not dead, is she?"

"Only by damned luck. Christ almighty. It's like talking to a wall."

"I resent that. I have been an exemplary contractor. I have standards to uphold."

The argument tumbled out of an open door, following a spill of yellow light from inside the council chamber. Cady and Daisy cubbied up against the wall, the doors opened inwards so if they craned even more they'd be sure to be seen.

Carver made a loud exasperated noise, "I said none of it should be traced back to me!"

"It won't be."

"Rubbish. Bullets? Casings?"

"The gun was a one-off. No serial number. I used gloves. This is a hick town, with hick police, not South London. No-one will give a tinker's cuss."

Cady, looked down at her phone. Could she turn on the recording function on it without it beeping? She daren't risk it.

"Where is the gun?"

"Gone. Don't you worry about that. What you should be worrying about, is the fact that there's a clever young girl out there, who's seen me, who's seen you."

Cady froze. Did he know they were out there? He couldn't, surely. He was slimy and clever, but he wasn't supernatural. Must have just been a turn of phrase.

"So?" said Carver.

"She's a loose end."

"I said no-one gets killed."

"I don't believe you did. She's a witness and even in a hick town like this, they'll believe an actual flesh and blood witness."

"Will they? With the wheelchair? It'll be easy to—"

"Both of us do time for this, if we're connected, you know that, right?"

"I'll deny everything."

"Deny what you like, I've kept insurance. If I go down, you're going too. Then where's your precious memorial?"

"I thought you understood."

"I understand business—contracts, completion. You clearly do not."

"Then I contract you not to do it! I'll pay you twice the money!"

"Firstly, you don't have that kind of money anymore, you spent it on me. Secondly, you can't undo what's been done once the wrecking ball has been set in motion."

"I told you to stop."

"I heard what you said, but it can't stop until it's finished."

"You're insane." Carver's voice was barely a whisper.

Cady could hear her own breathing. Daisy put a hand on Cady's arm, when she looked at her, she pointed back at the lifts. Cady nodded and slowly wheeled backward, keeping the yellow light from the council chamber in view. Behind her she heard the beep of Daisy calling the lifts. Even with the shouting going on it sounded like the loudest sound in the world. When the echoes of it died down, the machine it had called answered from the bowels of the building, rumbling and grumbling as cables and drums sticky with old oil woke reluctantly to their summons. Cady wheeled backward faster.

"No Cade! No!" But Daisy's shout was too late. Behind Cady, her back wheel caught the bin and the whole thing fell behind her with the crash of a hundred drum kits onto the shining face of the wood block floor. A flash of a shadow in the doorway and out stepped Tic-Tac, with a film-noir shadow mockery of him spread across the floor.

"Oho! And what do we have here? Two little maids from school."

Cady spun her head to see Daisy had come back into the wide hallway and was kneeling and trying to stuff the rubbish back into the bin. She flicked her head in time to see a flash at the end of

Tic-Tac's hand—a blade. He motioned with it for Daisy to stand. She tried to, slowly but her ballet pumps slipped on the floor. "Slowly now and hands up nicely. NO!" Daisy froze with the top of the bin in her hand. There was a blur or movement and a flash and Daisy shrieked. Between her feet, stuck into the floor was the blade. "Drop. It." She did. But if he'd thrown the knife; Cady looked over. In his hand was another, ready to go. She opened her mouth. Tic-Tac saw it and mocked her with a broken graveyard smile. "Tut, tut. What kind of amateur would have only one knife?" He beckoned Daisy again with the knife. "I was just leaving, but I believe my employer, wished to talk to you." He moved slowly, fluidly, his back to the large main staircase, blade glinting in the reflected amber light from the wood blocks. He narrowed the gap between them and the lifts. Daisy shuffled to join Cady and they edged back along the wall, to the open door of the council chamber. The smell of stale sweat and furniture polish met them in the doorway—the scent of democracy in Absdown.

Carver was inside, leaning on one of the enormous curved benches that the councilors presumably sat behind. Cady felt sorry for whoever's job it was to do the polishing, everything in here was either shiny wood or brass. Before she could address the scene in the council chamber, Daisy tapped her on the shoulder. She rolled back enough so her shoulders were out in the corridor. Tic-tac stood in the mouth of the lift passage, in one hand he now held a zippo lighter. In the other, he held a plastic bottle of purply-blue fluid with tissues stuffed into the top. His grin was as wide as it was possible to be, without any of his teeth actually falling out. The lighter flickered in the gloom of the lift area, making him into some kind of crazed homunculus. He waited till they were both watching him. "Goodbye girls." He lit the soaked tissue and dropped the bottle into the mess tipped across the wooden floor from the bin. They watched as it fell and as the flames danced across the rubbish. Then they looked up and Tic-Tac had gone.

Chapter 42

Carver leaned against the curve of desks, his hands behind him, gripping the edge, as if it were the only thing stopping him from pooling on the floor and never getting up. With the state of things outside, that was not an option. A bead of sweat ran from his thinning hair down to his eyebrows. He barely registered it. Maybe if he wiped it he'd have to let go. Cady sized him up. She could feel Daisy hopping from foot to foot behind her. He looked straight at her. Not as if she wasn't there, he nearly acknowledged her, but like she was a signpost in the way of his thousand mile stare. Daisy tugged on her shoulder. Cady, put a hand on hers. She smiled. Cady's smile always calmed Daisy and usually anyone she aimed it at. She'd always considered it one of her special powers. Daisy stopped tapping, but returned to glancing over her shoulder, leaving one hand poised on the chair. Cady looked back at Carver. His eyes hadn't moved.

"Well?" she said.

Carver's eyes sprang into focus, and he suddenly saw Cady "Sorry?"

"You summoned me, Carver. I'm your genie in a chair. What do you want?"

"I- I don't— It's all different now." He looked past her over Daisy's head.

Cady didn't want to break his gaze, partly because she didn't trust him, but partly because she could see he was on the brink, and she was damned if he was going to steal her Scooby Doo moment after all she'd been through. Best to keep him in focus.

"He's gone, Tic-Tac's gone," said Cady. Maybe that was what Carver was worried about.

"Sorry."

"You said that already. Tic-Tac, your friend? He's legged it."

"I meant I'm sorry. About him. I never wanted him to— He's not my friend," Carver's eye twitched. "I don't think he has friends."

"No," said Cady. "Figures."

She could hear hissing in the corridor behind them. Wood block floor catching properly? It sure wasn't sprinklers in this place. A listed building plus austerity, meant priorities. Carver looked, what? Empty. Cady wasn't sure what she'd expected. Defeat? His face didn't quite read that. Triumph? Not that either. Something else. Something crashed back in the corridor, she resisted the urge to twitch: she didn't want Daisy panicking, but she had to know.

"Why?" said Cady. Carver's expression zoomed back to her.

"Why, what?"

"I know what you did. Selling the school land to the frackers. But why?"

"Why, why, why? Why do you care? It's too late now, anyway."

"You tried to have me killed. I hate an unfinished ending. Humour me."

Daisy tugged on her arm, "Cady?" Cady turned. Daisy pointed over her shoulder. Smoke was expanding to their part of the corridor like a big grey balloon. She turned back. Carver was right on top of her. She shrieked, but couldn't even hear herself over the next *whoosh* of the fire. He forced himself past her, eyes wild and turned right into the cloud.

"I did it all for her!" he shouted, and disappeared into the fumes.

"No, no, no, no!" Cady was half-turned in the doorway, where Carver had pushed past. She twisted her wheels the rest of the way around. Across from them, was the grand staircase. To the side of the door her eyes fell on a lonely water cooler. Daisy saw her clock it, then look back into the smoke.

"No Cady, leave him, he's not worth it."

"No, he's not," Cady said. "Grab me a pad outa my bag will you?"

"Is now the time for—?" Daisy sighed and got a pad out of Cady's satchel anyway.

Cady took the pad to the water-cooler and doused it thoroughly. Then she pulled it across her mouth and nose and used the sticky tabs to secure it behind her ears. She looked like the kind of bandit that might hold up an A&E department.

"Daze, get downstairs and phone for the fire brigade. There's no alarms gone off in here. Find a panel down there and smash it. Other people could get hurt. Go!"

Daisy backed towards the staircase as a new billow of smoke engulfed Cady, and hurried off downstairs. Cady scrunched her face and dived in. She pushed her wheels forward till her face was in the smoke and her eyes stung. Whatever was burning here was acrid. Years of polish on the wooden blocks? All the rubbish from the bins and plastic signs on the walls? The smoke was hot, she didn't expect that and she'd not seen a lick of flame yet. Where was that wretched councilor? She couldn't see a damn thing, in front or behind her now. Cady rolled forward. She remembered something about getting

down low when there was a fire, but fat lot of good
that advice would do her. If she got out of the chair
she'd never get back in. Then she'd be screwed. It was
getting hotter by the second. Her forehead was
uncomfortably hot, head-in-the-oven hot and was this
smoke in front of her glowing? Loud ringing echoed
from everywhere at once. Either the smoke had set
the alarms off finally, or Daisy had smashed a panel.

Bump. Her chair stopped dead, she leaned
forwards, a dark shape. Carver. Now what? She
couldn't drag him and wheel herself. Shit. She looked
down again, eyes streaming now. If she was going to
do anything, she'd need to do it fast. She reached over
and grabbed down. A shoe, a leg. If she could get
enough of his weight onto her chair, then maybe she
could— Ahead of her was a mighty smashing noise—
a window shattering?

"Come on you, let's get you up he-re!" she
groaned, one leg up and then sorry she'd spoken out
loud, started to cough. When she'd finished, his leg
had fallen back down. She hooked his leg up again
with her foot and reached, at least he was on his back,
his leg bent the right way. Cady pulled his leg over her
lap and reached behind her for the chest harness
straps of her chair, hooking Carver's foot into one to
secure it. The second leg was really heavy. She tried to
lift Carver's backside off the floor. The smoke roiled
again. As it tumbled over and over itself, she could
see the fire just ahead and felt a massive wall of heat.
Her eyeballs were drying out. The streaming had been
better. She closed her eyes against it and heaved for
all she was worth. Carver's foot lurched and she had
enough on her lap that she might be able to move.
She unclipped the other shoulder strap from behind

her and wrapped it round Carver's foot and tied a
makeshift knot. That would have to do for now.
She'd need her lap strap still buckled if she was to get
any purchase at all to pull. She clipped her feet into
the shells on her footplate. She hated the damn
things, they looked too 'wheelchair', but damn if they
weren't going to be handy today.

"Right you bastard," she said, then coughing
and pulling and coughing she tried to gain some
leverage on the dead weight. With some sharp tugs,
she started to feel his bulk shift. And then once he'd
moved, if she could keep going she could beat the
inertia and keep him sliding slowly across the
varnished floor. "I. Bet. You're. Glad. You. Went.
For. The Cheap. Suit— Now." She hoped she was
pulling in the right direction, she sure couldn't tell in
the smoke. Her muscles were starting to burn, but not
as much as they would if she stopped, she knew.

"Man. You're heavy for. A. Little feller."

Was she just really slow or was the fire
creeping faster than she could drag? Either way, the
heat didn't seem to be abating much. Dragging Carver
backwards, meant that with every pull she was still
facing the fire. God, where was she? Surely she
should have found a wall by now, but all she could
see was smoke and the block floor underneath her.
She shook her head and then regretted it, it was like
her brain banged against the front of her skull and left
an imprint.

"Shit, you are a proper pain in the arse."

Once she'd stopped coughing, she pulled on.

"Cady?"

She jumped before she realised it was a
woman's voice calling her, and not Carver. It sounded

like Daisy, but where was she? Where was Cady for that matter? What was she doing again? She stopped.

"What are we doing here, eh fella?" She slapped the leg laid across her lap. "What's a nice guy like you doing in a place like this, eh? Whatsyername? Not very chatty are you. Hey!" She prodded him in his thigh. Then felt a huge welling up in her throat. "No, no, no—"

She was comprehensively sick, all over Carver mostly, but over herself too, "Eurgh. Sorry mate," she said. "Let's get you cleaned up."

"Cady?" this time the voice was nearer. Perhaps chucking her cookies had cleared her ears. The voice was behind and to her right. She leaned what energy she had left to pulling that way. What was wrong with that voice, the Daisy voice? Something was wrong. Something was terribly wrong. She struggled closer. Then the world lurched and time slowed down.

Chapter 43

Cady opened her eyes. She still couldn't see. Everything was grey. Her eyes felt like they were too big for their sockets. Her wrist hurt even more. Where was it? How long had she had her eyes closed?

"Cad-ey?" Daisy's voice, insistent, and did it stop suddenly?

She traced the feeling to her hand. It was gripping something cool and rounded—metallic maybe. She leaned, but everything lurched. What the hell was going on? A wall quickly hove into view and then away again. She looked down and saw one wheel of her chair floating above a ledge, and below that another parallel ledge. Shit was she on the stairs? How the hell? She'd lashed out instinctively and caught the bannister. That and the fact that most of Carver's bulk was still on the landing, legs still strapped to her chair, stopped her from toppling. Shit, she was re-enacting the closing scenes from *The Italian Job* with an old greasy councilor, possibly dead, certainly corrupt, in the middle of a public building which was burning down. Could her life get any more surreal?

There was a gust of cold air from below and for a moment the smoke cleared. Things did not look any better at all. Halfway up the stairs below her, climbing slowly was Daisy, with a knife to her neck, held by the crouching form of Tic-Tac. What was it with that guy? Didn't he think he'd killed them already?

"Stay very still, Cady," he said. What was she supposed to do? "You have someone I want, and I've got someone you want. Stay till I get up to you, we can all swap and no-one gets hurt."

"Yeah or you get up here get what you want and everyone gets hurt! Tosser."

"So much cynicism in one so young, Cady!" he spoke as he climbed.

She knew if she waited, they were all done. She had one idea left. A boom on the balcony belched more choking smoke at her. She had one chance. She leaned so she was perched on two wheels on the top of the stairs. When she disconnected Carver, too much of her weight was leaned over for her to right herself. She unclipped one leg from its plastic restraint. Now was not the time to wonder how that stuff would ever work in a car crash. Now Carver had fallen off the side of her chair, one of her legs, could reach the floor. She reached down to unclip her foot. Crap, where was Tic-Tac now?

"Why are you bothering with us?"

"Oh, y'know, loose ends." He was about eight steps below her.

"Don't bother," she shouted back. "Carver's dead."

That stopped him. How long for she couldn't count on. With one foot on the second step down, she undid her lap strap and slid so she could balance properly. She quickly undid her other foot. Now there was just Carver's other leg. Damn him if the clip hadn't jammed. Even unconscious, this guy was determined to be a pain in the arse.

"I don't believe you," Tic-Tac had his usual swagger, but the voice came no nearer.

"Wasting your time," said Cady. "Why bother killing me now?"

Click

"Oh, I don't know—"

Crash

The wheelchair careened down the massive staircase. Cady had aimed it at the talking—at least that had stopped—and hoped for the best with Daisy. It was all she could do. The smoke still billowed and Carver was still at the top of the stairs. If she left him there, the lie she told Tic-Tac would become true. Daisy would have to deal with the rest herself, she was a smart girl.

The smoke coiled in a weird way: the heat was making it rise, but it was trying to expand into all the space it had. It made it look like fluid—a moving, living thing, writhing, seeking to spread and consume. Well, it wasn't getting Carver. Not on her watch. She craned her neck from the top stair to see what was going on. Below, there was enough haze to see nothing, but no sign of Tic-Tac at least. Looking up, she started at Carver's legs: his shoe had fallen off. She could just pull from there, but if she just held his legs and dragged him down the stairs, that would definitely finish him off, poor sod. She felt up his trousers, trying not to let it creep her out any more than it already had. If she bum-shuffled across the step she'd find his head. If she could drag him down holding his head, the rest of him would have to come on down by gravity. His hair was thinning and smelt of hair wax. Why did he bother? There was hardly any to wax. Cady sighed and cradled his head in the crook of her arm. Oh god, she hoped Daisy was okay. Even Carver's head and shoulders were heavy, what had he been eating? She pulled him over the top step, now one leg, and his torso were over. He was still breathing at least, but they were all winging this, so anything past not-dead was a win.

A siren, louder than the fire alarm itself, joined the orchestra of chaos.

"Oh, you clever girl, Daisy!" The bundle in her arms groaned, as if in reply. "Oh you're back with us, are you?" But the groaning stopped. Cady returned to the job of carefully hauling Carver's dead weight without bashing him. By the time she'd gotten him to the bottom of the stairs, she found her chair lying, base over apex in the lobby, and Daisy returning with two large square-looking fire officers. They leapt into action, one running out the door again, presumably to the trucks that Cady could now see strobing blue outside, the other, a woman, she noted, on her phone/radio summoning an ambulance. The fire officer found a stretcher and someone else to help move Carver and before she had time to say thank you, another had come in, helped her back into her chair and wheeled her out, down the front steps. Throughout, there was no sign of Tic-Tac.

Once she was outside, she was summarily wheeled to the back of an arriving ambulance, and after Carver had been taken in and put on oxygen, they came out to triage her. Daisy was brought over by a police officer. This was becoming quite a night on the town. Daisy had a red line and a smear on her neck. Cady wheeled forward, ignoring the instructions of the paramedic, and threw her arms round Daisy. "Shit, Daze, are you okay?"

"Yeah," she said. "He caught me with the knife, when he was trying to duck your chair!"

"Oh, shit, I'm so sorry."

"It's okay. It's not bad. I kicked him in the shin while he was leaning and he fell down the stairs."

"Where is he now?" said Cady.

"Dunno. I guess he ran away when he heard the sirens?"

Slowly, they were embraced by the emergency service team. First aid was administered and statements taken as the shock set in.

Chapter 44

Cady reluctantly returned to hospital. Despite her protestations, even the most junior doctor was not prepared to let the gunshot wounds and smoke inhalation girl go home. Cady was grumpy. She was in a mixed ward of grown-ups, due to bed shortages and Daisy had gone home. At least she still had her phone. She called her dad.

"Hey Dad."

"Hey lovely. You okay?"

"Yeah, all good, well—anyhow can you come in and bring me some stuff. These clothes stink from the fire and they're torn and—"

"Sure, I'll be straight in. Wait, what fire?"

"I'll tell you when you get here. Princess Margaret ward, bay four. Bring my laptop and some wash-gear too."

"Okay?"

Everything shook. The windows rattled in their frames, Cady's bed lurched. There was a moment of silence. As if everyone in the hospital ward had held their breath at the same time. Then a massive amount of noise as everybody delivered a panicked version of what-the-hell-was-that? including Cady's dad.

"You felt that there too?" said Cady. Their house was the other side of town to the hospital.

"Yeah, did you hear the boom?"

"No, I guess I was listening to you. I felt the shake, though. What the hell was it?"

"Probably a little earthquake, they happen sometimes."

"Oh, god. Hey Dad, love you, gotta go."

"Ok see you in—"

She was already in mid-dial to Daisy. Daisy must have done the sensible thing and gone to bed. "Come on, come on, come on pick up." After thirty odd rings, she did.

"Huh?" said Daisy. "Cady? It's four in the morning—"

"Did you feel the shake? Hear the bang?"

"I woke up, then you phoned and the phone fell off the table and I had to look under the bed for it."

"So no?"

"Why?"

"I think they're fracking."

"Okay."

"No, not okay. World of not okay. If they start and they find anything, that's it game over. The whole school shut down. Carver said it was too late, the bastard."

"We can't do anything about it tonight, I'll come over in the morning and we'll chat then."

"Okay, tomorrow then."

After her dad had left, Cady tossed and turned so much, that in the end, one of the nurses gave her something to help her sleep, probably to stop her disturbing the other patients. She still woke at dawn, but added chemical grogginess to her list of charming symptoms. She was also a mass of bruises from the staircase, only distracted by coughing up lumps of brown phlegm from the fire.

She was stood up, drinking her fourth glass of water of the morning when Daisy arrived.

"Shouldn't you be resting?"

"I'm bruised, not pregnant."

"I'm not sure, but I don't think you need to rest for that either?" said Daisy.

"Oh, sod off," said Cady. They hugged. "Ow," said Cady quietly. "No grapes?"

"You hate grapes."

"It's the thought that counts."

"I thought 'You hate grapes.'" Daisy threw a desultory chocolate bar onto the bed.

"Awwww, thanks," said Cady with genuine rather than sarcastic appreciation.

Cady inhaled the chocolate, one of those supermarket own brand, fair trade touches. Daisy knew her stuff where chocolate was concerned. She was then left with a sticky wrapper and a dilemma of which hospital bin to throw it in. Once she'd read all the bin instructions, and complied, she turned to Daisy and smiled a chocolately smile. A nurse came in and did Cady's obs, complaining that her oxygen saturation levels still weren't over ninety percent in air. She made Cady sit back on the bed to check that her levels would go up with oxygen. After having her sit there for another five minutes until the stubborn monitor read ninety, then unhooking her again, the nurse set to checking the dressings she had on the scrapes and bruises from the bullet wounds. Having satisfied herself of enough progress, she issued Cady with painkillers and bustled out.

"So," said Cady.

"So."

"What do we do now?"

"About what?"

"The fact that those bastards have started fracking anyway."

"You know who we should ask."

"No Ed."

"Cade, he's mortified by all of this."

"I don't care, he was an arse."

"Yes, he was. But you weren't blameless were you? No-one was."

"You were."

"I was there too."

"I guess. It's still too soon," Cady poured herself another glass of water, drank half and swirled the rest round in the bottom of the clear plastic beaker. If she was hoping for divination from that particular body of water, none was forthcoming. She swirled more vigourously, until a wave spilled out and slopped onto her gown where it covered her legs. Daisy grabbed a paper towel, looked at the spill and then grabbed a couple more.

"Have there been any more?"

"Bangs? No."

"Maybe they've stopped."

"Unlikely," said Cady, mopping, "I reckon, more likely they're only doing it at night in the hope nobody notices."

"It's a big thing not to notice."

"You didn't."

"I sleep well, it's a gift."

Cady slipped down the bed and into her Totoro slippers. She shuffled over to the bedside cabinet, pulled out her camo sweatpants and hoiked them up then sat back on the bed. She realised that she'd forgotten any means to tame her hair, and rolled her eyes. Daisy clocked the expression and threw over Cady's comb and fished a small mirror from her bag. Cady spent the next half hour teasing at hair and swearing. Perhaps no day in a hospital was ever going to be a good hair day. Perhaps that was a rule. She thought that maybe she should cut herself a bit of slack, considering the last week. There had been people trying to kill her. It was bound to be hell on personal grooming. The smell of the food trolley wafted over, a smell that was always difficult to resolve into individual foods, but there would be a fair chance of some kind of custard associated desert. And the trolley meant the end of visiting until the evening. Daisy gave Cady a big hug and a smile, and she left.

Chapter 45

"Jesus, you look rough," said her dad.

Cady was sat on the edge of the bed hands tucked under her legs, swinging her feet.

"Say it like you see it, Dad," she said, laughing.

"What's with the coppers outside?"

"Oh, they laid me a guard on, since they never found that guy Carver hired."

"Shit. Are they worried?"

"Just a precaution."

Her dad sat heavily in the visitor's chair.

"Doesn't anybody bring grapes anymore?" Cady said.

"You don't like grapes."

"That's not the point."

Don Grey ferreted in his bag and produced a slightly dented bunch of flowers. The price sticker was still on them.

"Awww," said Cady. She placed them on the bedside cabinet. "I'll get a nurse to find me a vase in a min."

"Oh, your mum gave me this," Don produced a card. It was terrifyingly pink. It smelled of her mum—the three C's CkOne, Chardonnay and Ciggie smoke. She opened it. It was a Forever Friends bear with a bandaged head, saying *Get Well Soon*.

"Huh," said Cady, and put the card with the others on her dresser. Her dad's was there already. It read *Please Don't Die!* Most of her friends had sent cards with messages in a similar vein.

"The chair will live," said her dad.

"Oh, good."

"Despite your best attempts to kill it."

"Someone did try to shoot me."

"Yeah, plays hell with the electronics that does." He stood, crossed the distance to the bed and sat next to her on the covers. She reached across and put her arms round him. He hugged her back, fiercely. "Just be careful, okay? You're messing with some scary people."

"Carver?" she said, "He's a bit of a sad sack really. Wants to memorialise his daughter. He was the one who got involved with the wrong crowd in a way. Those developers are pretty ruthless."

"No, I meant the asshole he'd hired to hurt you." Her dad still had tight hold of her.

"Oh, him. Yeah. I can't breathe now, you're crushing me."

"Sorry."

Her dad held her at arms' length and looked into her eyes. Cady blinked. He had more wrinkles on his forehead than she remembered, and were those grey hairs at his temples?

"Where does a fella get a decent cup of coffee round here then? Is there a League of Friends Shop?"

"Welcome to the twenty-first century, Dad! There's a Costa down by Outpatients and everything now."

"Huh," he said. "Usual?"

"You know it."

As the door closed behind him, Cady found great big tears on her grey joggers. Go figure, she didn't feel sad, or much else these past few days. She stood and reached to the box of tissues above the sink by the door. It had been a long, long week. She blew her nose loudly at the mirror over the sink. Her dad was right, she looked like hell. She spat in the sink and then went up to the window onto the ward behind. She'd had the side room for privacy, but she knew they meant security. The curtains were drawn at all times and the room was bathed in that odd extra bright fluorescent light that hospitals seemed to specialise in. She tweaked the corner of the curtains. Blocking her view even then, was the black uniform jacket of the poor bobby who'd been tasked with protection for her today. It had been twenty-four hours. Surely Tic-Tac had legged it, or gone to ground if he knew they had an APB out for him, or whatever the hell they called it in the real police? Did he really believe all that bullshit about finishing the job? He must have had some sense of self-preservation, which would mean she'd be safe for a couple of days, at least. And the school was still in deep shit. The developers weren't going to stop for someone with influence like Carver. There was going to be real serious money involved if there was oil, or gas there. So what the hell were a group of kids from a special school going to do in the face of big money? Her life had gotten really weird really quickly and she wasn't sure she was enjoying any of it. She missed the innocent days of getting into trouble from the head for mop-jousting or whatever hi-jinx they could get up to, to keep from getting bored. Now boredom was the least of her worries, and an interesting day might just get her killed. And she was the only one who could hold all of this together long enough to stop these bastard developers—if she could hold it together for long enough. And if she could think of a way to stop them. When did being a grown up fall on her so quickly without her noticing? And why did it have to be her? There were enough adults in the council, but what the hell were all of them doing? Not protecting the town's best interests that was for sure.

A tiny knock at the door interrupted her reverie. She opened it reflexively and then regretted it, leaving the door open a crack in a weird compromise and her foot in the way. She peered through the gap, but no-one was there. Perhaps it had been one of those innumerable weird hospital noises that seemed to go on day in, day out with no explanation or purpose except to keep the reluctant guests awake. She felt an odd tap on her slipper and looked down. At her feet was a small blue thing on wheels, a robot? It had a grabber arm in front of it, presumably what it had knocked with, but it held a piece of paper. She let it in, closing the door behind it. It hurried into the room, stopped and held the note up using its grabber arm. The thing was tiny, so even at full stretch she had to lean right down to it. When she pulled the note it backed off a little as if to give her space to read. It had two tiny chrome cameras on its front that were positioned to look like eyes. She shook her head, resisting the urge to address it directly.

The note was a simple piece of copier paper folded into quarters. It had been typed or printed in one of those fonts trying to be an old school typewriter. It read:

sorry I was a dick. can we talk. please. Ed.

Chapter 46

Cady gazed in the bottom of her cup at the cold dregs of her mocha. Her dad had long since gone and Daisy had arrived. Neither had precipitated a response to the message that she'd just had from Ed and the robot had gone from whence it came when she'd led Daisy in. She'd worried briefly that the printed note could be from someone more sinister, but who else would have sent the sodding thing by robot?

Daisy now sat in the visitor seat, "Are you—?" Cady raised her hand to cut her off, then folded her arms.

Daisy opened her mouth, Cady glared at her, she closed it again. Then there was a knock at the door. Cady still twitched with every loud noise. Daisy was already most of the way across the room to the door.

"NO!"

Daisy froze, hand outstretched to the door, and turned wide-eyed to face Cady. Cady had her hands in front of her mouth then removed them and went to speak, but Daisy burst into tears. Cady closed the gap between them and enveloped her in a huge hug. Her friend clung on as if she was the last life belt. They both cried hard tears, neither of them able to stop once they'd started. There was a small, patient, knock at the door the second time. They were halfway through Cady's box of tissues when the knock came again. Daisy and Cady looked at each other, then laughed.

"I'll get it," said Cady, smiling. She still had to peek behind the curtain first, though she was pretty sure she knew the visitor this time. She held the door open while the small blue robot drove itself in. It was wearing a small cardboard cut-out of a frown underneath its camera eyes and in its claw, as much of a big bunch of grapes as it could carry. Her phone buzzed.

The message from Ed said "*?*"

Cady replied, I fucking hate grapes.

Ed: I know.

Cady: You're forgiven.

Ed: PHEW ;)

Cady: You're still a dick.

"What?" asked Daisy, with an expression as if she already knew.

"Ed."

Ed: What now?

Cady: Come here.

Ed: Visiting's nearly over.

Cady: Screw that we've got a town to save.

"Is he coming over?" said Daisy.

"Yes," growled Cady.

"Good."

"Your handiwork, I presume?"

"I told him to apologise, but he was really upset that he hurt you. You know he was only jealous?"

"What?"

"God, Cady, for someone so clever, you really can be dim."

"What?"

"He fancies you, you idiot. He has done for years."

"But he never—"

"Because he's a boy and he's an idiot too. You'd be ideal together."

"But I don't—" Cady flushed to her eyebrows.

"He's apologising, not proposing."

"Wha—? I—"

"Just say you accept the apology. We've got a town to save?"

****

They sat in the near dark now, the glow of three laptops and an iPhone on the bed shining up at three faces, each the point of a triangle, like some kind of 21st Century coven. Cady rubbed her face and took a massive swig of water from a china mug saying *NHS* that she'd got a nurse to sneak her from the kitchen. Daisy reached over and patted her knee. Cady smiled and looked up from her screen.

"Can't we just report all this to the council? Get it stopped?" she said. "Carver cheated to get it through. We can prove that now, right?"

Ed had been a busy boy.

"Yeah, but it still doesn't help us. Carver told you, 'Contracts have been signed'. And the developers and the company doing the fracking? They're huge. Billionaires. They don't care how they got the contract as long as they did. Any local problems, like democracy, they've got money to make people go away, to buy people off. It wouldn't surprise me if that was where Carver's evil little thug came from. He might have cheated to get there, might even be looking at a jail term for attempted murder and conspiracy but, the contracts are still binding and—"

A massive boom shook the earth beneath them. The glass rattled in the frames, every pipe and bolt in the bed shook against its neighbour. That eerie in-breath of silence. Then several cars in the street whooped as if in distress. Machines beeped in the hospital to say they'd need adjusting and nurses rushed to calm agitated patients. Cady's water mug was a centimetre from the edge of the cabinet.

"Shit," said Cady and Ed in chorus.

"Whu-what about—protesters? There's a group for this isn't there? Frack this? Frack you?"

"Yeah, but fat lot of good they did up north. Loads of them got arrested. Even though they voted against it. It's legal see? Shit, but legal."

Then another boom. It was like some demon knocking on the earth from underneath, asking to get in. Cady's mug fell, she saw it tip, flashed a hand out to it, but it fell, slowly and dashed on the hard floor, spilling its contents. Cady felt her stomach lurch and stared at the mess, felt Daisy's hand on her knee again, heard her say something, she watched the water trickle away under the cabinet, the small pieces had stopped moving almost immediately.

"Hey!" said Ed, and waved a hand in front of her eyes: once, twice, three times.

"Sorry," said Cady.

"Dude, it's only an NHS mug," Ed said, "They've got frigging millions of them."

"I know. I— Sorry."

"It's cool, Cade. Focus. We need to find a lever. Something to stop those fly bastards, before they do something we can't roll back. When the bulldozers arrive, that's it, game over."

"Hey Cady, you okay?" Daisy was watching her gazing into space again, this time out of the window. "We'll think of something, right? Cady?" She leaned on her arm with both hands.

"Yeah," said Cady, turning slowly, a grin spreading, "I think we will. Or Ed will."

"What?" asked Ed.

"You already said it! Just now. How do you fight crazy? More crazy?"

"Okay?"

"Fly!" she pointed at Ed, miming flight. "You said 'fly'."

"Yeah, I did? You're gonna fall out of bed."

"Bats," said Cady. "We'll send up the bat sign."

Chapter 47

With a plan agreed, Ed headed off to the school, to repoint his hidden camera, Daisy went home to ask her parents about the Bat Conservation Trust and Cady to bed on Daisy's orders. She couldn't keep her eyes open. Whether it was the amount of weird hospital food she'd eaten or the additives in the massive bag of Skittles that Ed had insisted on bringing, the moment sleep came, she dreamed.

There was a massive fire in a twisted building that partly resembled the school and partly the town hall, but every single room was stuffed with filing cabinets. Some were locked and as much as she pulled on them or kicked them, they wouldn't come open. When she did get them open they were full of infinite amounts of paperwork that when she looked at it was all gibberish and only served to fuel the flames that surrounded her. She pulled screeds of it out, throwing it over her shoulder in the search for… well she'd know what it was when she found it. The fire was burning her now and though it was searing her clothes from her back, she couldn't turn round to put it out. She ran back out of the door, into Ed's arms, who was really Dave, who spoke in Daisy's voice. She was saying something about having found a way upstairs. Cady turned, but the fire was still behind her and she followed Ed/Daisy/Dave out of the door.

They ran along a smoky corridor that people were racing wheelchairs along in the opposite direction. She waved to the racers as they passed. There was Charlie Whizz and Jasmine Jones in a fierce battle for the tape with David Weir and

Batman. She turned and it was Daisy's back she was
following. She ran faster to catch her, but Dream-
Daisy had gone on into the smoke, yelling 'it's okay,
there's a lift'. As she rounded the corner, the smoke
thinned out to reveal the lift. It was an enormous
hand, white and puffy and clammy like Carver's. Its
fingers were curled in front of her, barring access.
One of the fingers wore a massive masonic cygnet
ring with the odd symbols enormous in relief on its
surface. She reached forward and touched it. It lit up,
reflecting the fire behind her, and made an enormous
lift *bong*. She reversed hastily as the hand uncurled.
She bumped up onto the fingers, her chair seemed to
have squishy wheels to make that possible. Then
when she put her brakes on, the hand lifted her into
the air, through a massive atrium that seemed to
occupy all of the building at once, and was full of
pillars and statues and gothic windows with light
streaming in, sliced into coloured beams by the
smoke. God knew where the sun was—wasn't it still
night-time?—because the coloured lights were
coming from all sides at once like a massive disco.
Massive gothic windows loomed in front of her and
as the massive lift-hand approached, they opened
inwards onto a massive marbled hall where everyone
was dancing. All of her cousins and friends were there
dancing with people in worn business suits. The lift-
hand deposited her gently on the floor and she
moved into the room. Despite more beams of light
everywhere, in this room they were all white, there
was no noise. She coughed politely. All the people in
suits turned round to face her, then coughed in a loud
chorus, mocking her. They advanced towards her
coughing in louder and more phlegmy bursts until the

noise they made was deafening. She could feel their hot breath jetting at her, flecks of spit landing on her cheeks and hands, their faces becoming more and more distorted as they lost control of the coughing, and it doubled them over. She closed her eyes and screamed.

The coughing stopped. Then into the silence came beeping. She opened her eyes and she was on a hospital ward that seemed to stretch away as far as she could see. Beds contained patients to her right and left, old and young, people she recognised, strangers and people who hardly had faces at all. Nurses with fixed smiles hummed their way between the beds. Each bed had a monitor on a stand with multi-coloured wires trailing off it to stick all over the patient ending in tubes or clips or cuffs or stickers. She moved closer to the nearest bed. It seemed to contain someone who might have been her mum or Barbara Wintle. She looked at the monitor at the top of the stand. It seemed to contain a grainy picture of bats flying, but in a huge cloud like starlings do, then just as she could resolve what was going on the picture broke up. As she gently lifted the tubes to see what was going on, the patient grabbed her hand and shouted "Save me!" Cady looked back and said, "I'm trying!" She adjusted the tubes and pipes—one with blood in it felt warm as she laid it across her legs. She felt a tickle in her ear and she wafted at it—a wasp. She could hear it buzzing now, she waved it away again. It seemed to be getting louder the more she wafted, though she was so concerned with the pipes and wires that she couldn't turn to swat it properly. The screen was still juddering. If she could just get it into focus, then she'd be able to resolve all of this.

She realised there was a smell: sweat, male sweat and cologne, coming from her. She knew if the wasp could smell it he'd attack more. She snatched up a *Hello* magazine lying on the bed. Typical reading for her mum that. She tried to turn, but all the pipes caught in the spokes of her chair wheels. She pulled to free herself as the wasp hove into view again, it was massive, the size of a bird and it was wearing the smug face of Tic-Tac. She swiped at it with her improvised weapon, and struck home. The wasp sputtered, and fell back to the floor. She pulled herself loose to finish it off, but behind her the machine beeped to tell her she had pulled pipes and wires free. Blood was starting to spill onto the floor. She determinedly wheeled herself over, the wasp rose again buzzing loudly, its thorax bent to point it's stinger at her. She stood from her chair, magazine in two hands like a rounders bat and swung again. Again she hit it and it fell into the spreading pool of blood, still buzzing. She took her chance and strode after it and stamped on its prone form on the floor, her purple DM's crushing it. She could feel it under her boot. '*Buzz-buzz.* She stamped again *buzz-buzz,* why wouldn't the damn thing die? *Buzz-buzz.*

Chapter 48

She woke in a muck sweat, with her phone vibrating somewhere in the bed. Ed's name came up on the screen, but her phone had a message from Daisy too. What the hell time was it even? She focused her eyes on the top of the screen. 3:17. a.m. She answered the call.

"Frig, Ed."

"Hey Cady. Listen, I'm here at the school and I'm tweaking the cameras. The sixth form's been locked up for a whole day and no-one's in."

"Course no-one's in, you headcase. It's three o'clock in the frigging morning."

"Anyway, I'm moving the camera from the library—"

"You broke into the school." It was a statement, not a question.

"—and they've got loads more kit here. Tanks with chemicals, pumps. God knows what they're up to."

"Woah. Hold on there a min, Ed, I've got a message from Daze too, stay on the line and let me check it."

"Hurry up, it's freezing in here, they've not had the heating on."

Cady prodded her phone, opened up several apps she didn't need and some variety of settings. She poked frantically at it while a tiny voice came from the speaker hurrying her along. She held the phone at arm length and shouted encouragement back. Ed went quiet. The message came up finally and read:

****

Daisydoo: The bat signal has been sent up.

****

Cady chuckled, there was no time to check what kind of reality that represented, with Ed presumably stood on a rickety pile of books leaning out towards the window, with his usual degree of laser focus. But she hoped against hope that there were still bats for them to send a signal for. She moved the phone back to her ear.

"Kay. Back."

"There's loads of kit here now."

"Describe kit."

"There's a ten-foot-high steel fence all the way across the side of the sixth form centre, I've had to perch the camera on top, and as far as I can see, it runs all the way down the side of the block and school, and then it goes on round the back. Hold on."

He went off-mic and, carrying the phone, grunted and swore his way down from where he was, and then Cady heard footsteps and doors. Where the hell was he going now? More doors.

"Hold on. What's—? No. Wait on."

There was a weird hollow clunking noise and a bashing. More swearing, then he was back.

"Christ."

"What?"

"Lookit the size of that thing," he said it reverently, quietly, in awe. Like a prayer or a supplication. So much so Cady didn't feel comfortable taking the piss out of him for the obvious quote.

"Where are you?"

"In the loo. The window looks out over the back playing field. The site is all the way down there and there's a massive blue tower thing."

"Is that the drilling rig?"

"I guess."

"Frig. They've been proper busy."

"Ruthless."

"Can you go and check?"

"No, I'm as close as I dare. I don't think there's anyone working tonight or they've gone, but I reckon there'll be security. I need to put another camera in here. I was gonna swap the library cam for an IR one, but it's not come from Amazon yet."

"Did you see any bats?"

"I can see the tree they were coming out of, it's the wrong time of day, though to see anything properly. If they're going home when the sun comes up, then we'll catch them then. Camera's ready."

"Cool."

There was another *bing* from Cady's phone, "Hold on." She moved it from her ear again, to look.

****

Daisydoo: *h*

****

Weird. The message send and received times were ages apart and it was an hour ago. Probably close to the time she'd sent the other message. One of those stupid messages that gets lost in the ether and winds up super late.

****

Cady: Why are you even up still? Haven't your folks tucked you in?

****

She couldn't resist the dig. Daisy's folks were always super-protective, and it pissed her friend off no end. It might turn out yet that super-protective was exactly what they'd need. She heard Ed swear, and an intake of breath.

"You okay?" she asked.

"Shh—"

Before she could ask him what was going on, her phone *binged* again.

****

Daisydoo: *:)*

****

Weirder still. Daisy never, ever sent emojis. Hated them. She stared at the smiley face. She'd never felt less like smiling back. And now she couldn't talk to Ed either. She stood, pulled on her grey sweatpants. Then searched for her boots. She just felt she'd be more comfortable with them on. Armor against uncertainty. She lifted the phone to her ear. She put on splints and zipped up boots, they were lace-ups as well but if they didn't have a zip, with trying to get them over splints, all she'd spend her life doing was lacing. And right now, that was something she could do without. She stood, checked how they felt, then walked to the window. A twitch of the curtains revealed her protector, he was shifting from foot to foot. The bored night-shift. She padded back to the bed and picked up her phone. Silence.

"Ed?" she whispered. "Eddy?"

"Guard." he whispered back. "Gone now I think."

"In the school?"

"No, outside. Went past under where the camera is, looking with a torch. It's all set up now, though, I've checked the feed."

"Then get the hell out, Ed. The last thing we needs some asshole security guard catching you."

"It's okay, I'll play dumb. It never fails."

Cady sighed. Such a double-edged sword that. She felt the same way about that as she did about fluttering her eyelids and how much of that had she done recently.

"Wait, he's back. I saw a flash of his Hi-Vis. Shit."

"Bugger," said Cady, "Hide in the loo."

She heard a weird burble from her phone, Ed was video-calling in, so she could see what was going on without asking him or him replying. Clever boy. The camera came to bear on what? The doors of the sixth-form common room. He must've been crouched behind the bar, poking his phone out round the edge. She could see the torch beam of the security guard, but not a lot else. Why hadn't Ed rammed something between the door handles and crashed out of the fire exit on the other side? All very well for her to be having *espirit descallier* when she was here and he was there.

"Come out, come out wherever you are." Odd thing for a security guard to say. And an odd tone of voice. Familiar tone of voice? The massive bulk of the guard was lit by a splash of newly installed security lamp from the site, shining through the back windows. That was an odd-shaped torch. Shit. The way he was holding the torch and moving. He was holding a gun. Tic-Tac. Had to be. *Shit Ed, get out get out get out.*

"I can *accidentally* shoot you through there, or you can put your hands up and come quietly."

The camera didn't move. Had he placed it down? He didn't sound like he was for surrendering, very un-Ed-like.

"Five, four, three, two—"

The mic on the phone cut out, but there was still picture. The shaped loomed over the camera, then the picture lurched and blackness. The sound came back.

"Good boy. Hands nice and high."

There was a weird plastic buzz: zip ties? Then silence. The picture lurched back. "I bet I know who's on here." Filling the screen was the smug, resinous smile of Tic-Tac, framed by a security guard uniform, complete with hat. He said nothing, for what seemed like a minute, but was probably seconds. "I have both your friends. But you know that, don't you? You will meet me at the building site by the bridge in town at," he looked theatrically at his watch, mostly off screen, but she guessed what he was doing. "Four o'clock. That gives you twenny minutes, if you wanna see your friends alive again. No police. You know I'm not bluffing."

That much was obvious. She had very few ideas and very little room for manoeuvre.

"This is the bit where you say, 'Yes, Dominic'." Shit, he'd told her his name.

"Chop, chop, you've not got long."

He didn't care about remaining anonymous.

"Yes Dominic."

He was going to kill them all.

Chapter 49

She rolled her chair towards the building site hoardings, all decorated with graffiti of the neat and artistic variety that only councils could arrange. The mesh gate was open, like a great mouth, one or two rogue cones like a crone's teeth, either side. There were no lights on, and no guards here—no surprise on a council site. She had no idea what they were supposed to be building here, just that it had been there so long, had become such a town fixture, that when Tic-Tac had mentioned it, she knew exactly where he meant. There was a reasonable amount of actual building going on around town, a new shopping centre, a new multi-story and of course Carver's new hospital wing, but on this site, not so much. She gazed across the abandoned ground—vandalised Portakabins, a couple of rusty containers, several hoops of that ubiquitous blue pipe, but no actual work in progress in any way. The only recent anything there was a silver-grey transit van. The van was silent and unlit, but had clear tyre tracks leading all the way from the gate on top of some kind of temporary road surface. No sign of Tic-Tac, but he was here, somewhere. Was there a noise? She cricked her neck both ways to try to hear better. There were late night seagulls skreeing and scavenging, but not that. A voice? She rolled herself slowly towards the van, checking for movement in her peripheral vision. She stopped to check in her peripheral vision more than once on the way to the side of the van, but moved on each time, drawn by the muffled noise that was getting louder. She felt like a fly walking on a pitcher plant, walking but drawn by instinct, but unlike a fly, she knew what the pitcher could do and who was already in its depths. What she didn't know was when she would slip. She could definitely hear Daisy's muffled and panicked voice now. Was she gagged? Cady approached the van. There was enough makeshift roadway for two big diggers to pass each other, so she should be able to go round the front of the van to check Tic-Tac wasn't there. She wheeled slowly, so she made as little noise as possible. Passing the door of the van, she sat up, then used the door handle to lift herself to see in. No keys. Nothing to tell her of a recent occupant. She carried on around, reached out and felt the bonnet. No rain on it and warm to the touch, not hot, but warm. She stopped. Could she smell that god awful cologne that he wore? She inhaled gently through her nose. Maybe it was a false alarm, she leaned forward in her chair, till her head was out over her knees and wheeled inch by inch so she could see round the bonnet and down the van's long side. No sign of him there, either. But it did look like there was a sliding door on that side, too. Maybe all was not lost. She wheeled along the side to the handle and grabbed it. She pulled with as much force as she could muster while still being quiet. The handle moved towards her, then the door too, with a loud *clunk*.

Now she'd have to move fast. She peered into the van, could see nothing in the gloom, so risked booting up her phone light. Shining it inside, she saw two prone and now silent forms—Daisy and Ed, bound hand and foot and gagged. Daisy was on her back. Ed was lying facing away from the door. They both looked bruised around the face. That bastard. If they were quite now, had they lost consciousness or were they just playing 'doggo' thinking that it was Tic-Tac holding the door not her. She tried to hiss to them in a reassuring but quiet manner.

"Hey, it's me."

Daisy's head snapped towards her, her eyes flashed open and she started yelling into her gag.

"It's okay, it's me." But the yelling got louder, and Daisy was struggling against her bindings almost like Cady was her captor and not Tic-Tac. "What's wrong, Daze? It's me?" Then Daisy stared at her wide-eyed. "What?"

She felt a sharp jab in her neck. Then twisted to see what was going on. Shit, that hurt. Tic-Tac. That was what Daisy was trying to tell her. Then her head exploded into a million stars.

Chapter 50

Cady dreamed insane dreams. Colours upon colours, shapes exploding into shapes, morphing into things she'd never seen, giving birth to inexplicable beauty, dissolving into bottomless horror, running at the speed of a YouTube video, cut together by a million children. She opened her eyes with a gasp. It was dark still. She smelled damp carpet, dogs and rust. The carpet was under her, thankfully not as damp as it smelled. She went through a systems check. Head, banging with the worst hangover she'd ever had, but still intact. She felt as if she'd been under a lawn roller. She sniffed and got a faint whiff of something else, that shitty cologne.

It all started coming back to her. That bastard had drugged her. What the hell had he used? Judging by the high she'd had before she blacked-out, some kind of street drug. Was that what heroin was like? Shit, no wonder people became addicted to it. Scary, properly scary. She was on her back, her hands were behind her—tied? She couldn't feel them. Well, lying on her ass wasn't going to save it. She lifted her knees, oddly there was circulation there. She could lift either one at a time. The cocky asshole had assumed that she couldn't use her legs at all so he hadn't tied them. She leaned her knees over and rolled. Then she was nose down in the van's side well. She could see something a glint down there—a drink can and a tyre iron. Now that, she could work with.

Her feet wouldn't fit in the well. She couldn't point her toes wearing splints. She started to get some pins and needles in her hands. Could she get the thing on her back? With a little twist of her hands, she could feel that what was holding her together was thin but flat, hard—a wire or cable ties? That would do nicely. She rolled till her arms were in the well, and fumbled for the biggest bit of the tyre iron. The tips of her fingers could feel it. Then her arms went slack. Shit, she'd rolled across this van twice now, where were Daisy and Ed? If that bastard had harmed a hair on them. She rolled back into the well. Now she was wedged there, but her hand was flat on the tyre iron. She picked it up. Cold. Heavy. Reassuring. She fed it down her palm—then slowly between her wrists. This was gonna hurt, but she guessed after a heavy dose of narcotics was the best possible time to do this. She wriggled her knees up to start to twist the bar. Half a turn and she managed to stuff the socket end of the tyre iron over the edge of the well, then she leaned her weight back to pull. Shit, that hurt. She let the pressure off a quarter turn so the blood flowed briefly. Then outside she heard a scream from the end of the van that could only have been from Daisy. She glanced round the van, desperately. Next to the well was a small round finished hole in the panel of the van, just before the wheel arch. If she could jam the end of the tyre iron in there? With a forward roll either the tie would snap or her wrists would. She knelt, knees apart and found a place to wedge the thick end of the iron. Another scream, Ed this time. She didn't have time for nerves, her friends were depending on her. She took a deep breath, held it then—

As she exploded her breath out, she tucked her head between her knees and let the rest of her body tip over by momentum and gravity. Then there was a snap that echoed round the inside of the van. She looked down at her arms. The left one had a red circle round it where the cable tie had been, the right one had a bizarre bulge where her arm stopped and her wrist began. That was gonna hurt like hell when the drugs wore off. She shook her head and instantly regretted doing so. Okay, next plan.

She looked along the back door for anything resembling a manual locking mechanism and found a tiny, black, plastic lever. She flicked it over. His voice was still droning from outside. Had to make a speech didn't he? Arsehole.

Now what? Weight was not gonna be her friend, she was still rough as the proverbial badger, from whatever Tic-Tac had drugged her with and now she had a broken wrist. Plus column: he was a cock-sure bastard, he thought she was still immobilised, couldn't use her legs and she had a tyre iron. It could be worse. There was another scream. *Think Cady.* A roll towards the door? It had worked for her just now. If she could tuck her hand in somehow so she didn't snap it right off, then she'd have some momentum at the door. And a tyre iron. It was a shit plan. But it was the only plan she had. She measured out how far she thought she'd go in a roll. She tucked her right hand back in her hoodie arm and secured the end of the sleeve with a cable tie she'd found in the bottom of the van. She stood, slightly stooped, tyre iron clutched in her left hand. Not her favoured hand, but then none of this plan was favoured. Or non-shit. Time to go anyway.

"Hey asshole!" she yelled at the back doors of the van in a fake slur. "You missed one!"

Chapter 51

There was sobbing and a slap from outside the van. Then Cady yelled again, "Hey asshole!" She heard those click-clack shoes across concrete, even from inside, then fumbling with the doors and she threw herself forward, head over heels towards the crack of light.

The assassin opened the door with one hand. Cady crashed into it with a bang, whipping the door out of Tic-Tac's hands with a hiss. A gun-shot went off, she heard it clang into the van somewhere. She only hoped it hadn't gone through her first. She'd paced her roll perfectly, she was back on bum and feet facing forward, holding the tyre iron to her chest as if it was a crucifix. She let her motion carry her to the open door and went to stand as if she was going to leap out. She had to be too short to bang her head on the top of the van, right?

As she rose to leap out, ever so slowly, Tic-Tac was bending his head down, was he looking to fire again? He never got the chance, the tyre iron connected with his chin and the full force of that, whacked his head backwards.

"Watch out!" A loud male shout came from her left. Ed was kneeling execution style, with Daisy by his side, both of them cut and bruised. The warning was about where exactly they were kneeling. They were perched on the edge of something massive and high up, an unfinished building, the new car park? And at the edge, there was nothing except some tape fluttering in the breeze to warn people of the long drop down. Cady flung an arm out to try and catch hold of the door, but the arm she flung was her right. It hit the door with a wet thump. Cady, with pain knifing through her, fell to her knees, momentum still carrying her forwards towards the edge, in a mockery of the position her friends were tied in. Above her, arms raised, windmilling and trying to regain balance like the ugly duckling, trying out for *Swan Lake*, was Tic-Tac. Facing towards her, his face contorted in concentration and panic as his balance shifted: he took a step back. Poised on the edge of the building, one foot on the edge one foot over, arms still flailing but finding no purchase, the fulcrum beneath him and gravity taking its grim hold. He thrust his arms forward—plaintive or rebalancing? It was all too late. Even if Cady wanted to help him—and did she?—if she took hold of him, they'd both go over. There was nothing she could do. She was powerless. Again.

He stared straight at her, then, right through her, mouth open in a scream the wind sucked away. He drifted backwards like a boat untied. Cady skidded to a halt, her knee smashed into a concrete re-bar. A foot long piece of twisty steel saviour when most she needed one. She held on to it for dear life, though she'd actually stopped two feet from the edge. Funny it looked like one of those stupid candy twists. She wondered what kind of really camp building you'd be needing to throw up for one to be in pink.

Then slowly, oh so slowly, he became smaller, diminishing, arms still held out. Cady found herself reaching back with her lame right hand, still gripping the post with her left. Nothing she could do, but did she need him to know she would? Did she need to know that? Why? He'd tried to kill her three times now, why? Wasn't that enough? To stop forgiving?

She couldn't. She wasn't a killer. Cady could feel the other two on the ledge beside her but she couldn't tear her eyes away from the falling man. The wind lifted, blowing her coat, but even that seemed thick and slow like being pushed by sponge. She'd need to help Ed and Daisy, when, after—

Cady heard a boom. She was still staring at his eyes, tiny now in the distance, but his body had stopped. It seemed like his eyes, or maybe what was in them, continued to fall, back and back and farther in. A pool formed under the dashed head on the concrete. She watched the blood trickle away under a stack of pallets. The small pieces— her stomach lurched.

"A little help here?" said Ed.

"Oh. Yeah." Cady relinquished her hold on the re-bar and ushered her friends from the edge of the building before the wind picked up too much, and began to gently untie them. Daisy and Ed were a proper mess. She reached into her pockets, of course he'd taken all the mobiles. She left Ed and Daisy sitting on the back of the truck and limped to the cab of the van. She rifled the glove box and found their three phones, the contents of Ed's pockets, all stuffed into Daisy's bag. Her phone still had charge in it. She called an ambulance. She figured they were all going to need it. All maybe except Tic-Tac. No ambulance was saving him. She couldn't bring herself to look again. She took Daisy her bag and handed Ed his phone. Daisy busied herself with extricating Ed's belongings from hers. Cady sat on the passenger seat of the van, feet out of the door, head in hands and shook. In the pockets of her jacket was a pouch of tobacco, papers and a lighter. It took her thirty minutes to make a roll-up. By that time, the ambulance was there and she had to begin explaining what had happened to paramedics and then police. She was damned if she was going to stub it out now she'd rolled it and got it lit in the wind.

Chapter 52

The courthouse in Absdowne was busy for six months with the to-ing and fro-ing of the whole affair. The Bat Conservation Trust came in super quick off the back of the tip-off and the impressive footage that Ed had captured of the cloud of bats leaving the roost in the wake of a huge boom from the fracking site. It looked like something from a film, the massive cloud of mammals swirling and swarming like living smoke. There was even a satisfying half-moon in the sky to set it all off. The tip had even been to a Bat Emergency Helpline, about which Ed was over the moon. He was disappointed when the two retirees who turned up, did so in an old silver Volvo. However, that was to underestimate the power of the Bat Team. Within an hour of their arrival at the site, there had been a suitably impressive stand-up row with the site manager. After some argy-bargy with a rather burly pipe-fitter and the Bat Team's temporary removal from site, they returned with police officers, a local ranger and a small pick-up van containing civilian staff, one of whom wore the tell-tale suit, hi-vis and a helmet combo sported by high ranking council officers. Suffice to say, work on the site stopped after that and the whole thing wound up on the front page of the local paper. Cady was rather pleased with the rather racy headline: *Bat-Shut Crazy*. It seemed like whatever contract had gone on there, was irrelevant in the face of the Barbastelle Bat. Who knew?

Cady was just pleased the whole thing shifted the awful business of the car-park incident from the front page. Two front pages in the same month was more publicity than she had ever had in her life, or ever wanted again, for that matter. Daisy, conversely thrived in the limelight. Always better with feelings and people, it was good old reliable Daisy who'd dragged her out for coffee after not having seen hide nor hair of her for a week. After Cady had taken a few weeks' sick from school, Daisy had been texting, if not visiting, twice or more a day. They sat under a brolly, outside on an unusually cold day, sunny, but cold all the same. Cady was leaning over the arm of her chair pouring a pool of mocha onto the ground beside her, and watching as it dribbled under her chair.

"Hey, Charlie Whizz made it into the England under 18's chair racing team, did you know?"

"No."

"Ed says he wants to apply to UMIST next year. That came out of the blue…"

"Mm-hmm."

"And oh my god, there's Prince Philip come to buy his stuff at Wilkos…"

"Mm-hmm."

"Oh no, now he's taking all his clothes off! No! Phil don't do it!" Daisy pantomimed shock and stopping motions with large waving of her hands. When she'd finished, Cady was looking levelly at her. Daisy put a hand to gently right the cup. "Need more marshmallows in that?"

Cady smiled. She'd been there throughout all of it, and Daisy wasn't making half the meal of coping that Cady was. Daisy moved her hair over her ear. What in the living hell was wrong with her? "That would be lovely."

Some council suits on their lunch break sat opposite her. Two women and one bloke, all in those cheap-as-you-can-afford-on-council-wages suits that seemed to come only in grey or blue, but were available in men's or women's styles. The two women seemed to be mocking the chap over some parenting fail. The whole thing was producing the kind of great hilarity that Cady hadn't felt in months. No, that was wrong. Hadn't been able to feel. Stuff had gone on around her that she could have found funny, would have maybe? But she just couldn't. It was like she was living through a thin haze. All the time. Everything took longer to focus on, longer even to work out what it was, before she could move on and react to it. It made her feel tired. The last round of court appearances had been for Carver's trial. It had taken a while to unpick the financial skulduggery he had been up to, since it had been longest in the preparing. He was going to go to jail for a long time. In the court hearing Cady had been called as a witness. They hadn't heard the half of the things that Carver had had to endure with his daughter. She already felt sorry for him, but that was the only time in six months that she'd cried. Cady hadn't even appeared in court over her own incident. The Coroner had pronounced on Tic-Tac as a death by misadventure. Even though Cady had insisted on telling the police and the coroner's office everything that had happened. She'd had to phone the coroner's office back to double check that they'd noted the bruising under Tic-Tac's chin and exactly what had caused it. The very kind pathologist who came to the phone, said that she understood, and she was pretty sure she knew what had happened, and that Cady shouldn't feel guilty about it. Cady remembered replying that she was okay and didn't feel guilty. And that much was true, she didn't feel guilty. Or anything else for that matter.

"Extra marshies! For you madam, no charge." Daisy grinned. "I chatted up the barista." She held out overflowing cupped hands full of white and pink mini-marshmallows of the kind too small to put on a stick. She released her hands over the top of Cady's paper cup. The marshmallows went everywhere, down her legs, in her chair, on the floor, all over the table. Daisy was still grinning from ear to ear. They were starting to attract the attention of pigeons. For the first time in six months, Cady wore a smile she could feel.

Chapter 53

Her dad's shouting usually heralded something exciting. He was quite proud of his usual Gen-X laconic exterior, so shouting, whatever it was, heralded something big. Half-awake getting dressed, especially with achy, uncooperative legs was always a drag. Dad yelling from downstairs didn't make any of that less stressful. Sweatpants, and bare foot, she threw on her Disturbed T-Shirt and steered herself to the banister, trying not to overshoot.

In the kitchen, she headed for the fridge, where the diet coke lived and was half-way through a mid-air pouring, when her dad was behind her, pushing.

"Hey! Spillage!"

"Put the glass down, come see this."

He walked her to the window. There was a strange van on their drive. She shrugged. Her dad nodded towards the door. Miming was always a pursuit best done after enough caffeine, in Cady's opinion. He flapped his hands in frustration. For a brief moment, Cady considered torturing him and drinking her coke unbelievably slowly. But she took pity, took his arm and steered him to the door.

"Show me the nasty person who blocked the drive with their tatty van, then Daddy."

Her dad said nothing as they walked down the ramp. The van was blocking the drive. The van was not tatty in any way. It was pristine. It had a great big purple bow on the front. Cady looked across, he hadn't had he? No, with the amount of money he made from fixing up people's second hand cars and doing M.O.Ts, there was no way on earth he'd be able to afford something like that. It was a brand new, pristine VW Caravelle. It was metallic purple and it was beautiful. When she glanced over, her dad seemed as confused as she did. She walked over and tried the handle. Locked.

"Oh," He fished in his pocket. He gave her a bulky DL-sized envelope. "Came through the door."

She fished inside it. It was already open. It contained car keys and a letter on crisp expensive paper. She left the keys in the envelope and handed it back, reading the letter while he bustled to open the doors on the van.

****

For you.
  Thank You, Cady.
  Frog.

****

Followed by the pen and ink version of that masonic dividers and set square symbol. What the actual? Her dad sat in the passenger seat. There was no driver's seat. It seemed to have rails for a chair instead. He was examining how all the controls seemed to be on and around the steering column.

"I can't accept this." Cady leaned into the van.

He reached over and placed a pink post-it gently on her nose. She crossed her eyes, which made her dad laugh. She peeled it off and read it. It said *Yes you ca*n, in Frog's beautiful handwriting. There wasn't a curve or a loop in her script that was unbalanced or out of place. She wondered what a handwriting expert would make of it.

"Shit Dad. Did you read this?"

"What, the letter? Yeah."

"I—"

"Come on, whatever happened to not looking a gift horse in the mouth?"

"You know that's referring to Troy, right?"

"Yeah," he grinned. "You gonna come and give this a spin or not? Look! Look!" He pushed a button inside the cab and there was a *clunk* at the back of the van. Slowly, the back lifted up. Then he pressed another, and a ramp lowered itself down and gently landed on the driveway. The van was genuinely beautiful. It had every bell and whistle imaginable, and plenty Cady had never dreamed of. The cluster of controls around the steering column made it feel more like a helicopter than a car.

"Wanna hand up?" He helped her up into the driver's seat and excitedly talked her through how the crazy twirly seat functioned to do a transfer over from her power chair. Then he went on to try to explain what each of the controls on the steering column did and how cool he thought they were. Cady held the steering wheel and gazed out of the windscreen. Her dad segued onto how awesome the entertainment system was, demonstrating with a rather impressive blast of *Monkey Wrench* from his phone via Bluetooth. It did seem like the van had speakers everywhere, and she wasn't so far gone that she didn't notice what must be a massive set of bass bins somewhere in the back. He tapped her arm. She leaned forward till her head was on the steering wheel. "What's up love?"

"What exactly is this?"

"Err, it's a van, love."

"Not what I meant and you know it." She lifted her head mock heavily and stared. "I mean what am I getting into by accepting this, if I do?"

Her dad poked the flat screen at the centre of the massive control panel and the sound system went quiet. He swung his knees back into the well where the gear stick was. He then leaned forward, sandwiching his hands between his knees. He pursed his lips, then blew a puff of air up over his face, ruffling his receding fringe.

"I mean, is this paying me off? Paying me for—? Paying in advance for—?"

"Honestly, I don't know, Cade. I really don't, but what I do know is, life is—" His face went red from his chin to his scalp. "Well, you know."

"I know what you mean, Dad."

"You've been working so hard on, all of this, you gave so much, kid. I was so proud of you. I guess what I'm trying to say is that if someone says thank you, it's sometimes okay to just say you're welcome and stop worrying about it."

"Yeah maybe."

Cady adjusted the rear view mirror, which was as massive as the van, presumably allowing for people with restricted neck movement. Someone was standing on the other side of the road. She couldn't quite work out initially whether it was a woman or a man she was seeing, but in the end she decided from the way they were holding themselves it was a woman. The clothes were extraordinary. She was wearing a wide brimmed black hat and an enormous baggy three-piece suit. It was dark blue with white stripes, not the conservative pinstripe of someone who wanted to appear individual and unremarkable at the same time. This was the suit of someone who didn't give a toss. No, even that wasn't accurate enough, it was someone who took time and effort and care over their appearance, but didn't give a rat's ass about what anyone else thought. Cady closed her mouth and moved the rear view mirror to get a better look. The woman lifted her head enough for Cady to see her. She was old, maybe even over fifty, but she looked way younger than her mother, who was had only just turned forty. She had beautiful skin, but pale, even from this far away Cady thought she almost glowed. Cady didn't go in for make up much, unless she was going out but when she did, she'd always been fond of that weird esoteric 'goth-y' thing, influenced by vampires and Egypt and tubercular poets. But this curious woman had a flick of kohl in the corners of her eyes and dark red lipstick and she caught Cady looking. Cady fought the flinch that rose in her, gazing harder, rather than looking away. The woman's eyes crinkled and she smiled, a deep smile. Then she touched the brim of her hat, and she was gone. Cady moved the mirror but she wasn't there. She opened the driver's door and slid her feet out onto the drive. The rush of the rest of her weight catching up with her nearly made her buckle. She was kicking herself for not having brought a stick out. She walked as fast as she could manage to the back of the van, leaning with one hand for support, reaching there, she scanned the road, but no sign. In the near distance she could hear an unusual roary car engine, was that Frog? She wanted to walk across the road to where she'd seen her, but that was not going to happen today. And she wasn't going to collapse in the middle of the road and get pity bombed for anyone.

Her Dad pipped the horn in the van. It was a good robust-sounding horn. She turned to go back, then felt the wind rustle her hair behind her. Something tiny and white caught her eye, a cigarette butt, long and thin, pushed to her on a faint scent of flowers.

THE END

Afterword

Wow. This one was a whirlwind. Many thanks to all the people who stopped me getting swept away.

Thanks to Cheryl Arvidson-Keating for awesome formatting, website building and general patience; my awesome editor Sue Laybourn at No Stone Unturned Editing; @betibup33 for the awesome cover art, (catch them on twitter) and to thanks to my and insightful sensitivity reader Fuschia Aurelius, she's an actor and a model. Find her on Instagram as @fuschiaaurelius.

Thanks to Mik Scarlett for help and advice about sensitivity reading, to Joe T Redneck for police procedural tips and to Sara Horsman and Phoe Tanabe for tips on what the insides of a WAV looks like. And lastly but not leastly thank you to Kelly Ohlert and the street team for all their help, Lauren Roberts and the SWAN_UK lot for helping keep me sane and to Tracey Freame and everyone at CHSW for picking us all up when we're at our lowest.

***

50% of the proceeds of this book are getting split between two charities that have helped my daughter from the get go:

- Syndromes Without A Name (SWAN_UK) the support group for Genetic Alliance UK, they help families without a diagnosis (SWAN's). Find out more here: https://www.undiagnosed.org.uk/

- Children's Hospice South West (CHSW) who run three amazing hospices in the SW of the UK for families with life limited or critically ill children. Find out more here https://www.chsw.org.uk/

***

And lastly many thanks to you for buying it and reading it. I'm hoping that this is a massive success and we can donate a load of money to two charities that our family really couldn't be without, but that depends on you lot: if you loved it, plug it before you forget, write me a review, mention me to your mates!

You can join my mailing list at http://paularvidson.co.uk/cady-grey/ for 'Crocodile Rock', a free short story about Cady and her friends and to keep up to date with future releases in the series.

Contact Me

Web: paularvidson.co.uk
Twitter: @realarvo
Instagram: @realarvo
Facebook: facebook.com/paularvidsonauthor

Other Books: The Dark Trilogy

An abandoned colony, a mysterious quest, strange heroes and a world like no other. Read on for the first few chapters of Dark…

"This is Lt. Myrch Weston, service number NXBF-105345-GDT. Not that that matters overmuch now. I'm the last of the mission to Deepspace Colony Sirius 4, though the natives here call it Dark."

Excerpts from <Distress Beacon SN-1853001>. Found by E.S.V Vixen Terradate: 26102225.

Chapter One

Dun sat bolt upright in the darkness. Eyes open. Heart battering. He could still feel it coming.

Churning cold metallic water, spray everywhere, his sinews twanged tight, heart banging, ears singing. At least that's blocking out the sound of… What? What is it? What in the Gods is it? It's coming, still coming. It's like it's, it's a hunger. Driven. Want and hate. Blood and bone. Closer. Closer and … He inhaled a final struggling breath and shoved the horror in his head away.

He could hear his brothers and sisters making small stirring noises not far from him. He hoped he hadn't woken Mother too; he'd never hear the end of it. Since Father had disappeared, Mother had changed. Not close to him. Not warm. He'd become the man of the family and that was that. He still felt too young but what could he do? Someone had to hunt and forage while Mother cared for the little ones and he was the eldest. And now he was waking everyone more nights than not with these blasted dreams.

All that was familiar trickled into his brain: his bed of reeds underneath him, the drone of the fans, and the warm mammalian smell of his family. A new span in the Dark; time to wake up. The nightmares took longer to shake off. He dreamed of something pursuing him through tunnels, his calves deep in water. It was something horrible hunting him down. He ran and ran until his lungs felt like rags. Then, of course, as it got to him, he'd wake up. Every time he tried to get back to sleep, there it would be again, waiting.

He sighed. There was no telling Mother about his dreams. One day Father had gone out and had never come back. Just like that. It was like he'd ceased to exist. Once Father's smell had faded from their home, it grew harder and harder to remember he had ever been there.

Thinking about Father always made him feel a sharp sadness, even though it had happened two ages ago. Mother had pined, of course. Crying at night once she knew the babies were asleep. Hearing her weep in the darkness, Dun knew he'd be growing up faster than his friends. He couldn't talk to most of them about his concerns, except Padg. The others were busy playing and chasing each other as if nothing had happened; for them nothing had.

Padg, though, he had his own responsibilities. Being the son of the Shaman could do that. They'd known each other since they'd been the two youngest pups in the village. Padg had always been the most worldly of all their group, not averse to getting into trouble with the rest of them, but certainly averse to getting caught. He'd saved them all from many a beating. Now with Father gone, it felt to Dun like Padg was the only one he could talk to. Odd. The sense of responsibility Dun felt he'd had thrust upon him, Padg had been born with.

***

After breakfast and helping Mother feed the little ones, Dun went out, slamming the rush door behind him. He walked to the wooden span across the massive river pipe; the crossing that gave the Bridge-folk their name. From there, it was easy to follow the rope path to the village. He needed to reach the Shaman's compound on the opposite side of the village if he wanted to talk to Padg about why he'd been feeling so odd.

Out of the burrow, he was enveloped by the hum of smell and noise from the village. Some kind of auction of a new piece of found tech seemed to be taking place in the market. He heard raised voices, oddly (usually trading in Bridge-town was a good-natured affair). He couldn't process any of it today. It was all he could do to follow the rope guides underfoot without walking into anything. His head buzzed. He was relieved to finally reach the woven gate and the wisps of incense and worked wood told him he'd reached his destination.

"Dunno..." was all his friend could muster after Dun retold his dream.

"Well, thanks for that; great help."

"I mean, it might be something, it might be nothing."

"Somehow, none of today is working out how I'd planned," Dun sighed.

A breeze outside stirred the wooden wind chimes beside the lean-to shed Padg used as his workshop. Dun stretched out his arm to feel along the rack that held his friend's work in progress. He felt twisted bamboo staves that would be made into sword-spears, preferred weapon among the Bridge-folk. A shup-shup-shup sound indicated Padg had resumed work with sanding the sword-spear at his bench. The sword was made out of the extremely hard, woody stem of one of the larger fungi growing in the depths; it didn't stay sharp for very long, but long enough. The hunters usually carried two or three strapped to their backs for good measure. Padg carved particularly well; he was especially good at forming the helical twist in the shaft of the weapon that made it fly true when thrown.

"Padg? Hello?"

"Hush, I'm sanding."

"Oh."

The rhythm of the sanding was a reassuring odd kind of tune with the wooden, just musical, clunking of the chimes.

"Padg?"

"Sanding? Tricky. Needs concentration."

"Sorry, it's just..."

The sanding block clattered to the floor.

"Right! I give up," Padg said. "Grab a rod from the rack; there's some scraps in the bucket. You need something to occupy your hands."

Fishing was always Padg's go-to in a crisis. They left through the back flap of Padg's workshop and headed to his favorite spot: a rusted through hole at the top of the massive pipe. They scrambled up the side using massive bolt heads in the metal surface of the pipe as a makeshift ladder. Once at the top they gathered their kit, baited the long lines necessary to get down far enough and let each one fall through the hole with a satisfying 'plop'.

They fished for a while in companionable silence. A lazy breeze, scented faintly with vinegar, drifted up through the hole.

"Detail!" Padg cried suddenly.

"Eh?" Dun cocked his head, bewildered.

"Detail, my friend. That's what was bothering me."

"Good, I'm glad. Care to tell me why?"

"Your dream. Most peoples' dreams are vague, full of confused smells, feelings, sometimes sounds. You know, the I was there with my friend but it was really my sister and then the tunnel became my house, kind of thing. Yours felt like you were there."

"You can say that again," Dun said.

"Maybe you were."

"What do you mean?"

"Just what I said. Maybe you were there. Or at least maybe you will be."

"You're talking in riddles."

"Might be I'm not explaining it right. Listen, Dad talks about this kind of stuff all the time. You sit around and hear enough of it, and you kind of get a feel for it. Let's go back and find him; I think he'll be able to help. Besides, the fishing's rubbish today."

Chapter Two

"Do you know what foretelling is, Dun?" The voice of Barg the Shaman was deep and reassuring. Dun guessed that came with the job.

"No."

Dun, Padg, and his father enjoyed the warmth of the small air vent in the hut. Many of the shared buildings and all homes had a vent somewhere. They all came out of the ground or walls and delivered air in varying temperatures and smells, ending usually in a metal grill or mesh. The vent in Barg's floor had the unusual combination of a warm air flow and no smell other than a slight tinge of metal. This allowed Barg to place bags of herbs on the grill, which warmed by the air flow, would permeate the hut. Dun felt wrapped in perfume: the sweet and the spicy, the nutty and the resinous; too enveloped and overwhelmed to work out one smell from the next. It was a warm blanket of aroma, comforting and welcoming.

"Have you been sleeping well, Dun?"

"Well...er...no. Not really."

The Shaman didn't reply. Dun felt he had to fill the void, but his brain skittered to work out exactly what to say, without sounding foolish.

"I've been dreaming quite a bit. Every rest. Usually several times each rest."

"And you've been remembering them all, in great detail?"

"Yes. How did you..."

"Getting more compelling, more vital?"

"Yes."

Somewhere in the depths of the vent Dun could hear the ping of metal expanding. The Shaman made a non-committal humming sound.

"When they first started, they were weird. On the inside of my head. Noises and scents but really vivid, quite random. Then there was this odd sensation... Like tingling or prickling, waves of something, blankets maybe but not, sometimes filling the whole of the inside of my head and hurting. I'm not describing this very well."

"Those are called extra-sensory factors."

"Oh?"

"Things that you can't describe in sounds, touch, smell, taste or air-sense. It takes a while to get used to those, but you will. They're something that you won't really make a lot of, unfortunately. We don't know what they mean. They come in different types; some foretellers have called them flavors; it helps to categorize them, but ultimately it's hard to tell what they might mean. Historically, foretellers tend to ignore them, to be honest."

Dun was so lost in his own thoughts in the effort to take everything in. Barg filled the gap this time.

"Have the dreams been getting more consistent? Recurring?"

"I've been having one dream that has, yes."

"What happens?"

"I'm running along one of the rivers, in a tunnel and I'm being chased by something. A horrible something. It's hunting me. It won't give up and it's gaining on me. But I can't smell it or air-sense it; I just know it's coming. Almost, but not quite like, I know what it's thinking... A horrible 'other' thing."

"The same every time?"

"Yes, well, starting the same every time, but it seems like there's some more each time. Like a story?" Dun had intended his tone to be rhetorical, but Barg answered.

"Yes, like a story. Except this one may be real. And you may be in it."

"Hey, I said that," Padg chipped in.

"Thank you, Padg," his father replied. "You have been listening all these years. It is a shame, though, that you've never had the foretelling gift."

"Curse, more like."

"Padg!" The Shaman could crack his voice like a whip.

"Sorry, Father."

"What do you mean, 'curse?'" Dun asked, worried.

"Some people find the responsibility that comes with the gift of foretelling too much for them."

"That's the folk it doesn't drive bats!"

"Padg! That's quite enough. This is a serious discussion of a very serious matter. If you can't listen seriously then go outside. Young Dun here has the gift of foretelling whether he wants it or not. What matters now is that he understands it and what he does with it."

"Sorry."

"Hmm."

A distant clang echoed up the air vent with a sigh of acrid air.

"So is it the future then? I'm experiencing the future?"

"No. Not exactly. Sometimes it may be the future, sometimes it can be the past, sometimes it is a foretelling from far away. Neither your future or your past."

"So what use is that to me? Or to anyone?"

"That is for you to decide," Berg said. "That is what makes the difference between a good Foreteller and Mad-folk. That is the riddle that is foretelling."

"So you can't tell me what my dream meant?"

"No. Only you can know that. All I can say is that you do have the gift."

"But this dream," he corrected himself, "foretelling seemed so real. And it's not happened to me yet, so it must be my future, mustn't it?"

"Each foretelling appears from the mind of someone there, sometimes many minds. All of that appears in *your* mind. It seems like it's come from you. This is a lot to take in for one day, my young friend. Go home and think about it. Return to me after the next rest, and we'll talk some more."

Dun left the hut in a daze, foretelling, multiple futures, madness, extra-sensory-whatever-the-hells-they-were. He already had way more responsibility than ever he felt ready for, and now this. It was a long while before Dun realized Padg was still there walking alongside him, and to be honest with himself, Dun hadn't the first idea where he was going. He let his legs and the noisy current of folk carry him, while his conscious brain wasn't occupied with the task of directing him. The smell of Dodg's sweet-food stall on the market hit him just before he hit it.

"Dun!" Padg laughed.

"Sorry—in another world there."

Feeling guilty for dragging his friend halfway across the village, Dun felt in his shoulder bag for some trade strips he knew still carried some credit. He could smell the Sweetcrackle dried mushrooms on the stand. He asked for two handfuls and handed over the wooden trade strip. The sound of a few brief scratches followed as Dodg made tallies on it, before handing it back to Dun.

"Thanks."

The friends walked on munching side by side for a while. They tried to give the bowl in the center of the village, where auctions usually took place, a wide berth. The rowdy market that Dun had heard earlier seemed to have descended into a full-blown row. The raised voices of Bridge-folk seemed to be interspersed with the nasal shrieks of a group of River-folk traders.

"You don't think that'll happen to me do you?" Dun said.

"What?" Padg said. "Foretelling? Sounds like it already has."

"No, not the foretelling or whatever it's called; the going mad."

"Don't know. Probably not."

Probably. That was reassuring. Well, he'd have to settle for that for now, while he worked out what exactly was going on inside his head. Until then, he was supposed to do chores. Mother would need him by now. It would be chaos there, though; the pups fighting, Mother shouting. It wasn't much better staying here, whatever the hells was going on today.

He needed time alone to think. He said good-bye to Padg. Maybe another go at some fish?

***

Dun crept back through the rush door of the family home at River-hole. It was eerily quiet. Maybe Mother had taken the little ones to crêche in the village; it was about that time. He searched for his hunting bag. His mother had made it for his father, and Dun felt awkward using it. The bag was a traditional folk woven one from reeds, as opposed to the recent trends of making bags out of materials from found-things. Dun didn't have much to do with found-things. Not particularly because of the inherent danger or because of any traditionalist streak in him, but mostly because they were usually so damned expensive. The market traders and traveling visitors from the Machine-folk who collected and sold found-things made plenty of trade tallies to offset the risks they took, but on the whole, Dun didn't get it. For most problems, there was a folk generated solution available, cheaper or free, and that suited him fine. He swung the bag over his shoulder and made for the passage that led from the family room down to the river. The texture of the bag in his hands was strangely comforting today.

He could feel the cloud of fresh moisture many strides before he reached the river. The sensation was something he took for granted. It permeated the whole tribe's life, his family's especially since of all the tribe, they lived closest to it, their home called "River-hole" due to a convenient tunnel to the bank. The noise of the water rose and fell with the seemingly random levels of the river, quieter today as it happened, but it was always there. He walked down to the edge of the water; there was the walkway along the edge of the river. He walked the familiar route to his favorite fishing place, underfoot the textured metal mesh lightly crunching with rust. Stopping at his usual place, just after the air grill on the wall, he lay down on his belly, arm in the water, to wait.

Patience was one of his strong points. He was always able to distract himself in one part of his brain, working out what he'd do next, planning ahead, while another part of him lay in wait, wired and sprung to pounce. A swish in the water and a fish would be caught, stunned and in his bag. That is, if a fish came along. He twitched his fingers. Funny, it seemed like he was having to reach farther down today, to even reach the water. Ah well, everything today seemed like more effort. Maybe, it was his attitude he should be focussing on...

"Aaaaaaaang!"

In the water, the blood, his hand, the pain. Something churning in the water. Angry, cold, alien. He snatched his hand out, sure to feel blood dripping down his arm but no. His hand was fine, wet with water, but fine. He wiggled his fingers. What the hell was going on? His pulse hammered. The dreaming, foretelling, again? While he was awake? He could scarcely cope with it every night. Would it be every night? Gods, he hoped not. He forced his breath slowly through his teeth.

Whether or not he could stand it, he was starting to understand the folk who couldn't. When he was very young, there was someone from the village who had started behaving oddly. Beng? Or was it Teng? Dun couldn't recall, but he could remember that the poor unfortunate became more and more strange and disassociated, talking to himself, arguing with absent demons. Eventually, you couldn't smell him in the village and no one talked about him anymore. Now Dun knew why. He was beginning to imagine how this new "gift" could easily crack someone. The sleeplessness alone was enough to fray him at the edges.

He slowly clenched and unclenched his hand. He had the gift, want it or not, and he was just going to have to cope. There was no one else.

A cramp in his shoulder told Dun how long he'd been there. It never normally took this much effort to find a catch. He moved his spot to somewhere farther upstream, a spot he liked less but nearer the village bridge where the pipe turned. It was busier there. Dun didn't like the disturbance, people going into the village, the noise of the market more obvious, but it was a sure place to catch something. He waited again. Slowly a chilling feeling crept up his insides; he carried on fishing, trying to quell it, but in the end, he had to let the obvious overwhelm him. No fish. There were no fish.

There had always been fish. How could there not be? He sat back on his haunches, head in his hands trying to think. The family would be fine—there were mushrooms he could find if he wanted—but that wasn't the point. They'd be fine for now. All the Bridge-folk would be fine for now. But fish were an important part of what everyone had to eat. And then there was trade, although the woven weed bags that the Bridge-folk produced were very fine, by far the most important trade good was the fish. And there was something else he couldn't put his finger on. A tickling in the back of his mind. Something important. He had all the fragments, but he couldn't make them into one piece. Something was terribly wrong. One of the Elders in the village needed to know. Now.

He went straight to the Shaman's hut. All he heard when he got in earshot was the snick-snick of Padg whittling. Dun could tell the noise of Padg's carving from twenty or thirty strides away.

"Padg!"

"Hey! What's wrong? You're panting."

"Where's your father?"

"Some meeting of the elders in the Moot-hall. Why?"

Dun grabbed Padg by his shoulder and pulled him up to standing. The sword-spear he was working on fell to the floor with a clatter.

"Hells! Do you know how long those things take to sharpen?"

Dun kept pulling. "Come on, we've got to go there. Now!"

Padg stopped resisting and fell into an easy lope, alongside Dun. "Why?"

"Fish!" Dun shouted.

"Eh?"

"There's no fish. In the river. None."

"Gods!"

They slowed only as they reached the Moot-hall, a long low building built like the rest of the village hut dwellings from reeds and mud, but this was the largest building in the village and had the added feature of double-skinned walls, stuffed on the inside with fur to damp down noise from inside and out. However, no amount of auditory dampening or protection was going to hide the raised voices heard when the friends arrived.

"...care how important this is. He's too young!"

Padg grabbed Dun and pulled him down into a crouch, just around the edge of the Moot-hall from its door.

"He's wise for his years."

"But not many of those!"

"He's perfectly capable."

"Enough!" The voice of Ardg, the village Alpha, was heard loudly, and then more quietly he said, "We have no choice."

"But we would be sending him to certain... danger. Why can we not send a fully grown band of hunters?"

"You know why, Greng. We and only we of the Elders-moot know of the other threat that faces us. We must act with that in mind."

"How goes the discussion with our River-folk 'guest?'" Dun made out the odd, deep tones of Myrch, the Alpha's most recent advisor.

"He still won't tell us what he was searching for." A female voice was Swych's, the head of the Hunter's Guild.

"Though clearly up to no good, poking through the Bibliotheca. All of our records and maps?" Myrch said.

"We have nothing to hide," Ardg said.

"You say that like it's a good thing," Myrch said.

Both Padg and Dun were lifted off their feet swiftly and silently, gripped by the scruff from behind.

"People who listen at doors, get bent noses."

The quiet, precise voice carried almost no scent. It could only be Swych, head of the hunter's guild and tutor to both Padg and Dun in fighting and tracking and stalking food.

Dun and Padg, in mid-air, were still too stunned to reply. She had come out of nowhere, like a wraith, without even disturbing the air.

"Now what should we do with a pair of ear-flapping vagabonds, eh?" Swych said, hauling them up effortlessly. "I think we'll let Ardg decide what punishment is fitting."

With that, she swirled them around the corner and kicked the door to the Moot-hall deftly, so it swung inward.

"Friends, Elders, our meeting is adjourned. I have found some skulkers at the door jamb. What punishment do we deem fit?"

"Ah," the Alpha said when the scent of Dun and Padg quickly followed them into the hut. "I suspect what we have to say to these young rogues may be punishment enough."

Chapter Three

"But the fish?" Dun tried not to stutter. "Pardon?"

"Fish." Facing the Alpha it was all Dun could muster. So far his day had not worked out at all how he'd planned.

"I think for all concerned here, you'll need to be just a little clearer."

"Gone. They're all gone."

"The fish?"

Ardg, despite winning his role as village Alpha in combat, had spent many years in his position perfecting his diplomacy and forbearance against, what some would consider, extreme odds.

"Yes."

"Ah."

The low muttering next to Ardg was Myrch, the advisor, but it was too quiet for Dun to hear.

"That is worrying. We will investigate the matter of the fish in due course. We're glad you came, Dun; we wanted to talk to you. About another matter." He paused. "There's something you can do for us, for everyone."

"Me?"

"Yes," Ardg replied simply. "It has come to our attention that some old neighbors of ours, the Machine-folk, have gone very quiet. They are not near neighbors—they live far upstream—but we have not had a whisker-twitch of them for some time."

Dun and Padg listened intently but still weren't sure where they might come into it themselves. After all, they were the first to realize that in terms of the tribe, they were very small reeds in a very big basket.

"We usually meet them once a cycle at the tribes-moot fair," the Alpha continued. "They have occasionally missed a cycle; some tribes do sometimes; it isn't unusual. However, they send traders here all the time but no one has bumped into any of them for nearly an eon and now, pieces of found-tech are making their way here, brought by River-folk. That is troubling."

Dun twitched. From his tone, what the Alpha said was true, but equally, there was something he wasn't saying. He tried to think of what he knew of the Machine-folk. They came to the tribes-moots, of course, bringing some kind of clever mechanical toy or more often beautiful and useful pieces of rare metal. There were rumors about them being the custodians of wonderful machines. They could predict the future, could read your mind, that kind of thing and more. Dun was starting to realize that most of what he knew was conjecture and rumor; that was going to be of little help to him. Dun furrowed his brow. Not enough to go on.

"The tribe needs to send a small hunting party to check that all is well. We have chosen you, Dun, to fulfill this task, and you must choose who will go with you. Also, you must decide what provisions and equipment you need to fulfill your task. This will be provided by the tribe. Consider this wisely. Tonight there is feasting for Old Gryr; he has hung up his hunting spear this cycle, and it is time to celebrate his victories. Tomorrow we will talk again. Until then you must speak of this to no one."

"But, why choose me? There are plenty of older, smarter, tougher folk than me," Dun said

"There are. It is you we have chosen, nonetheless." Again, there was more that Ardg wasn't saying, but his tone brooked no argument.

"Mother and the little ones? Who will take care of them? Since Father..."

"The tribe will keep your people safe, rest assured, young Dun."

"May I go and think about it? It's ... a lot."

"We would expect no less."

***

"It's a lot..." He didn't finish his sentence in the tent. He didn't finish it as he stumbled outside. He couldn't finish it later, as he wandered through the village. There was just "a lot". A lot in his head. A lot of fear about what he was getting into. A lot he didn't know, and that frightened him most of all. There were many, many pieces to this puzzle, and he only had one or two. He felt like he was walking straight into the jaws of some horrible cave hunting predator. Something that sat with its jaws wide open and waited. Waited till someone was right on its tongue and then...

A pain seared through Dun's leg. Padg was laughing.

"Ow! What was that for?"

"Well, you've been such great company today, I had to entertain myself somehow."

"Ow," Dun said again, more quietly this time. He sat and rubbed his shin.

"So," Padg said. Half-question, half-statement.

"So?"

Padg left a gap in the conversation that a cart could've been pulled through. Then, as Dun was drawing breath to reply, he said as quickly as he could, "So are you going to take me with you on this stupid errand or what?"

"Oh. That."

"Oh! Yes of course that. What have you been brooding but not talking to me about, for gods' know how long?"

"Sorry," Dun said, back-footed. "I didn't know if you'd want to."

"Hmm...the biggest adventure of either of our lives and you're not sure if I'd want to? Did it ever occur to you that you need to take someone to prevent you getting your miserable hide eaten or lost?"

"Well, yes."

"And so?"

"So?"

"You still haven't asked me!"

"Oh. Sorry. Will you come with me?"

"I might be busy..."

Dun sprung on Padg shouting "ratbag!" and they rolled over the ground, crashing into a fence and earning a stern "hey!" from its owner. The play fight lasted some time, until Padg got the better of his old friend and sat astride his neck. Dun tapped his leg in a gesture of defeat. They sat on the ground panting.

"You know it's going to be really dangerous?" Dun said.

"Yes?" Padg replied.

"No, I mean *really* dangerous."

"Come on," Padg said. "Let's work while we talk. I know a secret Myconid-folk cave a good walk from here. No one goes there; there are good pickings, and it means you're not going back empty-handed to your mother if there's no fish."

"Ever the practical one, eh?"

"I just know your mother. She scares me."

So the friends walked and talked, keeping air-senses open for anyone else near, but Padg's cave, just as he'd said, was some way from the village. The passage was accessed by squeezing through a damaged grating at floor level, just large enough for the two friends. Padg was right; a full-grown adult would not fit. Sometime after all sound of the village and the river had died away, Dun began again.

"I don't think I'm explaining this well. By dangerous I mean, endangering-the-whole-tribe dangerous. More, if that were possible."

"How do you know? The dreams?"

"Not the dreams exactly. At least, not what's in them. It's just a feeling I get when I'm in the dream. And now, when I'm awake too."

"What kind of dangerous? You know, I wouldn't let you go alone. Death doesn't bother me; I've been trained as a hunter. So have you."

"Not death, at least not just death. Worse than that, somehow. It's really not that clear in the dreams."

"Great. Already I'm not enjoying the role of 'Foreseer's companion'. You get to scare the hairs off me and then say, 'Oh, it's really not that clear. Just worse than death.' Great."

"Listen, I'm not very good at this yet. I'm just saying I hope you know what you're agreeing to before you get too far in."

"You haven't really agreed yourself yet, from what I remember in the Moot-hall," Padg reminded Dun.

"True. But I think I have to. You've got a choice."

"Not if you're going."

And so it was decided.

***

The first two members of the party to hunt and find the Machine-folk sat in the warmth of the Moot-hall and listened to the village skald, Ebun, sing the Ballad of Yarra and Jaris. No one knew how old the song was, but it was old indeed. They'd heard its strains scores of times since being small; it was a favorite at festivals and feasts, but somehow this time there was a new romance to it; a frisson of knowing that they were on the verge of the kind of journey that was worthy of a song.

Ballad of Yarra and Jaris

In the place of long ago, outside the egg upon its back
Yarra looked upon the deep—and her shimmered hair was black
Resplendent in the void and deep—and her shimmered hair was black.

Jaris came and warmed her heart—he came to her along the track
Came from the deep and warmed her heart—he came to her along the track.

They loved as one an eons breadth—and half was warm and half was black
They loved as none before or since—and half was warm and half was black.

And then a one came in between—she felt her heart begin to crack
The darkest face came in between—she felt her heart begin to crack.

Then he was gone and never seen—and none was warm and all was black
He faded went and never seen—and none was warm and all was black.

Then we climbed back inside the egg—how long to wait till he came back
Returned ourselves inside the egg—how long to wait till he came back?

Dun heard no more of the ballad that night as the strain overtook him and he slept. Padg hadn't the heart to wake him.

Chapter Four

Dun's family had always been unusual in that they didn't live in a hut. "River-hole" comprised two dirt-floored rooms near a short tunnel which led to the pipe and the river. Why they had wound up there Dun didn't know. He supposed there might have been a story if he pestered his mother, but he couldn't bring himself to. She still seemed lost in her own world.

Living there certainly had its perks. Besides the obvious benefit of being so close to the river, something the family had always made the most of, there were odd storage compartments on the walls and nooks and crannies for the children to play in.

The floor beneath them was always strangely warm but without an air vent. Not a huge difference, but noticeable when you went outside. Beneath a covering of packed soil in their rooms, the base floor was a metal; Dun had dug down in a corner one day as a child.

Mother and Father must have moved earth in from elsewhere to make things more comfortable. Thinking about it now, their home had so many advantages, it was strange that an Elder didn't live there. They must have done something to be allowed to live there? Dun started to think life was turning out like the floor in their house; scratch the surface a little and something odd laid not that far below.

"Oi! Dozy!" Padg shouted at the rush door, rattling the door in its frame.

"Oh sorry," Dun said.

"Rough sleep?"

"No, not too bad..." Dun began absently

"Good. Let's go back to our hut," Padg said. "Father's not in. He's off having another Elders' meeting. We need to plan."

Dun grabbed his bag and off they went.

On the way through the village, passing the edge of the market stalls, Padg piped up, "If I'm providing the venue, you're providing the provisions."

"Sounds fair."

Dun dug out his tally sticks and bought two cups of burnt-smelling, bitter-dry Racta in wooden cups from one vendor and two handfuls of sweet crackle from Dodg. The middle of the village was oddly quiet. A hiatus after something? He was clearly thinking too hard. Dun shook his head, and they went back to the hut. Padg sat Dun down on a log, then rustled off into distant corners, searching for who knew what. After a few moments and a grunt of satisfaction, he returned to the log and prodded a stylus and a bark-roll into Dun's hands.

"What's this?" Dun said.

"List," Padg replied, with that tone of certainty that previous times even Dun had found annoying. Oddly, this time, Dun found it comforting. More than that, he had a creeping suspicion the traits in question could just save their lives.

"Check these off."

"Go ahead."

"Firstly, weapons: me." The low scraping of stylus on bark filled the tent.

"You?" Dun asked, slightly too surprised.

"Yes," Padg returned. "Even Orsn the Maker said my stuff is really good now. I can carve a sword-spear that flies true, make pipe darts, knives, bolas. I've been collecting stuff."

"Stockpiling? Whatever for?"

"I was going to start trading them, but it seems like they've got a different fate now. I've got knives and a stack of sword-spears that I'm really pleased with. I spent ages foraging the plants for them but I found this odd group of plants way out toward where the Myconid-folk live. Took me ages to get them but they're rock hard and sharpen up really well. There's a bit more weight to them too so they fly really good."

"Wow," Dun said. "What's next here? Food."

"Food: We've got to guess this, but say, twelve spans there and twelve back; allows six spans to explore."

Thirty spans; that was a whole cycle. The scale of this whole undertaking was slowly sinking in for Dun, and it was one of the many things he wasn't comfortable with.

Padg continued his train of thought. "We probably want something we can eat easily; something we don't have to cook and that doesn't weigh much. Dried mushrooms, caked fish—that kind of thing. We might find fresh stuff on the way, but we can't count on that."

"And there's no fish," Dun reminded.

"Okay, true. Next: bed-rolls," Dun said. "I can get us some from home. We've always got spares. Mother weaves them when she's bored."

"Add some packs with shoulder straps," Padg said. "All this stuff won't carry in just bags; there'll be too much. Plus it keeps our hands free should we need to fight."

"Who in the gods would we fight?" Dun tried to hide the rising tension in his voice.

"Dunno. Bandits maybe? It has been known. There are supposed to be big arachnoids in the deepest caves, not that I know anyone who's met one. And then there's whatever the hells that thing in your dream is. That hardly seems friendly, does it?"

"No." Dun swallowed. "I don't suppose it is."

After a pause, Padg pushed on. "What else? Rope? We'll need to go to the weavers for that. Is your Aunt Danya still the weavers' guild leader?"

"Yes, she'll recommend us something good. She may have backpacks too."

"Clicker-beetle and grubs for timekeeping; got those back here somewhere," Padg said. There was a scratch as Dun ticked the scroll.

"Healing stuff from the midwives?

"We should probably pay them a visit. There may be things we've not thought of."

"Padg?"

"What?"

"There's been something bothering me this morning," Dun began hesitantly.

"Well, if it's about supplies or equipment, I thought we were going out now to collect the last bits we need and then sleep on any final 'forgets' and pick them up before we leave next span?"

"No it's not that; I think we're on top of most things and between us, I think we know what we need later. No, I had another dream last night."

"Oh good, more doom. I was beginning to miss that."

"No, not doom this time. More a feeling."

"Go on."

"Well, this is going to sound odd, but we were in a particularly dull part of our journey, sometime soon, plodding along. I wasn't sure exactly where we were, or even what our surroundings were..."

"Sounds like one of your foretellings; I'm beginning to enjoy their particular non-specific, not-all-that-helpful nature."

Dun ignored the jibe and continued, "But one thing I *was* sure of. There weren't just the two of us."

"What? We were being followed? Didn't you cover that part of the foretelling in the bit about the slavering monster?"

"No, it wasn't that at all. There was someone else in our party. Someone with us. Padg, I think we need to find someone else."

"Oh," Padg said, a bit floored. "I know Father's already said this to you or something like, but you know not to take all of this too seriously, right? I mean, some of the things you dream might not be our future, or yours. Some of the possibilities don't come true because of your choices—all that kind of thing. Because if you do take it too seriously, pretty soon you can't take a pee without having dreamed about it first."

"No, I know." Dun giggled, the tension released. "I was just saying, is all. I guess it just feels like an unanswered question."

"Hmm. Come on, let's go find some questions we can answer—to the midwives," Padg said.

The eBook of Dark is free. You can download it via Paul's website at paularvidson.co.uk/dark-series

Thanks for reading!

Printed in Poland
by Amazon Fulfillment
Poland Sp. z o.o., Wrocław